MW00413837

YIELD UP THE DEAD

AN EXCITING DETECTIVE THRILLER WITH A
TWIST YOU WON'T SEE COMING

DEREK FEE

Copyright © 2016 by Derek Fee

All rights reserved.

No part of this book may be reproduced in any form or by any electronic or mechanical means, including information storage and retrieval systems, without written permission from the author, except for the use of brief quotations in a book review.

Publisher's Note: This is a work of fiction. Names, characters, places, and incidents are a product of the author's imagination. Locales and public names are sometimes used for atmospheric purposes. Any resemblance to actual people, living or dead, or to businesses, companies, events, institutions, or locales is completely coincidental.

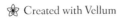 Created with Vellum

For Aine, Bobbie and Sean

PROLOGUE

M arch 1984, County Down

ALAN EVANS LEFT the village of Saintfield behind and was heading towards the town of Carryduff. The meeting in Downpatrick had been a huge success and he had attracted his largest, and most enthusiastic, crowd to date. Maybe his message was catching on. Unfortunately, the success of the public meeting meant that he was late on the road home. He didn't much like travelling in the dark. It was something to do with his night vision being bad. Also, he was beginning to lose faith in his ten-year-old Peugeot 504. The road ahead to Carryduff was pitch black and the headlights of the Peugeot must have been designed to be measured in candlepower. He looked at the young woman in the passenger seat. She was the best-looking woman at the meeting and he was more than a little surprised when she sought him out when the evening was winding down. She put herself in the group that surrounded him afterwards and as people drifted away they had found themselves the last two present in the hall. It was at that point

that she asked whether she could have a lift back to Belfast.
Evans had been more than pleased to oblige. She was at least
twenty years his junior and he assumed that she must be a
student of politics in Queen's University. Given the way the
attendances were going, he supposed that he should expect to
attract more attention from the fair sex. He wasn't exactly an
evangelical preacher but his stage presence was improving,
and he was getting better at projecting himself. The young
woman had made no secret of the fact that she would not be
averse to spending the night with him. She lay back in her seat
listening to the music on the radio. Her eyes were closed and
she was humming along to the song that he recognised as
Karma Chameleon by Culture Club. Evans flicked his eyes
back to the road but his mind was on a potential sexual
coupling with this beautiful woman on their arrival in Belfast.
He had phoned his wife from Downpatrick to let her know
that he might not be home due to his aversion to travelling in
the dark. All in all, it was turning out to be a most satisfactory
evening. They were about three miles from Carryduff on a
dark stretch of road when he saw the roadblock directly before
them. Bloody hell, he thought, this was just what he didn't
need. These roadblocks had become a feature of the Ulster
landscape and were generally manned by people with IQs
measured on the Richter scale. He peered through the wind-
screen but his high beams made no impression on the scene in
front. He slowed down as he approached the makeshift roadblock. So far, he saw no sign of movement. Eventually, he was
obliged to bring his car to a stop. When he had done so, he saw
two men in what he took to be Ulster Defence Regiment
uniforms approaching from behind the roadblock. He looked
quickly at his watch and saw that it was almost midnight. The
young woman beside him, whose name he had forgotten,
stirred and sat upright.

'Why have we stopped?' she asked.

'UDR roadblock by the look of it,' he replied. He was

concentrating on the man approaching the driver's side of the car. He was of medium height, a trifle overweight and was wearing some kind of army fatigues. Evans wasn't an expert on army uniforms but in Ulster there were three kinds of road-block: British Army, UDR or IRA. Since the men were not wearing balaclavas, he assumed one of the former two.

The woman was now fully awake and sitting forward. 'I don't like it,' she said simply.

'It's no problem. We've nothing to hide. We'll show them the papers for the car and we'll be on our way.' He wound down the driver's side window.

Willie Rice approached and at the same time shone his torch across the occupants. There were two and he had been led to believe that there would only be one. The second occupant was a young woman. Wrong place, wrong time, Rice thought. 'Good evening, sir,' he said as he came level with the driver's window.

'Good evening. 'Evans looked at the marking on the man's jacket but didn't recognise any rank. He decided to play to the man's ego. 'Eh, sergeant,' he added.

Rice smiled displaying two rows of tobacco-stained teeth. 'You're out late, sir,' he said.

'Just driving back to Belfast from Downpatrick,' Evans said. He could feel the young woman shifting in her seat.

'Do you have any identification?' Rice asked. He was looking at the woman who was staring back at him.

Evans pulled his wallet out from his pocket. 'My driver's licence.' Evans withdrew the document from the wallet and offered it to the man who he assumed was in charge.

'Thank you, sir.' Rice took the licence, examined it and handed it back to Evans. Then, in one swift movement he removed a .22 calibre pistol from his holster and shot Evans in the face. Evans slumped over the steering wheel, blood already pouring from his mouth. Rice then turned the gun on the woman.

'Wait,' she shouted. 'I'm....' She didn't get to finish the sentence. A .22 calibre bullet hit her directly in the face, entered her skull and bounced around destroying her brain in the process. She slumped forward in her seat.'

Rice returned the gun to its holster. 'Jimmy,' he shouted.

A small thin man came forward dressed in similar fatigues to Rice. He looked into the car but didn't say a word.

'Get rid of that fucking roadblock. Then get in the car and be ready to follow me.' Jimmy immediately disappeared and started dismantling the roadblock.

Rice pulled Evans from the driver's seat and put him in the rear of the Peugeot. He pushed the woman back into the passenger seat. Her face was a mess. She'd been a good-looking biddie before he'd changed her looks. There wasn't much blood in the front of the car and Rice settled himself in the driver's seat. One more job to do and he'd be back in Belfast.

CHAPTER ONE

Wilson looked forward from his seat in the fourteenth row on the left side of the nave in Belfast Cathedral. The church was filling up as the great and the good of Ulster, and beyond, came together for the memorial service for the recently-deceased Chief Constable of the PSNI. The corpse had already been laid to rest in his birthplace of Great Malvern on the border of England and Wales. Therefore, the only representation of the man was his cap sitting on a pedestal directly facing the congregation. The first three rows of seats on the left side of the nave were reserved for the deceased's family. The third to sixth row contained members of the Ulster Assembly led by the Chief Minister, her deputy and representatives from all the political parties. Directly behind them were seated the newly-appointed Chief Constable, Deputy Chief Constable Royson Jennings and four Assistant Chief Constables. Behind them was the officer commanding the British Army in Northern Ireland accompanied by several heavily-braided officers. Then came the Chief Superintendents and finally the row where Wilson sat among the Superintendents. Behind them were the Chief Inspectors, Inspectors and a scattering of other ranks displaying that the

PSNI was an egalitarian organisation. The PSNI cohort was resplendent in its dress uniforms. Across the aisle from the Wilson sat the representatives of the sporting fraternity headed by the former Chief Constable's golfing buddies, the business community, the cultural community and local government. Sitting in the middle, and no doubt representing the financial community, sat Helen McCann conservatively dressed in black suit and matching hat. Wilson had received his invitation for the event the previous week and his first reaction had been to bin it. He had been on leave for a month. The first two weeks were spent in Nova Scotia reconnecting with the mother he had excluded from his life for more than twenty years. The reconciliation had been a great success and he enjoyed exploring the Canadian island with his mother and her husband. The second two weeks were spent having chats with a counsellor. Wilson preferred the word counsellor although the diploma on the wall used the word 'psychotherapist'. Wilson wanted to avoid that word and its more colloquial 'shrink'. He thought psychotherapist ill-suited since his counsellor dispensed no therapy at all. Wilson had endured six sessions in which he spoke and his counsellor listened and wrote what looked like copious notes. Wilson was looking for answers as to why his relationships, including that with his mother, generally ended in disaster. Thus far, this effort at self-examination had proved fruitless. The counsellor's future as Wilson's listening post was bleak. While trying to find enlightenment, Wilson had more or less convinced himself that he and the PSNI were on separate paths and it was time they made the change in direction permanent. He didn't really know why he hadn't binned the invitation to the Chief Constable's memorial but he had no intention of attending when he tossed it onto his coffee table. His hand was forced by a phone call from Donald Spence, his old boss at Tennant Street. Spence was several months into his retirement and had used all his emotional blackmail to convince Wilson to attend. It was evident that Spence had an agenda but Wilson had no idea what it might be. By the end of the phone call, Wilson had not only promised to attend the memorial but also agree to join Spence for a post-event lunch at his new home in Porta-ferry. Looking at the number of PSNI officers present, Wilson wondered who was keeping Ulster's criminals at bay. He had searched the faces of his uniformed colleagues for Peter Davidson and Harry Graham, his former colleagues in the murder squad. But they were conspicuous by their absence. Ten minutes before the memorial was about to begin the empty seat beside him was taken by Donald Spence.

'Shouldn't you be sitting with the other head buck cats up front?' Wilson said offering Spence his hand.

'Nothing changes.' Spence shook hands. 'I asked for this particular seat.'

'Trying to make sure that I don't make an early exit?'

'Something like that.' Spence smiled. 'How are the sessions with the shrink going?'

Wilson winced theatrically. 'You mean my counselling sessions. I'm beginning to see what an absolute shit I am. Next week we're going to explore how I managed to get you bumped with only a few months to retirement.'

'So you're making progress then?'

Wilson smiled.

'I don't blame you for having to retire a couple of months early,' Spence continued. 'Jennings took advantage of the Chief Constable's illness.'

On cue Jennings turned and looked at Wilson and Spence.

'The bastard must have exceptional hearing,' Wilson said. 'Either that or his antennae are set to vibrate every time his name is mentioned.'

'Maybe he's in league with the Devil.'

Wilson had no doubt about that.

At that moment the Archbishop of Armagh and a coterie

of clergymen suitably cloaked for the solemn occasion entered stage left and the congregation fell instantly silent.

THE CONGREGATION SPILLED out of St Anne's and stood in groups on the stone steps or the area in front of the cathedral, which had been kept clear of cars. The lesser ranks of the PSNI group had already departed for their day jobs while the higher ranks paid homage to their new boss. Chief among the group surrounding the new Chief Constable was DCC Jennings who was doing a more than passable impression of Uriah Heep. Wilson and Spence had moved to the side and both were watching the fawn-fest. Wilson let his gaze fall onto the latest group spilling out of the large wooden doors. Helen McCann had latched on to the group of Assembly Ministers as they exited. It was obvious that she was well-known to them all. For a second, her head turned and she looked directly at Wilson and Spence. It was not a look that conveyed affection. Wilson had not heard a word from Kate, Helen McCann's daughter and his former lover, since they had made their 'break' definitive. He half expected Kate to be part of the congregation and was disappointed when she hadn't shown up. As a leading light of the legal fraternity she would certainly have received an invitation.

'Let's get out of here,' Spence said. 'We'll travel in my car. On the way you can regale me on the details of your latest investigation. I understand it was particularly personal.'

CHAPTER TWO

Portaferry is a small town located at the southern end of the Ards Peninsula near the narrows at the entrance to Strangford Lough. It has become a mecca for retirees with a desire to brave the Northern winter rather than fly south to the Canary Islands. Spence had done well in the selection of his retirement property. His five-bedroomed house stood on a small incline facing a beach and the ferry port.

'I understand why you decided to engage a shrink,' Spence said as he drove his car into the driveway and parked in front of the garage. He was enthralled by Wilson's recounting of the Lafferty investigation. 'A lesser man might have gone under by proving that their father was a murderer. Someone badly misjudged you.' He switched off the car but didn't move. 'You shouldn't be too hard on your father, Ian. It was a strange time. People did things that they ordinarily would never have done. Try to remember that your father was a victim. There were plenty of others.'

Wilson stared straight ahead. He had covered this ground with the counsellor already but had received less therapy than Spence had given him. 'It's all in the past. Right now I'm concentrating on the future.'

'I'm glad you said that,' said Spence as he pushed open the driver's door. 'Come and look at our new palace.'

'If this is retirement, I can't wait,' Wilson said when the tour of the house was completed. They were standing on the small patio to the side of the house and looking across Strangford Lough. Miriam, Spence's wife, stuck her head out of the kitchen door and told them that lunch would be ready shortly. During the tour, Wilson noted that the dining table was set for three and assumed that he was Spence's sole guest. He was, therefore, a little surprised when Spence told his wife to hold lunch until their guest arrived. They were settled with a pre-lunch drink in the living room when Wilson saw a large black Mercedes coming up the drive. He was more surprised when he saw the occupant of the rear seat emerging. He had never met Chief Constable Norman Baird and he had no idea what he was doing at the Spence residence. He turned to look at Spence but his former boss was already on his feet and heading for the front door. Wilson stood and waited for the two men to enter the living room.

'Superintendent Wilson,' said Baird as he came forward with his right hand extended. 'I've been looking forward to meeting you.'

'Sir,' Wilson said shaking the proffered hand. Baird cut an impressive figure in his dress uniform. He was several inches shorter than Wilson but he was obviously into fitness. His slim figure could have been that of a model for the uniform. His steel grey hair was cut short and his blue eyes showed a keen intelligence behind them. His face was narrow and his high cheekbones were more Scandinavian than Celtic. What Wilson noticed most was something he learned from his sporting life, Baird had the charisma associated with good leaders.

'Norman today,' Baird said. 'But if you ever call me Norman on business, I'll be quick to reprimand you.' He beamed a smile at Wilson and started to remove his jacket. 'I'm famished. I hope Miriam hasn't forgotten how to cook.'

During lunch Wilson discovered that Spence and Baird went way back and that Spence mentored Baird as a young copper. Wilson was obliged, as he often was, to tell some rugby stories but he had the feeling that the objective of the lunch was to give him and Baird the opportunity to get the measure of each other. They reached dessert without any mention of why Baird, or indeed Spence, had gone to the trouble of wasting a lunch on a meet-and-greet.

'I understand that I owe my job to you,' Baird said as the coffee arrived.

'I had no idea I was so influential,' Wilson said. He saw that Spence had left the table unobtrusively, and he and Baird were alone.

'Jennings was a shoo-in until he shat on his doorstep trying to screw you. So, in a perverse way I owe you for getting me the big job.'

Wilson smiled. 'Don't say that in front of the Deputy Chief Constable.'

'I daresay the DCC has a doll representing you some-where into which he regularly places needles,' Baird said. 'Donald tells me that there's no love lost between you. I have no doubt that situation will be acerbated by my elevation to the job he covets.'

'I'll try not to worry too much,' Wilson said.

'Has Donald told you why I wanted to speak to you in private?'

'No.' Wilson shook his head.

'I understand you are contemplating your future in the PSNI.'

'Things haven't been going too well.'

'I've looked at your record and I definitely don't want to lose you. You may have heard that the former Chief Constable was undertaking a reorganisation.'

Wilson nodded.

'I've cancelled it.'

Wilson suppressed a smile. It was so true to form. He thought Baird might be different but the reorganisation upon taking over the job was par for the course.

'I see you're a cynic,' Baird smiled. 'The proposed reorganisation had some good elements but there were some aspects I couldn't live with. One of them might involve you. If you're still interested of course.'

'What do you have in mind?'

'I want you to head up a squad which will investigate murders throughout the province. It will be a specialist squad dealing only with homicide.'

'So, the Serious Crime Squad idea is being scrapped.'

'Precisely, we need specialist units not generalists. We already do it for drugs and fraud, and it works. Most rural coppers may see one homicide in their career. They don't have either the tools or the skills to carry out a professional investigation. We only have to look at the way some of the historical crimes were investigated. The RUC were rightly criticised for the slipshod way some of the homicides were treated.'

'That wasn't only the case in rural areas.' Wilson could speak from experience.

'So are you interested?'

'Where will we operate out of?'

'Do you have a preference?'

'I'd like to stay in the centre of Belfast. What about personnel? I'll need a minimum of five detectives. There are two still active so that means three new officers. One of them should be a sergeant.'

'Done. I'll have some names for you soon.'

Wilson scratched his head. He'd been threequarters of the way to making a decision to leave the PSNI. He wasn't sure he should say yes to a new challenge. Maybe the time was right to make a break from his old life. Go somewhere new and make a start doing something else. Who was he kidding? He wouldn't fit in anywhere else and he'd spent twenty years putting miscreants behind bars. Was he ready to swop a career he had built up to run a bar in Tenerife? He didn't think so, but he also wasn't sure that his new big boss was on the level. 'How long do I have to make my mind up?'

'I have to say goodbye to Donald and Miriam.' Baird stood up and took his jacket from the chair before heading in the direction of the kitchen. 'Shall we say five minutes,' he said over his shoulder.

Wilson smiled. He'd been right about Baird. He was a leader of men. Maybe it was time to toss his hat into the ring. -- again. And there was always Sammy Rice to find. *One last try*, he thought, before he switched to pulling pints for holidaymakers.

Baird had already put on his jacket by the time he returned to the dining room.

Wilson extended his hand. 'I'm on board.'

'I thought as much,' Baird shook hands. 'We'll expect you back next Monday. I'll have the files of your new recruits on your desk. I'm looking forward to working with you.'

'I doubt you'll be saying that in a few months,' Spence said joining them.

Baird looked at his watch. 'I'm already late.' He turned to Wilson. 'I saw you play. You were something else.' Then he was gone

Spence saw Baird to the door and returned to Wilson. 'I knew he was set for the top the first day I met him. He's got that ability to concentrate on you and make you believe that you're the only person in the room. But don't be swayed by the easy manner. Norman is as hard as nails and he's one hell of a politician. If it's ever his neck or yours, then prepare to lose your neck. Whatever you do, do not underestimate him.'

'Was all this your idea?' Wilson asked.

'I'd like to take the credit but he wanted you anyway.'

'So, he ran it by you first?'

'He's not a man who takes chances. He wanted to know what I thought and he wanted to meet you outside the job.'

CHAPTER THREE

R ichie Simpson looked around his current lodgings, a downstairs room in a two up two down with a shared bathroom. It was a far cry from the suite of rooms he had occupied on the top floor of the building on the Shankill Road housing the Ulster Democratic Union office. He chuckled to himself. Had he really been so naïve? Had he really believed that the UDU was intended to live on beyond the retirement of the man who had set it up as his personal vehicle? The UDU was on life support from the day Jackie Carlisle walked out of its office for the last time. That life support had nothing to do with electricity, it was all about money and Carlisle had left just enough in the coffers to cover the next month's rent on the offices. Simpson looked at all the rubbish lying around his room. His restricted accommodation had put him in spring-cleaning mode, although spring was long past. He hadn't realised the amount of crap he had collected and that was now stuffed into every corner. He sat with a cup of coffee spying the two black bags full of rubbish he had already collected. Somewhere in the back of his mind he remembered some TV guru saying that one of the first stages of a prospective suicide was to start cleaning out their life. If that was the case, half of

Scandinavia must be on suicide watch. Simpson had no intention of committing suicide although he had plenty of reasons to contemplate an escape from life. He was broke, he had no job and was living on state benefits, and he realised belatedly that the gun he had used to shoot Sammy Rice was in the possession of Davie Best, the right hand man of the current biggest, in more ways than one, Belfast crime lord. To add to his level of despair, the only man who could have helped him out of his current mess was the man who put him in it. Jackie Carlisle, founder of the UDU and its principal beneficiary, had been put in the ground two months previously. Times had been hard for Simpson since the demise of the UDU. In contrast, Carlisle was given the funeral he'd dreamed of. A flag- bedecked coffin had been paraded along the Shankill Road before a respectful Protestant community. The people he had served so well had bid farewell to one of their heroes at a packed First Presbyterian Church in Rosemary Street. The Moderator had led the congregation in prayer for the soul of the departed son of Ulster. Membership of the congregation was by invitation only and Simpson waited until the last moment to receive his. When he realised that he wasn't going to be invited, he prevailed on Carlisle's widow. As soon as he heard that Carlisle was dead, he had harboured the hope that he might be included in some small way in the will of the Great Man. As the weeks went by, he realised that he had been nurturing a forlorn hope. Richie Simpson's salvation was not in the hands of his former boss. When he did a stocktaking of his situation, he wondered why he wasn't contemplating suicide. Perhaps he was but it was so deeply set in his mind that he refused to recognise it. He'd always thought of himself as one of those types who would get up immediately when knocked down, but that image was trashed two months after Carlisle left him in charge of the moribund Ulster Democratic Union. Simpson considered himself to be multi-talented. After all, few people could claim to have been a political fixer, a tout

for British Military Intelligence and a murderer. Well few
people except several inmates of Crumlin Road prison. Unfortunately, Simpson's attributes were not the type that were
currently in demand at his local job centre. In his mind, the
spring-cleaning was simply the first step in de-cluttering his
life and sloughing off the last vestiges of his former life as
Carlisle's dogsbody. During the weeks after the Sammy Rice
affair, he had scoured the newspapers for any mention of the
disappearance of the crime lord. Sammy had vanished off the
face of the earth and nobody appeared to give a flying fuck.
The last he had seen of Sammy was his corpse lying in a
disused warehouse. He assumed that Best and his friends had
incorporated Sammy into the structure of a new building or
perhaps they had gone all Mafia and Sammy was sleeping with
the fishes in the Lagan. Despite the silence as to Sammy's ultimate resting place, Simpson hadn't been sleeping well. Even a
dead Sammy Rice could throw the fear of God into you.
Whatever the future, Simpson knew that Best and McGreary
had him by the balls. They had the murder weapon and his
fingerprints were all over it. If Sammy's body did manage to
resurface, he would be securely in the frame for the murder.
Life was certainly pissing on Richie Simpson. He finished his
coffee and got to his feet. There was more crap to sort through
and get rid of. He started rooting around in the bottom of one
of his wardrobes. There were several boxes there that he didn't
recognise. He pulled out one and ripped off the sealing tape.
The box contained a series of files all bearing the logo of the
now-defunct Ulster Democratic Union. Simpson had no idea
how this box had made its way to his flat. The day that Carlisle
left their office in the Lower Shankill every scrap of paper was
boxed and delivered to Carlisle's house in Hillsborough.
Carlisle had overseen the operation himself, and when it was
completed there wasn't so much as a sheet of paper left in the
office. Carlisle was also abstemious in making sure that the
hard disk of his computer was wiped clean to the extent of

putting a magnet next to his computer. He obviously wanted to obliterate any evidence that could be used against him in the future. He didn't know at that time that the Grim Reaper had already taken care of his future. It appeared that somehow two boxes were diverted to Simpson's modest abode. He removed one box and carried it to his coffee table. He took out the top file and began to read the contents. Two hours later he had read every file in the box and had confirmed everything he knew about politics. It was the most venal of professions. Carlisle's constituents, who voted for him religiously, were in constant contact with the Great Man. His replies to their entreaties promised the earth, but were aimed at delivering nothing. He would speak to so-and-so concerning their problem and would let them know the result in the fullness of time. Simpson closed the final file and tossed the box on the floor. There was still one box of equally irrelevant trash to go through. He took the second box from the wardrobe and put it on the coffee table. He ripped open the sealing tape, and looked into a box full of black Moleskine notebooks. He had often seen Carlisle scribbling in these books. There had to be twenty of the small notebooks in the box. He picked out one and opened it. The front page had '1972' as its title. It was a diary of sorts. He turned the page and sure enough there was the scrawl he recognised so well. This was a treasure trove. These small black books contained the inner thoughts of one of the men who had been at the centre of the fight to keep Ulster British. Simpson went to the kitchen and made himself a fresh cup of coffee. He had a long day of reading ahead.

Six hours later Simpson's eyes were aching and his brain was addled at the banality of Carlisle's thoughts. Nobody would ever see a printed version of these scribblings on the shelves of Waterstones, or any other bookseller for that matter. Simpson was up to 1976 and there was not a single useable nugget. Carlisle had been neither a fighter nor a fucker so there was nothing that was even mildly interesting to either the historian or the seeker of lurid details. Why hadn't Carlisle hooked up with Margaret Thatcher or even some non-descript British MP? A male or female MP would have done. Simpson felt like a gold miner panning away hoping to come across that big nugget that would forever change his life. He picked up the next notebook in the hope that it would yield that life-changing titbit.

When the light began to fade, Simpson was obliged to put on the table lamp. Where had the day gone? The diaries had become a trifle more interesting as the 'Troubles' escalated, but Carlisle was always peripheral to the action and his personal life was still as dull as ditchwater. He was about to call it a day when a loose piece of paper tumbled from one of the note-books he was handling. He picked it up and saw that it was a map of sorts. It was crudely drawn and he laid it out on the coffee table. The area of townland was marked as Ballyna-hone. Simpson didn't know where it was so he consulted Google maps on his computer. He found that Ballynahone was in county Antrim and was famous as an area of natural bogland. What the hell had Jackie Carlisle to do with bogland? The rough map showed a road and some geographical features and most specifically a small cross and the name 'Evans' beside it. Simpson had no idea who or what the 'Evans' signified. The book dated from the 1980s so referred to a time long before he had become Carlisle's factotum. But it was during the time when Carlisle's star had been in the ascendant. It was strange reading the notebooks. Carlisle had been a nobody throughout the early 1970s, but suddenly in the 1980s he had found his mojo and began a steady climb up the political ladder. It was about that time that his influence with the Protestant paramili-taries increased. It was noticeable that around this period there was more money around to support Carlisle's election fund. The 1980s had been Carlisle's golden years. Simpson fired up his computer again and put in the name 'Evans' and Northern Ireland. At the top of the results was Jonny Evans the former

Manchester United and current West Bromwich defender. He had to scroll down several pages before he found a reference to Alan Evans, a minor Ulster politician who had disappeared in 1984 and had never been heard of again. According to several articles, it was assumed that Evans had been a victim of the IRA and had been "disappeared". Simpson finished reading all the articles. He closed the lid of his laptop and looked at the map on his coffee table. Could this possibly be the place where Evans had been 'disappeared' to? And if so how did the location of a man who had been "disappeared" by the IRA fall into the hands of a Loyalist politician? Perhaps Carlisle had left him a treasure map after all. He settled back in his chair. He needed to think how he could turn this information into money.

CHAPTER FOUR

'Morning, sir.' The desk sergeant smiled widely as Wilson walked into the station. 'Good to have you back.'

'Morning, Billy,' Wilson returned the smile. 'It's good to be back.' It was almost six weeks since he's been to the station; the longest period he'd been away in more than five years. He was gratified that nothing appeared to have changed. Well, physically nothing had changed but there was one major philosophical change. Donald Spence was no longer in charge. Wilson had, in his inside pocket, a letter signed by the Chief Constable appointing him as head of the regional murder squad. It was in effect his old job but with a regional focus. He would be required to assist police throughout the province in investigating murder on their patch. It was a challenge that he relished. As far as he knew, there were no impending investigations outside Belfast but that could change quickly. He already decided that his first priority would be to clear up the murders of Grant, Malone and O'Reilly. That meant that his first priority was to locate the whereabouts of Sammy Rice, his prime suspect for the crimes. He breathed in the air of the station. It was a strange mixture of stale beer, testosterone and the synthetic smell of the cleaning agents. His dead wife, rightly or wrongly, described it as his womb. It was true that he felt more at home there than anywhere else. He was about to make his way to the murder squad room when Billy put up his hand.

'The boss wants to see you immediately you came in.'

Wilson's smile disappeared. Donald Spence's replacement was Chief Superintendent Yvonne Davis. He'd never worked with her but he'd heard a lot about her. She was newly promoted to her post as Chief Superintendent. Like him, she was one of the new Chief Constable's personal appointments. Word had it that she was destined for the top. He went immediately to Spence's old office. Donald's name was already removed from the door and a new plaque announced it was now the office of Chief Superintendent Yvonne Davis. The guard was well and truly changed. He entered the outer office and the secretary asked him to wait. The Boss was on the telephone. Five minutes later, the secretary announced him and nodded at the door to the inner office.

Yvonne Davis stood as soon as Wilson entered and came out from behind her imposing desk. She was of medium height and was wearing a black regulation skirt and a white shirt with a diamond and star on the epaulettes. Her hair was cut short and was salt and pepper. She obviously had no desire to hide the grey. She had an open pleasant face and a pair of blue eyes that sparkled. She looked fit for her fifty something years. She extended her hand towards Wilson. 'Superintendent Wilson, I've been looking forward to this.'

Wilson took her hand. 'Congratulations on your new appointment, ma'am,' he said.

She smiled. 'Thanks, please take a seat.'

She moved back behind the desk while Wilson took the seat directly facing her.

She looked at Wilson half lounging in the seat. She been told that he was a handsome devil and that hadn't been a lie. If

she had been twenty years younger and without her experience of men, she might have batted her eyelids at him. But that
day was long gone. His posture exuded confidence. She
cleared her throat. 'I wanted us to meet before you get
swamped with work,' she said leaning forward. 'As soon as I
was appointed, I received several phone calls offering me
advice. One was from Deputy Chief Constable Jennings who,
after wishing me well, launched into a diatribe against you.
Apparently, you are a dangerous psychopath, a career wrecker
who must be carefully managed if one is to avoid disaster. The
second call I received was from Donald Spence. After congrat-
ulating me, he gave me a rundown on the station and the
personnel. He was exceptionally complimentary about you. In
his opinion, you are the finest policeman he's ever worked
with. So, Superintendent, what are you devil or angel?'

Wilson was smiling. 'I suppose a bit of both, ma'am.'

'My intuition tells me that you could be like a bold child.
Such children are interesting, but trying.'

Wilson laughed. 'No one has described me in those terms.'

'I've raised three bold children, and it took me twenty
years to get rid of what was a very bold husband. So I have a lot
of experience. How long do you think you're going to last?'

'I love this job and I do it to the best of my ability. I didn't
join the police force to win friends and influence people. I
joined to put criminals where they belong, behind bars.
Donald Spence and I were on the same wavelength as far as
why we did what we did. I'm aware that I ruffled the feathers
of some of the big birds but I am who I am.'

She had heard a lot about Wilson and she could see that
most of it was true. He had huge respect among the rank and
file but was detested in Castlereagh. She was ready to develop
her own opinion of him. 'I hope that we're going to get along.'

'I'm sure we are, ma'am.' It wasn't going to be the same as it
was with Donald but that had been special.

'I like to meet my senior officers early on Monday morning

for a general briefing.' She could see from Wilson's face that this didn't particularly please him. 'You don't do meetings, I assume.'

'Murder investigations are fluid. Sometimes I may not be available first thing Monday morning.'

'Then I'll be happy to excuse you. In the meantime, you will attend.' She looked at her watch. 'The first meeting is in twenty-five minutes.' She stood up. 'I'm looking forward to working with you, Superintendent. I have a feeling it's going to be a challenge.'

Wilson would have been slow to admit it but Davis had impressed him. She had displayed that she was in control and he had a feeling that she was competent. He didn't have a view on whether he would develop the same relationship with her that he had with Spence but it wasn't a bad start.

CHAPTER FIVE

D etective Constables Harry Graham and Peter Davidson were already at their desks when Wilson entered the squad room. He had contacted both of his former colleagues the previous week to bring them up to date on his new responsibilities. He also contacted Eric Taylor to invite him back into the squad but Taylor declined.

'When will the new recruits arrive?' Graham asked.

Wilson looked through the glass panel of his office and saw that the Chief Constable was as good as his word. There was a stack of files sitting on his desk. 'As soon as possible,' Wilson looked at his watch. 'You have twenty-two minutes to bring me up to date on Baxter, Weir and most of all Sammy Rice.' All three had international arrest warrants out against them for the murders of Grant, Malone and O'Reilly. A whiteboard in the corner of the squad room had photos of Baxter, Weir and Rice at the top. Beneath each photo was everything that was known about their whereabouts. Wilson noticed that there was very little change to the board since he'd left. The lack of momentum was the death knell of any investigation. After listening to Harry and Peter, it was clear that no progress had been made. It was self-evident that people cannot just disappear. Baxter and Weir would eventually resurface when they thought the hue and cry had died down. Sammy Rice was a different matter. Sammy had businesses to run and mouths to feed. If those businesses were neglected, cash flow would cease and the gang would disintegrate. According to Harry and Peter, Rice's main competitor, Gerry McGreary, was already encroaching on Rice's territory. Old Willie Rice, Sammy's father, had pulled himself out of the bottle and was trying to hold things together until his son reappeared. Wilson wasn't happy. The investigation had stalled so he needed to create some new momentum. He would need his additional recruits immediately. 'Sammy's car?' he asked.

'Stopped by the uniforms two days after Sammy disappeared,' Graham said. 'Being driven by two gobshites who claimed they found it abandoned in East Belfast.'

'Where exactly did they find it?' Wilson asked.

'Over by Queen's Road,' Graham answered.

'What the hell was it doing over there? Does Sammy own any property in the area?'

Graham shrugged his shoulders.

'Well, find out! You don't leave a BMW 7 series in the street over by Queen's Road if you don't have business in the area.'

Wilson's phone started ringing. He glanced at his watch and saw that it was just after nine o'clock. Shite, it was the first day of school and he was late for a meeting with the headmaster.

CHAPTER SIX

Jock McDevitt was sitting by the window in Clement's Café on Donegall Square. The crime business was slacker than usual, and McDevitt hadn't had a front-page story since Maggie Cummerford was sentenced. Maggie was the gift that was continuing to give. McDevitt had lodged an advanced payment of £10,000 in his account from a publisher who commissioned him to write a book about her case and trial. He contemplated making news out of Wilson's investigation into a thirty-eight-year-old murder, but his editor had laughed him out of the room. There was no traction in identifying who killed a couple of kids a generation ago. He took a bite of his fruit scone and washed it down with a mouthful of coffee. That asshole Richie Simpson was late. He must have been out of his mind agreeing to meet yesterday's man. Even in his heyday, Simpson wasn't capable of producing enough copy for a page five story. He'd probably been led astray by the excitement in Simpson's voice. He looked out through the window at the activity on Donegall Square. The girls were out in their summer dresses and you could forgive people for thinking that Belfast was like any other sun-kissed city in Ireland. You had to dig below the surface to find the bitterness that still drove the sectarian divide. Triumphalism made sure that the sectarian pot was kept boiling. McDevitt turned back to the inside of the café as Simpson dropped into the chair facing him. He'd heard that Simpson was on a downward spiral since Carlisle had retired and the UDU had imploded in his wake but nothing prepared him for the state of the man in front of him. Simpson looked like a derelict. He cursed himself for accepting the meeting. 'Coffee?'

'Aye, and a couple of them scones,' Simpson said. 'I didn't have time for breakfast this morning.'

McDevitt waved at the waitress and when she arrived gave her Simpson's order and asked for a refill of his coffee. 'So, how have things been, Richie?'

Simpson kept his gaze on the waitress's ample derriere as she walked away. 'Not so busy, Mr McDevitt. I'm on the lookout for a job but things are a bit slack right now.'

I'll bet, McDevitt thought looking at the state of Simpson. He looked like he hadn't washed for a month and that during that period he'd slept in his clothes. He'd seen tramps that looked more employable. 'Yeah, the modern economy is a bitch. What can I do for you?'

Simpson looked around furtively. He saw the waitress approaching with their order and he stayed silent.

McDevitt smiled as the waitress placed their order on the table. Simpson was making a credible attempt at piquing his interest. As soon as the plate of scones was placed on the table, Simpson fell on it like a hungry locust. The food had super-seded the purpose of the meeting. Hunger banished all other thoughts.

'I can do something for you.' Simpson was spewing crumbs of scone over the table as he spoke. 'I have information that could be very useful to you.'

'What kind of information?'

'Ever hear of Alan Evans?' Simpson had spent the

previous evening at Belfast Central Library in Royal Avenue reading everything they had on Evans.

McDevitt ran the name through his memory banks. 'Some kind of commie politician from the 1980s. He was a bit of a minor shooting star. Right in the middle of making a name for himself he disappeared.'

Simpson slurped some coffee into his mouth. 'He propagated the idea that the "Troubles" weren't a sectarian conflict but part of the class war. Some people thought he went a bit far when he called for Russian soldiers to replace the British Army as a peacekeeping force. The guy was a dingbat. How would you like to know where he disappeared to?'

McDevitt sipped his coffee while Simpson attacked his second scone. How far had Simpson fallen? At least he wasn't offering to divulge the resting place of Jean McConville. Alan Evans had been a nobody who was trying to whip up the working class to attack their betters and not each other. In retrospect maybe it wasn't such a bad idea. He wondered how much interest there would be if Simpson could actually provide the goods. It might just be enough to get him back on the front page. And there might even be a follow up book to his Cummerford tome. 'Tell me more.'

'I'd love to, Mr McDevitt but we'll have to discuss money first.' More crumbs of scone flew across the table.

'What did you have in mind?'

'£10,000.'

'You're havin' a laugh, Richie. You obviously haven't met my editor. He makes Scrooge look like Bill Gates. I think that he actually stitches his pockets. What sort of information are we talking about here?'

Simpson finished his coffee and called the waitress. He ordered a refill and two more scones. 'Say I could give you the exact location where Evans is buried.'

'I don't think it was ever proved that he was murdered.'

'I have a map showing where he was buried.' Simpson

stopped while the waitress deposited his coffee and scones. 'I mean the exact location,' he added as soon as she left.

'Yeah, and I have the original map to Flint's treasure.'

Simpson stopped attacking his scones. 'I'm not jokin' Mr McDevitt.'

McDevitt noticed that Simpson was ignoring the scones. He must really be serious. 'And the provenance of this map?'

'What?'

'Where did you get the map?'

'After we settle on the money.' He started on the first scone.

'I could probably get you £200.'

'You're jokin'. I'm not givin' it for less than £5,000.' Simpson spewed out more crumbs.

'Get real, Richie. You've got three big problems. First, you'll have to convince someone the map is genuine. Second, you have to find someone who gives a shit about digging Evans up and third, you go to the police with this and they'll give you their thanks and that's all. Maybe I can get you £500 but that would be pushing it.'

Simpson stopped eating and thought for a few moments. The mangy bastard was right. 'A grand, I'm not going lower than a grand.' He didn't think he was going to get ten grand but five had been his bottom price. Fuck Jackie Carlisle, he was continuing to screw him from the grave.

McDevitt was about to offer £750 but he was getting bored with the negotiation. 'OK, a grand it is.'

Simpson put out his hand.

'Stop kiddin', Richie. I don't carry a grand around in my back pocket. But everyone in Belfast knows that I'm a man of my word, and if I say I'll pay a grand, you can take it to the bank. Now where did you get the fucking map?'

Simpson explained about finding the stray boxes from the UDU office and how the map had, more or less, literally fallen into his hands.

McDevitt's mind was working overtime. He was trying to make the connection between Carlisle and Evans. He concluded that there wasn't any. Why then would Carlisle be in possession of a map showing the burial place of someone who had been 'disappeared'? The common perception was that the IRA was the organisation responsible for the majority, if not all, the people who had "disappeared" in Northern Ireland. Something here didn't gel. 'I want to see the notebooks,' McDevitt said.

'Not part of the deal.' Simpson hadn't had time to examine all the notebooks. He had no idea what nuggets might be contained in those he hadn't yet read.

'Five hundred extra if you deliver me all of the notebooks.'

'Two grand.'

McDevitt thought of the advance for the Cummerford book sitting in the bank. 'One grand extra.' He had no doubt that his editor wouldn't stump up more than a grand total so the investment in the notebooks would be his.

Simpson didn't reply immediately. The notebooks he had examined already were full of crap. It was a better than even bet that the rest would be the same. 'OK, two grand for the map and the notebooks.'

McDevitt signalled to the waitress and made the sign for the bill. 'We're off to the bank, Richie boy. Then we're off to whatever hovel you're inhabiting these days. I want those notebooks and the map asap.' He pulled out his mobile phone and called his assistant at the *Chronicle*. 'I want everything we have on Alan Evans, minor politician from the 1980s, on my desk in one hour. Hop to it.' He closed the phone and dropped a £20 note onto the metal plate containing the bill. 'OK, Richie, let's go and see what I've just bought for myself.'

CHAPTER SEVEN

Wilson was rethinking his decision to continue with the PSNI. The meeting with Davis and the other senior officers had left him wanting to eat his own head. Those participants who were not trying to climb up the new boss's behind were busy trying to show how bloody clever they were. Spence would never have put up with that level of fawning and self-aggrandisement. But Spence was gone. His fellow senior officers didn't seem to realise that they were employed to fight crime. They had subjugated that responsibility in their desire to climb the greasy pole of career. He hadn't said a word, praying that others might follow his lead and the meeting would be cut short. He was sadly mistaken. If this was the future, Wilson wanted no part of it. Then again, what part of 'adapting to change' hadn't he understood? He'd had bosses before Spence, and he had survived them. As soon as he returned to his office, he started on the personnel files. He was surprised to find a note on top from the new Chief Constable making 'suggestions' as to who might be suitable. There was no direct instruction. It was subtler than that. Nothing ever changes. He could select whomever he wanted but the boss had already reviewed the candidates and had a view. There were ten files in all, five for a new sergeant and five for a new detective constable. The Chief Constable's note had suggested strongly that diversity should be employed; one Catholic, one Protestant, one man, one woman. So be it. Wilson had reviewed the sergeants first and was forced to agree that the CC's proposal was the best. He had set that file aside. He now had his man and his Protestant. Now, he needed to find the perfect woman who was also a Catholic. There was only one woman among the candidates for detective constable and surprise, surprise, she was the candidate suggested by the CC. So, Wilson could have any candidate he wanted as long as it was the two suggested by the CC. That wasn't exactly true, but it was the way it had turned out. Wilson sent an email to each of them requesting their attendance that afternoon for interview one hour apart. He had just put the eight files of the unsuccessful candidates away when his phone rang.

'You have a visitor,' the desk sergeant informed him.

'For God's sake I'm only in the place five minutes and I have a visitor.'

'It's Willie Rice.'

'Put him in an interview room. Maybe he's come to confess to some crime. He's guilty of enough of them.'

Wilson went into the squad room. 'Harry, with me, we're having a visit from Willie Rice.'

'The Willie Rice,' Harry said.

'Is there another one?'

'Room one,' the desk sergeant said when Wilson and Graham entered the reception area. 'Tea and biscuits?'

Wilson gave him a look that would wilt flowers. The two murder squad detectives went down the corridor to the interview rooms. Wilson noticed on the door to the interview room that the top screw holding the number '1' had fallen out leaving the number hanging upside down. He made a mental note to bring this up at next week's senior officers' meeting.

Willie Rice was sitting at the table set against the side of the room. He didn't stand when Wilson and Graham entered. Neither policeman spoke as they took the seats directly facing their visitor.

'Morning, Willie,' Wilson said as soon as he was seated. Willie had cleaned up his act since the last time Wilson had met him. For a start, the room didn't stink of alcohol and stale farts. Willie's face, however, still bore the ravages of his addiction to the Devil's buttermilk. His nose was bulbous and purple, and his cheeks were lined with broken veins. Even in his cleaned-up version Willie looked like an overweight extra in an episode of *The Sopranos*. 'What can we do for you?' Wilson asked. 'I suppose it's too much to hope that you're ready to cop to something?'

'Fuck you,' Rice said. 'What are you doing to find my son?'

Wilson looked at Graham. 'What are we doing to find Sammy Rice?'

Graham shrugged. 'You mean Sammy Rice, the fugitive from justice? The Sammy Rice we have the international arrest warrant out for.'

'I think that's the one that Willie means,' Wilson said smiling.

'I don't think he wants to be found,' Graham said.

'Very fucking funny.' Rice leaned forward. 'You two should go on stage together. Sammy's been missing for nearly two months. He's never gone this long without contacting me. I've even filed a missing person's report. What the fuck are you people doin' about it? Bloody useless Peelers.'

It was as good an example of parental care as Wilson had seen. At least from someone with Willie Rice's pedigree. 'We're more than anxious to find Sammy. In fact, he could be the key to providing us with information that could clear up three murders. Maybe you could point us in the direction where we should concentrate our efforts.'

Rice slammed his fist on the table. His cheeks became more florid. 'Something's happened to my son. I can feel it in my bones. Sammy went off the rails a wee bit over the last year. That bitch he's married to screwed his head up. She's coke mad. But he takes care of his old man now that his mother's dead. He wouldn't leave me like this without a word. And he wouldn't leave the business.'

'What have you heard?' Wilson asked.

'Nothing, that the problem.' Rice sat back. 'If a flea farts on the Shankill, I'm the first to know about it. There isn't a word about Sammy out there. It's like he's vanished. Someone knows what happened to him but everyone's keeping a tight arsehole.'

'I thought that you people liked to advertise a kill,' Wilson said. 'In gang wars up to now killers have been rushing to claim their handiwork.'

'We found his car,' Graham said. 'Two idiots picked it up over near Queen's Road. They claim it was abandoned over there. They watched it for a few days before nicking it. They claim they know nothing about Sammy's whereabouts. They're just a couple of car thieves and their records bear that out. We have the car with the technical people but they haven't found anything useful in it. What would Sammy be doing over by Queen's Road?'

'He has some property over there,' Rice said.

'We're going through the property register,' Graham said. 'So far we haven't found any property in East Belfast.'

'It won't be in his name,' Rice said. 'It's probably in some company's name. I'll get his accountant to dig it out. '

'What do you think has happened to him?' Wilson asked.

'I'm scared he might be dead.' Tears welled up in his eyes but didn't flow.

For a moment Wilson was sorry for Rice. The man was a thug and had been involved in violence for most of his adult life. But he was also a father and in that moment the father dwarfed the thug. But it would be stupid to forget that the essence of the person was the thug. 'And?'

The tears vanished from Rice's eyes. 'McGreary's behind it somewhere. I'm not saying that he pulled the trigger himself but he's behind whatever happened to Sammy.'

'And if that's the case, where's Sammy?'

'Concreted into someone's floor, lying in a boghole or at the bottom of the Lagan.' Rice clenched his fists. 'If I find out for sure that McGreary's behind Sammy's death, this city will run with blood. And the first head to roll with be that fat bastard's.'

Graham straightened. 'I'd advise you that you are speaking to police officers, and making threats like that could rebound on you.'

Rice leaned forward again. 'You think I care. That crazy bitch Cummerford murdered my wife and now my son may also be dead. You think I care what happens. If you want to stop a bloodbath, you better find out what happened to Sammy before I do.' He pushed his chair back from the table. 'Personally, I hope I'm the first to find out. If I'm going to be killed, I want it to mean something. And I'm taking McGreary and his mob with me.' He turned and walked to the door leaving Wilson and Graham to look after him.

'I don't like the sound of that,' Graham said when the door closed. 'Back to the bad old days. What do you think, boss?'

'I don't think we're going to find Sammy Rice alive. We may not even find his dead body. But I sure as hell think we have to find out what happened to him, and why. Because it's not about lining up Sammy for the murders of Grant, Malone and O'Reilly anymore, it's about stopping a gang war.' He stood up. Willie Rice wasn't the kind of man who made empty threats. If he wanted the streets of Belfast to run red with blood, he had the means to make it happen.

CHAPTER EIGHT

Wilson ordered Graham and Davidson to follow up on the whereabouts of Sammy Rice. It was time to inject some urgency into the search for him. Although he would prefer it not to be the fact, he was forced to agree with Willie Rice that his son was probably no longer in the land of the living. He would have to establish that fact before moving on to investigate who might have ended Rice's life. For a start, Graham and Davidson would have to find out what Rice was doing in East Belfast and what caused him to abandon an expensive car in the area. That was priority number one. Priority number two was to get more bodies on board as quickly as possible. It was early afternoon, and he had asked the prime candidate for sergeant to come for interview at three o'clock.

Detective Sergeant Rory Browne arrived at three o'clock on the dot. The desk sergeant accompanied him to Wilson's office and then left.

Wilson stood to greet the new arrival and shook hands. The handshake was firm and strong. Browne looked younger than his twenty-nine years. He was slightly over six feet and had mousey brown hair stylishly cut. He was handsome in a manly way and the only feature out of place on his face was his nose that had been broken and badly set. His brown eyes were intelligent and his smile when he shook hands was full and engaging. A short beard of reddish-brown hair covered what Wilson thought was a weak chin.

'Please sit down,' Wilson said flopping back into his chair in a relaxed manner. 'Did you just come over from Coleraine?'

'Yes, I left just after receiving your email' Browne's accent was recognisable as mid-Ulster.

Wilson opened the file on his desk. 'Graduate entry,' he read aloud. 'Degree from Coleraine University in French and Psychology.' He looked up at Browne who was staring directly at him. He noticed that Browne was licking his lips to wet them occasionally. 'I doubt you'll be needing much French if you come to join us here.'

Browne forced a smile.

'Joined the force at twenty-three after two years voluntary service overseas,' Wilson read.

'I taught in a school outside Arusha in Tanzania,' Browne added.

Wilson nodded. He knew it was the fashion for young graduates to spend a year or two in Africa. 'Very fulfilling I'm sure.'

'Doing God's work is always fulfilling,' Browne said.

Wilson sighed inwardly. He had been born a Christian but somewhere along the line he had fallen off that particular wagon. What he had seen of sectarianism in the intervening period had convinced him that religious fervour was to be avoided like the plague. He reminded himself that he would have to be careful to observe the religious niceties should Browne join the squad. He continued to read. 'Three years on the beat, then two years as a detective constable and a rapid promotion to detective sergeant. What makes you want to join us here in Belfast?'

'I'm looking for a challenging position and your squad

seems to fit the bill. I'm not saying that Coleraine is not challenging it's just that Belfast is where the action is.'

'And you like action?'

'I love the work. I've always wanted to be a policeman.
University was only a way of getting in and on a fast track.'

'You didn't like being on the beat?'

'Some aspects I liked and some I didn't. I'm not into
community policing. I think it's important but I want to work
in the investigative branch.'

'And there aren't enough investigations for you in
Colerain?

Browne reddened. 'Some burglaries, muggings, car theft,
the usual crimes.'

'But no homicides?'

'No.'

'So you have no experience in investigating murder?'

'No.'

'So what can you bring to my squad aside from the ability
to converse with a suspect in French?' This was the point
where Browne would either sink or swim.

'I think I've been pretty successful in the investigation I've
led so far. I know I have no experience in murder investigation
but I'm a quick learner, and I'm here to learn from you. I am
one hundred per cent loyal to my superior and you can count
on me for backup. I came here to tell you that I absolutely
want this job and that you won't be sorry if you take me on.'

OK, so it was swim. Wilson slowly closed the file. Browne
might turn out to be another George Whitehouse and he
certainly wasn't Moira McElvaney but maybe there was
enough material to mould him into a decent investigator. 'I'll
pass the message to the administration that you'll be joining
the squad as soon as we can get the paperwork through. The
CC assured me that it would be more or less immediate so you
can start packing your bags. You start here next week. What
about family? I notice that you're not married.'

Browne shuffled uneasily in his chair. It was the first time that Wilson saw his confidence slip. There was something there but he wouldn't be the only officer on the force with family issues.

'I'll be coming alone,' Browne said.

'Well, see you soon then.'

'Thank you, sir,' Browne gushed. 'You won't regret taking me on.'

'If I do, you won't be here for long. How did you break your nose, rugby or boxing? And, by the way, I don't like "sir" or "gov", you call me boss.'

Browne smiled. 'Neither. I was playing with my nephew and I tripped and fell on my face.'

Wilson smiled. He would have preferred rugby or boxing. He stood up and extended his hand. 'Welcome to the squad.'

Browne took his hand and shook it vigorously. 'Thank you si. ... boss.'

One down, one more to go, Wilson thought. He knew he should have brought the young man to meet Chief Superintendent Davis but that would have to wait. Davis would be pissed off at him but he didn't have time to play the organisation game.

Thirty minutes after Browne left the desk sergeant showed Detective Constable Siobhan O'Neill into his office. Her name instantly recognised her as a Catholic. There would be no need for supplementary questions about school or area she came from. The woman who entered his office was in her early thirties, she had dark straight hair cut short and she was carrying more than a few extra pounds in weight. Her face was pale and round. Her eyes were the most striking feature in her face. Wilson had rarely seen such beautiful blue eyes. She was dressed in jeans and a loose jacket. He stood to greet her extending his hand. She took it in a loose grip.

'Please, sit,' Wilson said indicating the chair that had been so recently vacated by his latest recruit. 'Detective Constable O'Neill.'

She nodded.

'Fourteen years on the force,' he read from her file. 'Ten years in uniform and four years in Dunmurry, expert in computer systems. How come?'

'Used to be my hobby.' She was sitting upright. 'They needed a computer person and I was the only applicant. It was a case of "in the land of the blind the one-eyed man is king."'

'What's your investigative experience?'

'I've worked mainly as a member of a team. I'm not going to pass myself off as a potential SIO. I'm more a background worker bee and I'm a good copper with a lot of grassroots experience.'

He flicked through her assessments and saw that her view of herself was mirrored by her superiors. He thought that she might make a very suitable replacement for the departed Eric Taylor. 'We sometimes work strange hours. I notice that you've never been married.'

'I take care of my mother. She has Alzheimer's and we have a carer. Working odd hours isn't a problem.'

'I wasn't trying to pry into your private life,' Wilson said. He felt slightly embarrassed.

'I prefer to put all my cards on the table. I don't expect you to pass on that information immediately, but I'm sure that the other members of the squad will find out in their own way.'

'I can respect that. Your beat was West Belfast. You know most of the characters?'

'Since they were in short trousers.'

'Why do you want to join the squad?'

'You want the real answer?'

'Yes.'

'You. I heard you speaking at the police college. I wasn't in the class but I was at the back of the room. Your speech was funny and witty but what came across most was your passion.

I knew that if there was ever a chance to work with you I would take it.'

Wilson could feel his face redden. 'I'm glad I got my passion for the job across. I'd like you to join us here. Is there anything you'd like to ask?'

'Not really. I just want it clear that I'm not coming here to make the tea or fetch the biscuits.'

'Nobody comes here to make tea or fetch biscuits. I'll get started on the paperwork this afternoon. You'll be joining as soon as the papers have been put through.'

'Thank you for giving me the opportunity.'

'You may not be thanking me in a couple of weeks.' He stood and extended his hand. 'Welcome to the squad.' The handshake this time was firmer.

Wilson was satisfied with his first day back on the job. He'd injected a little urgency into the Rice investigation and recruited two new members of the squad. He was happy enough with Browne and O'Neill but squad dynamics are a peculiar thing. It was like sport, the team had to be more than the sum of the players. If the team weren't together, the results would be less than expected. Making sure the team operated properly was his job.

CHAPTER NINE

'I see that normal service has been resumed.' Jock McDevitt's head appeared in the snug several second before his body followed it.

Wilson looked up from the file he was reading and then closed it after carefully marking the page. He had lost almost two months of work and needed to catch up as quickly as possible. He put the file away in a tote bag that had the logo of a well-known British supermarket on it. He'd never owned a briefcase and he wasn't going to start now.

McDevitt sat down and dropped his messenger bag on the floor. 'How was your first day back at the grindstone?'

'Strangely normal,' said Wilson as he pushed the button signalling the waiter.

'Thanks, I could kill for a pint,' McDevitt said. 'It's been one of those days.'

'I have the feeling that with you every day is one of those days.' The waiter popped his head through the serving hatch and Wilson ordered a pint of Guinness for McDevitt and a refill for himself.

McDevitt picked up his bag and rooted around in it. He pulled out an A4 sheet of paper and put it on the table. 'I'd like to have your professional opinion on this.' He pushed the paper towards Wilson. 'It's not the original. That's back at the office.'

Wilson picked up the paper. It was a sketch of a rough map. Several geographical features were shown and there was a road marked in one corner of the map. Lower down there was either an 'x' or a cross and the name Evans beside it. He put it back on the table. 'Sorry, you'll have to give me more information.'

McDevitt took a slug from his Guinness. 'God, but I needed that.' He picked up the paper. 'As far as I can tell it's a map of Ballynahone bog. But the intriguing fact is the name Evans beside that cross. Ever hear of Alan Evans?'

Wilson shook his head.

'Some sort of Commie politician from the 1980s. A bit before your time, and mine for that matter. He was stirring things up. Going on about sectarian conflict being a cover for the class war. He disappeared on his way back to Belfast from a meeting in Downpatrick. He and his car were never found. This map purports to indicate his final resting place.'

'I think I've had a bellyful of historical crimes. I hope you didn't pay good money for this tosh.'

'My source wanted ten thousand. He settled for a grand.'

'Enough said. It's not like you to fall for a scam like that.'

'If I'm wrong, it'll be the first time my bullshit detector has failed me. So you think it's a hoax?'

'Remember Hitler's diaries?'

McDevitt smiled. Perhaps he had paid a grand for a pig in a poke but true or not it would get him back on the front page of the *Chronicle*.

'You're surely not going to run with this piece of trash?' Wilson said.

McDevitt took several sheets of paper from his bag. 'I spent the afternoon writing up the story. Of course, I've had to give Evans a little more prominence than he deserved but there's a lot of interest in the "disappeared". Mind you if it had "McConville" instead of "Evans" on the map it would be pure gold. But beggars can't be choosers. Most people have no idea who Evans was and what some of his dingbat ideas were. I had to create that picture for them.'

'Who's the source?' Wilson was close to finishing his second pint. It was approaching his cut-off limit.

McDevitt pushed the button and ordered another round. 'I assume you're not driving tonight.'

Wilson shook his head. 'I'm celebrating my return from the dead.'

'Yeah, how the hell did that happen? I was sure they'd hung you out to dry.' There's definitely a story in that. "Top cop returns to post after proving father to be murderer". 'The public would lap that up.'

'I just used up life number five, only four more to go. And the public wouldn't give a shit about my pathetic story. If you haven't worked that out, I'll bet that your editor has.' Wilson finished his Guinness and set his empty glass aside. 'Am I wrong or are you trying to avoid answering my question? Who's the source of this particular hoax?'

The waiter deposited the new drinks and took the empty glasses away.

McDevitt sat up straight in his chair and put a serious look on his elfin face. 'I am a professional journalist and I will never reveal my sources. You can put me in jail and throw away the key but I will never tell. Mind you, I'll cheat and lie to get a story but I'll maintain the only ethical stance that we journalists hold.'

'I thought so. Take my advice and don't run with this story. You're putting yourself out on a limb and someone will see through it.'

'Too late.' McDevitt proposed a toast with his glass of Guinness. 'Jock McDevitt hits the front page tomorrow with a scoop.'

'It's your funeral.' Wilson clinked his glass and drank. McDevitt was opening a box that many in Ulster would like to see closed forever. It was alright to talk about the "disappeared" as long as you were talking about Pinochet's Chile, or Argentina or even the drug wars in Mexico. It was part of Ulster's unsavoury past that paramilitaries, particularly the IRA, executed individuals and disposed of their bodies in a way that they would never be found. This practice only succeeded in refusing closure to the families of the dead. There could be no wake, no funeral and no grave to lay flowers at on the anniversary of death. There would only be uncertainty and longing. Like their co-sufferers in Latin America, the families of the "disappeared" in Ulster jumped on any excuse to remind the population of their suffering. This was the box that McDevitt was opening with his story on the map and Evans's disappearance.

'So,' McDevitt said, 'any news of the luscious Kate McCann?'

Wilson sighed. He had enjoyed the evening thus far but mention of Kate was like rubbing a raw wound with sandpaper. Kate had cut him off completely. He hadn't seen or heard from her since she had declared their break as final.

'Wrong subject,' McDevitt said. 'Not over yet?'

'Over and done with.' Wilson finished his Guinness and pushed the button.

McDevitt frowned. 'Like that, is it? As the man said, nobody ever found the answer to a problem in the bottom of a bottle.'

'Two Finns go into a bar. One points at the beer pump and lift up two fingers. The barman pours two beers and the men start to drink. Ten minutes later one of the men points at two empty glasses and the barman refills them. One of the men picks up his glass and says, "Skol!". 'The second man turns to face him and says, "Did we come here to talk or did we come here to drink"?' 'Enough said.'

CHAPTER TEN

Although Gerry McGreary depended on the people of Belfast as customers for his drugs, prostitution and protection rackets, he had chosen to live in a five bed-roomed mini-mansion in Upper Malone close to Dunmurry Golf Club. The house was reached by a leafy lane and one of his soldiers was placed strategically at the entrance to deter unwelcome visitors. Since he was in a phoney war with the Rice gang, he had added a second man as a precaution. Sammy Rice might no longer have been on the scene but Willie was a vicious old bastard who had very little to lose. And it would take a deaf, dumb and blind man not to work out that the prime suspect for Sammy's disappearance was his main rival. McGreary's advances into Rice territory had been steady and planned. It wasn't so much a turf war as a turf takeover. Nobody had died. Well, nobody had died yet. McGreary was not so naive as to think that there would not be an eventual repercussion to his territorial encroachments. He sat in his favourite chair in his lounge. The walls were festooned with memorabilia from his days as a football idol. There were football jerseys he had worn himself and several that more famous players he had played against had gifted him. Interspersed with the jerseys were photos featuring McGreary and famous footballers. Nobody who looked at the three hundred and twenty pound man sitting in the voluminous chair would believe that Gerry McGreary once had an incarnation as 'Slim Ger' McGreary.

'I don't like it,' said McGreary as he picked up his five ounce Waterford Glass tumbler and took a taste of his Bushmills twenty-one-year-old Madeira finish whiskey. McGreary was born in the backstreets behind the Shankill but he'd taken to the good life as a duck takes to water. 'Simpson is a loose end. He knows we're the ones that got rid of Sammy and now he's been seen talking with that little rat, McDevitt. I definitely do not like it.'

Davie Best sat in a chair directly facing his chief. The two men were physical opposites. Best was one hundred and eighty pounds of well-honed muscle. The muscles on his forearms stood out making his tattoos from his British Army days more prominent. 'Simpson's not a problem as long as we have the Beretta that put the slug into Sammy's head with his fingerprints all over it. We hand that gun over to the Peelers and friend Simpson is toast.'

McGreary savoured another sip of the golden liquid. 'McDevitt's a dangerous wee bastard. He's worse than a crab for gettin' under rocks. If he gets a whiff of who put Sammy away, he'll ferret out the rest of the story. And don't forget, Wilson is back in the equation. He's not just going to drop lookin' for Sammy.'

'I thought we were rid of that bastard. I'm surprised that someone hasn't put a bullet into him before now.'

McGreary held up his glass and swilled the contents. 'Maybe we were hasty in making Sammy disappear. We could have just shot the bugger and had him found down a lane in South Armagh.'

'The idea of dumping him was to make sure that the Peelers didn't come after us; no body no crime.'

'I don't like loose ends,' McGreary said more to himself than Best.

'You want me to get rid of Simpson?'

McGreary looked at Best. He used to think that the hard men from the Seventies and Eighties were the toughest he'd encountered but Best and the new recruits he'd brought along were something else. The majority of them had seen action with the British Army in Iraq and Afghanistan. They were a well-trained and murderous bunch of bastards. McGreary wouldn't like to admit it but they scared the shit out of him. 'You still think he might be useful as a patsy if the Sammy thing blows up?'

'We get the gun to the Peelers and he's the one in the frame for killing Sammy. He'll try to drag us into it but we've developed alibis for both Ray and me that'll be impossible to break. But a wink is as good as a nod to men like Wilson. We have two choices; we let the whole Sammy Rice thing die down or we get rid of Simpson.'

McGreary thought for a second. 'And if Simpson were to be found dead with the gun in his possession, there would be no way he could implicate us. Set something up in case we need it. The man's life is a train wreck; I've heard tell that he's depressed. Maybe he might commit suicide.'

Best smiled. 'Leave the arrangements to me. I'll handle it.'

'And what are we going to do about auld Willie?'

'Death by a thousand cuts,' Best said. 'We're taking him down brick by brick. His revenue is cut by forty per cent and we're pushing further into Rice territory every day.'

'There's goin' to be a reaction.'

'Then we'll get the guns out. Why don't you try to talk to Willie? He doesn't have the capacity to fight a war.'

McGreary smiled. Best had never seen a turf war in Belfast. As soon as the Good Friday Peace Agreement was signed, the paramilitaries were wondering what to do with themselves and all the firepower they had collected. The easy answer was to have a good old Irish turf war. Bodies littered Belfast for a few weeks until everyone came to their senses. 'I'll think on it.'

CHAPTER ELEVEN

W ilson picked up a copy of the *Chronicle* on his way to the station and saw that McDevitt was as good as his word. The front page was dominated by the map showing the burial place of Alan Evans, small time politician but more importantly one of the "disappeared". If the information proved valid, it would give hope to the families of other "disappeared" that someday their family members might be located. If the information proved valid. But that was a big 'if'. McDevitt was a newshound. He was the kind of journalist who lived and breathed the front page. And the *Chronicle* wasn't exactly the *Boston Globe*. So, he doubted that the process of checking out a Jock McDevitt story bore any similarity to that described in the film *Spotlight* that he'd seen during his 'holiday'. McDevitt could look forward to a few more days of front page coverage before something more newsworthy replaced his Evans's pieces. Wilson was more tired than usual. He had been burning the midnight oil bringing himself up to date on the investigation into the deaths of Grant, Malone and O'Reilly. Big George Carroll, the driver of the car for the first two killings and the man who had thrown O'Reilly out a window to his death, had been co-operating and the murders

were in effect solved to the extent that the murderers were
known. Getting his hands on Baxter and Weir for the murders
of Grant and Malone, and Sammy Rice for the murder of
O'Reilly was proving difficult. Baxter and Weir had fled Scotland for God knew where, while there was no sign of Sammy
either locally or at his villa in Spain. He would have to wait
until the men he sought raised their heads above the parapet
before he could sign off on the killings. He could use the down-
time to try to put some sense on his living arrangements. The
apartment in Queen's Quay was supposed to be a stopgap but
it was taking on an air of permanence. In a way he was happy
to continue as he was. There was a level of comfort having the
number of a landlord to call when something went wrong. He
wasn't, nor had he ever been, good at DIY. In effect, he had
been downright bad at it. He had just signed a lease for a year
and that meant that he could put a decision on whether he
needed to own his living accommodation on the long finger.
The Queen's Quay apartment had a second bedroom which
could be used by his mother and his stepfather should they
decide to visit Belfast. He was settling down in his office
steeling himself before opening his emails when his phone
rang.

'Good morning, Superintendent Wilson.'

He was not yet used to the voice of his new boss so he
didn't reply immediately.

'Superintendent Wilson.'

'Good morning, ma'am,' Wilson said. 'It's totally appropriate for you to call me Ian while I'm aware that it would be
totally inappropriate for me to call you Yvonne.'

'Ten minutes in reception, Ian. Our presence is requested
at a meeting in Castlereagh.' The phone went dead.

But she had called him 'Ian'. They were advancing. Maybe
it would turn out alright.

Half an hour later Wilson and Davis sat in a meeting
room in PSNI HQ in Castlereagh. The other participants

had not yet shown up and Davis did not know the reason they had been summoned. A uniformed female police officer served them coffee and biscuits. After ten minutes, Chief Constable Baird, his personal assistant and one of the newly promoted Assistant Chief Constables entered the room. Baird sat at the head of the table. They sat facing Davis and Wilson.

'Assistant Chief Constable Nicholson,' Baird said introducing the senior member of his entourage. 'Meet Chief Superintendent Davis and Detective Superintendent Wilson.' There was a general nodding contest between Wilson, Davis and Nicholson.

Wilson examined the new ACC. Nicholson was three inches over six feet and was rapier thin. His white shirt hung on his thin shoulders. His hair was fair and lank and his face had the pallor associated with alabaster. Wilson was reminded of Shakespeare's warning – *Yon Cassius has a lean and hungry look, such men are dangerous*. He decided that in this case Shakespeare had probably got it right.

'I have a busy schedule this morning and this meeting is an addition. We have how long?' Baird looked at his PA.

'Five minutes,' the PA said.

'You've seen the *Chronicle*?' Baird asked.

Wilson nodded but Davis shook her head. The PA removed a photocopy of the front-page from a file and pushed it across the table.

'What do you think?' Baird asked looking at Wilson.

Wilson hesitated deferring to his superior.

'Go ahead,' Davis said.

'It's a fantasy,' Wilson said. 'McDevitt is a sensationalist. He's been off the front page since the Cummerford trial ended, and that's not his style.'

'So you think that there's no basis to his story?' Baird asked.

'If there is, it's accidental. Nobody has even heard of

Evans. Why should someone have "disappeared" him? I'll check the missing persons file from the time.'

Baird looked at his PA.

'It's on your computer,' the PA said to Wilson.

Baird turned to Wilson and Davis. 'I want an assessment on this story before close of play this evening. The Minister was on the phone to me first thing this morning. He wants to know when we're going to start digging. Do either of you know what searching for this body could do to our budget?'

Welcome to the big time, Wilson thought. Baird might be learning that it's not so much fun being the top dog. 'No, sir,' said Wilson facetiously.

Baird raised his eyebrows and then smiled. He stood up. Nicholson and the PA joined him. 'An assessment by this evening, report to ACC Nicholson.' Without another word, the three left the boardroom.

'What the hell was that?' Davis said still reading the article.

'That was pressure from the Minister on our new Chief Constable.' Wilson picked up his coffee and sipped it. 'Nice coffee.'

'To hell with the coffee, how are we going to check out this story by this evening?'

Wilson took another sip. 'The difficult we do immediately, the impossible takes a little longer.'

'I hadn't marked you down as a comedian.'

Wilson continued to drink his coffee. 'It's the motto of the US Army Engineers. Now the new motto of the PSNI.'

Davis pushed her untouched coffee away. 'Finish up your damn coffee, it'll be my bum in the wringer if we don't report to Nicholson. What are you going to do?'

'I suppose I should start by having a chat with McDevitt.' He decided not to impart the information that he was friendly with McDevitt and that he had foreknowledge of the front-page story. He finished his coffee and stood up.

Davis folded the copy of the *Chronicle* story. 'I barely have my feet under the desk and I'm about to be landed with a major problem that involves the Chief Constable and the Minister for good measure. Jennings could be right about you. You're attracted to trouble like flies are attracted to ...'

Wilson cleared his throat. 'Ma'am, please remember that you're a lady.'

CHAPTER TWELVE

Since it was too early in the day to countenance a visit to the Crown, Wilson and McDevitt snared a table by the window of Clement's Café. It was the same table where McDevitt and Simpson had concluded their deal on the map and Carlisle's notebooks. But McDevitt had no intention of telling Wilson that little bit of history.

'I knew it.' McDevitt had a wide smile on his face. 'I knew the story would put them into a flap.'

Wilson thought that McDevitt did really look like an evil pixie when he smiled like that. 'You are incorrigible. I thought you might be winding me up last night. You should have checked the story out before you went to press.'

'Did Woodward and Bernstein check out Deep Throat's information on Watergate? My source is totally reliable.'

'I have a strange feeling that most professional journalists spend eighty per cent of their time checking stories out and twenty per cent writing them up. With you the percentages are probably reversed. I need to know who your source is.'

McDevitt put his right palm over his heart. 'Put me in jail, give me the rubber hose treatment, do with me what you will. I'll never give up my source.' He removed his hand and picked up his cup of coffee. 'Anyway the bugger would be absolutely no good to you. He can't even spell the word provenance.'

Wilson explained the situation with the Chief Constable. 'I have to make an assessment by close of play this evening. If I say your story is a heap of rubbish, there'll be an outcry that we could have returned one of the "disappeared" to their family. If I say that your story smacks of the truth, the Chief Constable will blow his budget. If I get it wrong and the budget is blown for nothing, I'll have to start looking for a new job. Do you really want to do that to me?'

'Are you willing to take my word for it?' McDevitt asked.

'I'd prefer something a little more concrete in terms of corroboration. But go ahead.'

'There's a lot I can't tell you because it would expose my source. I'm convinced that the map is genuine. I have no idea who murdered Evans or why but I think if you dig up the part of Ballynahone bog that's shown on the map, you'll probably find the body of Alan Evans.'

'You can't provide me with any corroboration that I can present to the Chief?'

McDevitt shook his head. 'Today the story is that Evans's body is in Ballynahone bog. Tomorrow's story is that the PSNI has decided or not decided to dig the body up.'

Wilson picked up his coffee and sipped. It was only marginally better than the coffee in Castlereagh. McDevitt wasn't helping him. The business about the source was pure bullshit. McDevitt wasn't giving him up because he had some further use for him. That meant that the source was someone who was 'connected' or who had been 'connected'. In six hours, Wilson would have to report to Nicholson and there was only one more person he could turn to for an opinion on McDevitt's story.

'Ian, I am genuinely sorry that I can't give up my source.'

'I know.' Wilson drained his coffee and stood up.

McDevitt watched the big man leave the café. He might

have been wrong but it seemed like Wilson's shoulders were a little more hunched than usual. The past few months had been tough on the PSNI man. The fact that his relationship with Kate McCann was history was bad enough but he had been obliged to prove that the father he idolised was involved in the murder of two young men in the 1970s. Those two setbacks alone would lead most men to look like they had the troubles of the world on their shoulders. On the positive side, the PSNI might soon be digging up Ballynahone bog that would give him lots of column inches and further endear him to the editor of the *Chronicle*.

CHAPTER THIRTEEN

W illie Rice wasn't big on either reading, listening or watching the news. He learned everything he needed to know from the people he met in the course of his daily rounds. That meant most of the patrons of the Brown Bear public house in the Shankill Road. His day was taken up by trying to maintain control of the territory his son, Sammy, had carved out in the new peaceful Belfast. The family business had moved seamlessly from managing a paramilitary force to managing a criminal enterprise encompassing drugs, prostitution and protection rackets. The Rice enterprise was worth millions of pounds annually, most of which Sammy had secreted overseas. Therein lay the major problem. Sammy was such a secretive bastard that he alone knew where the money was. But Sammy was gone and it didn't look like he was coming back. That meant that the accounts in Switzerland and Lichtenstein, or wherever the hell they were, were untouchable. Willie cursed when he thought of the money they had built up ending up in dormant accounts that would eventually be divided among the partners of some private bank. Their enterprise was still churning out money but in nothing like the volumes as when Sammy was in charge. Willie was seventy and he knew that he was not capable of maintaining his hold on their territory indefinitely. Maybe twenty or thirty years ago he would have been able to put up a decent fight against the incursions of McGreary. Drugs were the main source of the Rice revenues and drugs were a young man's business. Also the toerags involved in the drugs business were nasty bastards. McGreary wasn't the only threat to the Rice family. The vacuum left by Sammy's disappearance was being filled from both ends of the crime spectrum. Experienced operators like McGreary were at one end and new entrants to the drug business and prostitution were at the other. Willie Rice was being squeezed in the middle. And like a rat trapped in a corner, Rice knew only one reaction, and he was prepared to spill blood to reduce the pressure. He generally liked to walk from his home in Malvern Street to his 'office' in the rear of the Brown Bear. Given the phoney war situation that he found himself in, he was always accompanied by one of the younger members of his gang. His stroll along the Shankill Road involved passing several newspaper shops that he usually ignored. Today, he was stopped in his tracks by a hoarding advertising the *Chronicle*. The white poster screamed in large black letters '**Chronicle Reveals Burial Place of Disappeared Politician Evans**.' Rice stood transfixed in front of the placard for several minutes before entering the shop and buying a copy of the paper. He folded it carefully and deposited it in his pocket. Alan Evans. He tried to remember what the man had looked like but the image was unclear. Rice had, in his time, murdered many times. He didn't dwell on what he had done. The faces of the dead didn't interfere with his sleep. Many had died in reprisal for IRA attacks on Protestants. They had been nameless and faceless as far as he was concerned. Poor sods who had been in the wrong place at the wrong time. Others had been suspected IRA men. They'd been lifted and interrogated, then tortured and dispatched. They got everything they deserved. They had signed on as soldiers and their deaths had been part of the package. There had been very few like Evans. Willie Rice had been one of the elite hit men operating in Belfast in the Seventies and Eighties. He wasn't a 'Mad Dog' or a 'King Rat'; he didn't have a nickname, had never appeared in the newspapers and was known for his trade only by those who needed his services. Out and out assassinations were a rarity. So the Evans's murder was fairly unique. The order had come from someone higher up the food chain, and it had been accompanied by five grand in cash. In 1984 that was real money. Rice didn't know why Evans had to end up buried in the bog, and he didn't need to know. His involvement in politics was based on a simple premise -- the Taigs were trying to take over his country and if he had to kill every last one of the bastards to stop them then that was what he was prepared to do. As soon as he arrived at the Brown Bear, he made his way to the table at the rear that acted as his office. He ordered a pot of tea and removed the paper from his pocket and laid it out on the table. It took him a few seconds to recognise the copy of the rough map he had drawn after he put Evans in the boghole. He quickly scanned through the article. It was mainly about Evans's career and his disappearance on his way home from a rally in Downpatrick. Rice didn't appear anywhere in the story. And there was no reason why he should. It had been a clean kill and the burial went according to plan. But somehow the map he'd drawn had found its way into the newspaper. What class of asshole keeps something like that? Could that small piece of paper link him to the murder and disappearance? He doubted it. It was his handwriting but it was his handwriting from more than thirty years ago. He dumped the paper on an empty chair as soon as his tea arrived. He had more pressing problems. If Wilson didn't come up with something on Sammy's disappearance soon, the phoney war was going to be turned into a real war. Rice had nothing to lose. He poured himself a cup of tea. He always fancied going out with a bang. And he wouldn't be going out alone.

CHAPTER FOURTEEN

Before his meeting with McDevitt, Wilson had done some basic research on Alan Evans. His concentration was on whether Evans had been married and if so, what had happened to Mrs Evans? Harry Graham was a damn sight better on the computer than him so he had left Graham slaving over a hot computer while he had left for his meeting with McDevitt. The fact that he drew a blank with McDevitt made the location of the former Mrs Evans all the more important. As soon as Wilson left Clement's Café, his phone pinged indicating the arrival of a new message. He opened it and saw that Graham had been successful. The message was a name, an address and a telephone number. He stood on Donegall Square watching the people of Belfast going about their business while he punched in the number on Graham's message. The phone was picked up quickly and answered by a lady with a very correct accent.

'Mrs Karin Faulkner?' Wilson asked.

'Yes, who is this?'

'My name is Detective Superintendent Wilson. I was wondering whether you might have some time this morning to meet me.'

'Is this about the article in the *Chronicle* this morning?' she asked.

'Yes,' Wilson said.

'I don't think I can be of much help, superintendent. It was such a long time ago. It's like another lifetime.'

'I understand. But I would appreciate a meeting nonetheless.'

'Can you be here within the hour?'

Wilson looked at the address. 'Absolutely.'

Wilson returned to the station, picked up his car and headed for the Westlink. He felt a sense of loneliness as he drove east along the A20. It was one of those occasions when he wished that his former detective sergeant hadn't decided to abandon him for a new life in the US. He hated admitting it but he was missing her. After a twenty-minute drive, he turned into Castlehill Road and drove on to Castlehill Park before arriving at the Faulkner address in Stormont Wood. This part of Belfast was light years away from the narrow Victorian streets of the inner city. He drove into the driveway of the address that Graham had provided and surveyed the Faulkner residence. Karin Faulkner had certainly done well for herself. The house was an imposing pile. It consisted of two wings connected by a central area containing the front door. The ground floor of each side of the house had a large picture window that looked out on the well-tended lawn and mature garden. He parked by the front door.

The door was opened as Wilson was exiting from the car and an elegantly dressed lady with well-coiffed hair stood in the opening.

'Mrs Faulkner,' Wilson said covering the distance from the car to the door in several strides.

'Superintendent Wilson, may I have some identification please?'

'Of course.' Wilson took out his warrant card and handed it to her.

She examined the card before returning it and then stood aside to allow Wilson in. 'I was anticipating a visit from some journalist or other.' She led Wilson into a living room to the left of the large hall. 'Can I offer you some tea?'

'No, thank you.'

The room was decorated in the classical manner with a well-upholstered suite of a three-seater, two-seater and two club chairs. There were two coffee tables and several other pieces of classical Regency style furniture.

'Please, superintendent, sit.' She sat on one of the club chairs and straightened her skirt.

Wilson guessed that his hostess was in her sixties, her dark hair had turned grey at the sides and she made no attempt to hide it. Her face was open and slightly cherubic and her lightly tanned skin was smooth like that of a much younger woman. She wore an expensive sweater over a silk blouse. The Faulkners were not short of money. 'I'm sorry for imposing on you but I'm sure you realise that the article in the *Chronicle* this morning has caused some consternation in PSNI HQ. Your former husband is numbered among the "disappeared" and any information that might lead to the discovery of his body must be treated as a matter of urgency. I've been tasked with assessing whether the information in the paper is accurate.'

Karin Faulkner smiled. It was the smile of a sweet old lady. 'I understand your desire to speak with me but as I said on the phone Alan's disappearance seems a lifetime ago. It has a dreamlike quality for me. I'm sure there's a file somewhere with the interviews I gave at the time.'

'Why would someone murder your former husband and hide his body?'

'I have no idea. Alan had some fairly controversial views and he was beginning to be listened to in some quarters but he was on the far left of the political spectrum. The politics of the province at the time were sectarian and Alan was more concerned with social justice. I can't imagine that anyone felt threatened by him. He was beginning to develop a bit of an ego about himself but aside from that nothing.'

'I don't like to ask but might he have been involved with dangerous people on either side?'

She laughed. 'Alan would have run a mile at the first sign of violence. He was more anti-establishment than anything else.'

'I suppose there was no question of another woman?'

She reddened. 'Like I said, Alan was beginning to get an ego. He was speaking to bigger crowds and I'm sure that there might have been possibilities for him to wander. But I wasn't aware of anything in that direction.'

Wilson was disappointed at the dearth of new information that was forthcoming. 'Do you think that your former husband might have run away? Might he have wanted to get away from Ulster?'

She shook her head. 'Not a chance, his ego had clicked in. He was beginning to see himself as some kind of Messiah.'

Wilson stood. 'You've been very helpful.'

'What do you think, superintendent?'

'Thirty years is a long time. I think it's as likely that he's in a boghole in Ballynahone as that he is living in a shack in Bora Bora.'

She stared directly into his eyes. 'I'd prefer if you didn't dig him up. I've left that life behind and I don't want it brought up again.'

Wilson stood up. 'I appreciate you meeting me. I'll keep you informed if you like.'

She continued staring into his face. 'No, I'd prefer to forget that part of my life. I was left alone and destitute, a young woman whose husband had vanished off the face of the earth. You have no idea the thoughts that ran through my brain. It took an effort to pull myself up from the floor and get on with my life.'

'I can understand your reluctance to relive a horrible time for you.'

They walked to the front door together.

'Leave him where he is, please,' she said.

'It won't be my call.' Wilson walked out on to the tarmac drive and looked at the perfectly manicured lawn and the beautifully maintained garden. He could understand Karin Faulkner's desire to leave Alan Evans at rest wherever he was. And he supposed that she wasn't the only one feeling like that this morning. If Alan Evans was in a boghole, someone had put him there. If that someone were still alive, they would be wondering whether their crime was going to come to light. Digging up Ballynahone bog wouldn't be his call alone but if he advised against it then maybe Evans would be left where he was. On the other hand, every man should have his resting place recognised. He still had half a day before he had to report to Nicholson. He took out his mobile phone and called Graham. 'Did Evans have any brothers or sisters?'

'One brother, Robert Evans.' There was a slight pause while Graham consulted his notes. 'He works in a garage on the Ravenhill Road.' Graham gave him the address.

Wilson closed the phone. The address that Graham had given him was fifteen minutes away via the Newtonards Road. What did he have to lose?

CHAPTER FIFTEEN

The article on the front page of the *Chronicle* had included a photo of Alan Evans, and the man who sat behind the desk at the garage reception had such a strong resemblance to the photo that Wilson immediately assumed that he was Robert Evans. He took out his warrant card as he approached the desk.

'Robert Evans?' he asked as he stood before the man on reception.

'Who's asking?'

'Detective Superintendent Ian Wilson.' He held the warrant card up so that the man could read it.

'So bloody predictable, yes, I'm Robert Evans and I was wondering when someone from your lot would be around.'

Evans was probably in his late fifties, which would make him the younger brother. He was well built and his hair was cut so short that he appeared to be bald. A pair of spectacles was pushed up on the top of his head. His face was blotchy with red patches and Wilson assumed that he was a drinker. He was wearing a blue mechanic's overall.

'You've seen the story in the *Chronicle*?' Wilson asked.

'Who hasn't? All the lads have been at me this morning about it.'

'Is there somewhere we can talk in private?'

'The only place private here is the men's toilet and for obvious reasons I don't think we should go there together. At least this time they sent one of the head boys.'

'Meaning?'

'When Alan disappeared, the lad they sent around to interview us was a wet-behind-the-ears copper. Now that he's been missing for over thirty years, they send a detective super-intendent no less. Looks like they're taking things more seriously this time It's a bit late, eh!'

'You used the word "missing". You don't believe that your brother is dead.'

'It was part of the family mantra. Alan wasn't dead; he'd turn up any day now. God, but we were naïve.'

'So you think he is dead?'

'Of course I think he's bloody dead. We seen or heard neither hide nor hair of him since the day he disappeared.'

'And what do you think happened to him?'

'Who the hell knows! They were killing people for no reason at all around then. Every day you picked up the paper there was some fella or girl's picture on the front page. We were living in the Wild West.'

'You think he was a random killing? If so, why did the murderers hide his body? Why not dump him in a lane some-where he could be found?'

'Search me. All I can tell you is that his disappearance hastened the death of our parents. Why couldn't the bastards who killed him have given us the body to bury? It was the not knowing that preyed on our minds. Sick fuckers, the lot of them.'

'Why pick on your brother?'

'He was an uppity bugger, always talking about how

Russia was great and how we needed to set up a workers' republic for the whole island of Ireland.'

'That must have pissed some people off.'

'Are you kiddin'? Nobody took him seriously. Russian soldiers on the Foyle to protect the working people of Derry? He was my brother but I'd be the first to admit that he was off beam.'

'Do you think he might be in Ballynahone bog?'

Evans shrugged his shoulders. 'I have no idea where he is, but it's as good a guess as any. If he is there, I want him back so I can bury him properly.'

'I just spoke to his former wife. She'd prefer it if we left well enough alone.'

'Aye, she would. Made a pretty good life for herself has our Karin. She doesn't want anything to upset the well-stocked apple cart. Her and her new husband started the process of declaring Alan legally dead a few months after he disappeared. They demanded a coroner's inquest so that they could have an official death certificate. Karin said it would bring the family closure. Bullshit. She was in a hurry to get hitched. In the heel of the hunt, she divorced Alan. It was a much simpler procedure and it provided her with the closure she was looking for. Anyway, I never thought that Karin bought into Alan's Communist crap. They met at college before the real world hit them. '

So much for the prim and proper Karin Faulkner, Wilson thought. 'What does Mr Faulkner do?'

'He was an accountant. I think he now runs some kind of investment fund. I have no idea what that is but he seems to make lots of money from it. Have you seen the house in Stormont Wood?'

Wilson nodded.

'Then you know what I mean.'

'So, you think that your former sister-in-law and Faulkner were involved before your brother's death'

'It wouldn't surprise me.'

'Would Faulkner be involved in your brother's death?'

'What's this you people say, it would only be speculation. You didn't meet Faulkner?'

Wilson shook his head. Maybe that had been a mistake.

'He's a sad wee prick,' Evans said. 'I don't think he has the balls for murder himself but he might have found someone who was up for it.'

A crime of passion was a tempting hypothesis, but Wilson felt that if he accepted it, he would be grasping at straws. He was beginning to come to the conclusion that if there was even a possibility of finding Evans's body they should take it. 'Thanks for your time.' He extended his hand to Evans.

'What are you going to do?' Evans asked taking Wilson's hand and shaking it.

'Not my call, people beyond my pay grade will make the final decision.' Wilson removed a business card from his pocket and put it on the counter. 'Call me if you think of anything that might be useful.'

Evans picked up the card and put it in the top pocket of his overall. 'Alan needs justice.'

'He's not alone.'

CHAPTER SIXTEEN

R obert Faulkner spent the afternoon ensconced in his office. After instructing his secretary to hold all his phone calls and cancel his appointments, he closed his office door and took his place behind his desk. This was the day that he prayed would never come. When he opened the *Chronicle* on his arrival at the office, he felt an instant lump form in his throat as his eyes fell on the front-page headline. It was the first time in more than thirty years that the name Alan Evans had appeared in print. He read the article and realised that somehow a map showing Evans's resting place had come to light. How could such a thing happen? He had immediately called his wife and given her the news. As usual, Karin was not fazed. He often wondered what it would take to put her in a blue funk like the one he was experiencing. Her response was very much as expected, they had done nothing and they had nothing to fear. They were beneficiaries of his death but they neither planned it nor executed it. Her words did a lot to calm him and he could feel his heart rate drop as she made a rational analysis of the news. She was quite a woman. By the time he put the phone down, he had dismissed the *Chronicle* report and was ready for the purpose of the day – making money. His calm had lasted until almost lunchtime when Karin called to tell him that she had been visited by a detective superintendent looking into the report. The name of the superintendent had struck a bell with him and after putting down the phone; he went immediately to his computer and put the name into the search engine. If his heart rate had increased at the appearance of the report in the *Chronicle*, it had almost forced its way out of his chest. Ian Wilson wasn't any old PSNI detective. He was the head of the murder squad and was possibly the most famous detective in Ulster. As soon as Faulkner finished reading, he ran for the toilet and vomited the contents of his stomach into the bowl. It was all so long ago. His wife was right. They had done nothing wrong. But he had a good idea who was responsible and as long as Alan Evans stayed disappeared that knowledge wasn't dangerous. Now everything was changed. The PSNI would dig up the body. There would be a new investigation and God only knew what might come to light. He tried to calm himself. Over the past thirty years, he had made a bucketful of money and gained a lot of influential friends. Whatever came his way, he had the resources to stand against it. He thought about calling Lattimer but decided against it.

Sir Philip Lattimer had just finished a very agreeable lunch at Coleville House, the family pile on the north Antrim coast. It was a beautiful day and he contemplated a post-prandial walk with his two Weimaraners. That was as soon as he packed off his lunch guests back to Belfast. It had not only been a fine meal, it had also been productive. His developer colleague had managed to convince the two bankers present to finance their new venture. Lattimer was thus not only physically sated but was happy in the knowledge that the lunch would contribute substantially to his bank account. He was enjoying a post-lunch brandy when his wife entered the dining room and whispered in his ear. He sighed and stood up. 'Forgive me, gentlemen; I have an important phone call in the study. It shouldn't take too long.' He shuffled off in the direction of the study. He pressed the speaker button on the phone and sat in a chair. 'Yes,' he said, the sharpness in his voice indicating his displeasure at the call.

'Have you seen this morning's *Chronicle*?' The tension in Robert Faulkner's voice was palpable.

'Yes.'

There was silence for a moment.

'What are we going to do?' Faulkner finally broke the silence.

Lattimer rubbed his substantial chin. He was hyper about security and was aware that no phone conversation was secure. 'Your investment is safe,' he said finally. 'I suggest there is no need for disquiet at the moment.' He hoped that if Faulkner had even a modicum of intelligence he would be able to decipher the message.

'Are you quite sure about that?'

'Please don't worry old chap. Everything is under control. The most important thing now is that nobody should panic. All eventualities have been covered. Now be a good man and stop worrying. I'd prefer if you didn't call me again on this matter.'

'Sorry,' Faulkner spluttered on the other end of the line.

Lattimer pushed the button cutting off the call. He didn't rise immediately from his chair. He was more than a little annoyed at Faulkner's call. It dispelled the good mood that the meal and the possibility of a capital injection had created. He had put the article in the *Chronicle* out of his mind. He could not understand how a stupid piece of paper could have come to light. There were enough thirty year-old crimes in Ulster to keep the PSNI busy for a generation. So what if they dug up Evans? Every shred of evidence would have long ago disappeared. He pushed himself up from his chair. Faulkner might be a weak link. He remembered the wife had been made of sterner stuff. Poor old Robert Faulkner, he overestimated his importance in the decision to remove Evans from the scene. There were far more pressing reasons for the elimination of Alan Evans than the satisfaction of Faulkner's lust for his wife. It was time to get back to his guests. His developer colleague might drown the bankers with his enthusiasm. It was his experience that it took subtlety to separate bankers from their money, and he had subtlety in abundance. Who cared if they managed to dig up Alan Evans? That trail was colder than the grave he was lying in.

CHAPTER SEVENTEEN

W ilson downloaded the file relating to the disappearance of Alan Evans and printed it off. There was only so much time he could spend looking at a computer screen. He opted for having lunch at his desk. In an attempt at a healthy lifestyle he had chosen a tuna sandwich on brown bread and a cup of mint tea. The sandwich turned out to be a soggy mess and most of it found its way into his wastebasket. But he enjoyed the freshness of the tea and it beat the hell out of the station cafeteria coffee. The initial investigation into the Evans's disappearance was the usual 1980s sloppy RUC job. There were reports of interviews with his wife, his parents and his siblings. The SIO was a detective sergeant who was obviously hard-pressed to move on to something more concrete. The facts were clear enough. Evans had been holding a public meeting in a hall in Downpatrick. The meeting had finished at nine thirty but Evans hadn't left until ten thirty. He had stated a clear intention to drive directly back to Belfast. According to his wife, he never made it. Therefore, it was safe to assume that sometime between ten thirty and eleven thirty, Evans and his car disappeared into thin air. As Wilson read the reports of the interviews, he could imagine the desperation of the SIO to find a rational explanation for the disappearance of man and machine. Reading the documentation of the investigation, he could feel the momentum draining as nobody was located and no witness had been found who could indicate what might have happened on the short trip from Downpatrick to Belfast. Eventually, the investigation just fizzled out as the SIO had less and less time to spend on it. In the end Alan Evans became just another statistic, one of the three thousand unsolved murders in Northern Ireland. That was if it really was a murder. There was not a shred of evidence to prove that Evans had, in fact, been murdered. It was three-thirty when he finished reading the file and he felt that he was no further forward than when he started. A meeting was scheduled with the chief super at four o'clock so that they could discuss their joint approach on the advice to ACC Nicholson. He had thirty minutes in which to review the interviews with Karin Falkner and Robert Evans and the content of the file before coming to a conclusion that could cost the PSNI valuable budget. Faulkner wanted the matter forgotten while Evans wanted closure. Which side would he come down on? If Evans was dead why not leave him where he was? Did it really matter whether he was resting in a bog or in a cemetery? But why had someone bothered to hide the body? He could have been left for the early morning milkman to find, like so many others. That was the real mystery. And Wilson was attracted by mysteries. There was a knock on his glass door and he looked up before waving Harry Graham inside.

'News, boss,' Graham said. 'I spent the morning at the property register and you were right. Sammy owned a warehouse in East Belfast.' Graham put a copy of a property registration document on Wilson's desk.

Wilson picked it up and looked at the address. It was in an industrial estate not far from his apartment in Queen's Quay.

'Where is this place in relation to where the two idiots say they found the car?'

'It was more or less next door.'

'Nine o'clock tomorrow morning, make sure we have someone on site that can gain us entry. I'm upstairs now and then the Chief Super and I are at HQ. Whatever's in the warehouse will still be there tomorrow.'

'OK, boss. I'll make the arrangements. You think Sammy's inside?'

'That's what we're about to find out.'

CHAPTER EIGHTEEN

On the way upstairs to the chief super's office, Wilson was still juggling with what side of the fence he was going to fall on. He knocked on the office door and entered.

'Don't tell me it's four o'clock already,' Davis said looking up from a pile of papers on her desk.

Wilson sat facing her. It would be his nightmare scenario to one day sit in Davis' chair. Even the rise to superintendent bothered him. He had set his goal at arriving at chief inspector and would have been happy to stay at that grade. There was administration at that level but it was manageable. He was about to refuse the promotion to superintendent but accepted only when he was told that he would be remaining in his old job.

Davis moved the papers aside. 'I'm swamped.' She leaned forward on her arms and let her head drop.

Wilson smiled. 'It's early days. I'm sure you'll get the hang of it.'

'Right now I don't really want to get the hang of it. I don't have time to take a pee. Please tell me that you're going to reduce my administrative burden not add to it.'

Wilson shook his head. He had just this minute decided what side of the fence he had decided to come down on.

Davis put on a sad face. 'Tell me.'

Wilson started by going through the interviews he held earlier in the day and finished with his review of the RUC file of the investigation. 'McDevitt thinks that the map is genuine. By accident, we probably have stumbled onto evidence of the final resting place of Alan Evans. The question is what are we going to do about it? Walking away gives the impression that we don't really care what murderers do with the bodies of their victims. That PSNI is not the one that I want to work for. We're here for the victims and whether Evans is in a hole in Ballynahone bog or not, we owe him the effort of finding out.'

'Wrong answer,' Davis said. 'I've already had Nicholson on the phone attempting to steer us towards refuting McDevitt's information.'

'And saving the PSNI the cost of recovering the body.'

'If there is a body. And if there isn't a body, we're left with egg on our face. And I've screwed up the first major decision I've made as a chief super. I can see that working with you is going to be a challenge. No chance you could change your mind?'

Wilson shook his head. 'It's the right thing to do.'

Davis stood up. 'Let's get this over with, Nicholson's waiting for us.'

Assistant Chief Constable Nicholson sat back in his chair and made a steeple of his hands. There was a feeling at PSNI HQ that bereft of Donald Spence's support Superintendent Wilson would be easier to manage. Yvonne Davis was chosen because she had a reputation as a ball breaker and there was general agreement in Castlereagh that Wilson badly needed his balls broken. However, the discussion that had just taken place in his office convinced Nicholson that Davis had, like her predecessor, fallen for Wilson's brand of charm. The man undoubtedly had charisma and even the new chief constable wasn't immune to it. Nicholson, on the other hand, had been an acolyte of Deputy Chief Constable Jennings and had tied himself to that star. His mentor was currently doing penance with the Cumbria Police Force but would be rejoining the PSNI in the near future. In the meantime, it was up to Nicholson to jump on Wilson every time he erred. Wilson's support for an effort to find Alan Evans's body might provide a chance to change the Chief Constable's view. He had spent the day doing a preliminary costing of the project. It involved a preliminary survey using sophisticated ground-penetrating radar, followed by a costly programme removing tons of bog leading to a further programme of body clearing and removal. He looked at Davis concentrating his gaze on her. 'You realise we are putting the credibility of the PSNI at stake here. We are assuming that the *Chronicle's* claim is valid. You are prepared for the fallout if Superintendent Wilson is wrong.'

'Yes, sir.' Yvonne Davis was a thirty-year veteran of the police force. She had dragged herself up from the beat and into the management while being sexually harassed and denigrated by her fellow male officers. It was obvious to her that nothing would please Nicholson more than her falling on her face. There had been lots of Nicholsons on her way up the greasy pole of career advancement in the RUC and then the PSNI. The man sitting beside her was nothing like Nicholson. He could be just as deadly in finishing her career but at least he would do while he was doing his job.

'OK.' Nicholson smiled exposing two rows of small white teeth. 'We have limited experience in this type of operation. However, our friends in the Garda Siochana have considerable experience of unearthing bodies in bogs. I'll discuss your find-ings with the chief constable and make the necessary contacts with Dublin if he decides to go ahead.'

'I suppose that you will oversee the operation,' Davis said.

'Oh no, Chief Superintendent.' The smile faded from Nicholson's face. 'I am going to leave that pleasant task to you and Superintendent Wilson. It's on his advice that we will proceed so I think that it's only appropriate that he should be responsible.' He picked up his phone. 'Now, if you'll excuse me. I must arrange a meeting with the Chief Constable. He'll be anxious to make an announcement.'

Wilson and Davis rode down the lift in silence. They sat together in the back of the car.

'I think I need a drink,' Davis said.

'I have the necessary in my office,' Wilson said. 'So the only question is, your place or mine?'

She smiled. 'Spence told me that you were irredeemable. It doesn't bother you that Nicholson appears to have set his sights on us.'

'I noticed that it didn't seem to bother you.'

'Better make it my place. Bring the bottle to my office but make sure nobody sees it. I don't want to set the station rumour mill running.'

Wilson smiled. Maybe it was going to be fun after all.

CHAPTER NINETEEN

Wilson decided that an evening in was in order. He had already consumed a large whiskey in Davis' office. It was the first time he had worked for a female boss and while he had some reservations at the beginning, Davis had impressed him as a very competent officer. She wasn't slow at voicing her trepidation at managing him and his squad in her first role as the head of a station. But he was convinced that, while they would never have the same relationship he'd had with Spence, they were going to get on well together. He decided that he would continue to cut back on the visits to the Crown, and especially on the drinking sessions with McDevitt. That would prove easier than usual since McDevitt was into his new role as an author. Apparently, his publisher had an urgent need for the book on the investigation that had snared Cummerford and her subsequent trial. People like Cummerford had a sell-by date. The public's interest was constantly being tweaked by current events. And it was important to strike while the iron was hot. This all meant that McDevitt was not as available as usual and Wilson didn't like drinking alone. Being alone always brought his thoughts back to Kate McCann. He was so sure that she was going to be the "one", but he supposed that she would have to go down as the "almost one". She was beautiful, intelligent and came from one of the best families. Her father was a judge and her mother was one of the foremost businesswomen in Northern Ireland. It was a background that contrasted starkly with his own. His father was a police sergeant and a suicide, his mother a teacher who had fled to Canada to escape the disgrace. Perhaps he and Kate had been an ill-starred couple from the start, a ying and yang that could never work together. But he missed her every day. He had accepted that they would never be together again, and the longing that he had experienced during the first weeks of their break-up was fading. He had seen enough of life to know that it was pointless to pine for the past. Right now, he had a disappeared criminal to find and a possible body to dig up. He was about to make himself an omelette when the intercom sounded. He pressed the button.

'It's you know who,' Stephanie Reid's voice came over the line. 'Buzz me up.'

He smiled and pushed the button. Stephanie was the chief pathologist of the province and operated from the Royal Victoria Hospital. She was also the professor of pathology at Queen's University. It was impossible for a man not to like Reid. She was beautiful, funny and vivacious. They'd been "seeing" each other for almost a month. It wasn't dating and it wasn't regular. It was two people having a meal together, watching a DVD together and sometimes sleeping together. The word "love" hadn't been mentioned and he wondered whether it ever would be. He heard a knock on the door and opened it.

'Hi!' She stood on tiptoes and kissed him on the cheek. 'Have you eaten yet?'

"I was just about to make an omelette.' He closed the door behind her.

She had apparently just come from the hospital and she was wearing her normal day dress of white blouse and black knee-length skirt. Her blonde hair was tied back behind her head. She looked fantastic.

She made for the kitchen and dumped a Marks and Spencer bag on the counter. 'I spent the day cutting up dead bodies. For a change they all died of natural causes. It appears that crime in Belfast has taken a holiday. At least the kind of crime that leads to people being on my table.' She sighed. 'Today's was the kind of work that gives me an appetite for steak and salad.' She produced two rib-eyes and a packet of prepared salad from the bag. 'And I got this for afters.' She held up a DVD of the latest James Bond film.

He smiled. Kate would have to be chained to a chair to watch tosh like that.

Reid headed for the cooker. 'I'll stick the steaks on and you can get me a nice glass of Chardonnay. You do have a nice bottle of Chardonnay?'

He nodded and went to the fridge. He had gone through many years of not having friends. Now he had two, McDevitt and Reid. He poured her a glass of wine and handed it to her. She already had the ridge-pan on the gas and the steaks were sizzling.

She took a long drink of the wine. 'God, I needed that. It's been a long hard day. How was yours?'

'Long and not so hard, did you get a chance to read the *Chronicle* today?'

'You mean the article by your friend?' She flipped the steaks. Reid liked her meat literally as it came off the animal. Rare would be too well done.

'Looks like I'm going to be in charge of bringing up the body.' He had poured himself a glass of wine and was sipping it.

'Not your forte.' The steaks were reflipped and two plates were already covered in salad. 'Get the knives and forks. I suppose there'll be work for me when you bring him up.'

'I have no idea what shape the body would be in. It's been

in a bog for more than thirty years.' Wilson wrapped a paper napkin around a knife and fork and put them on the breakfast counter. He had just finished when two plates with a barely cooked steak and salad arrived on the counter.

'Refill,' Reid held out her empty glass. 'The body might be in reasonably good condition. Bogs have been known to preserve bodies. It depends on the soil conditions.' She sipped her wine and then cut into her steak. Blood ran onto the plate. 'Perfect.' She cut off a chunk and dropped it into her mouth savouring the taste. 'Steak, salad, a glass of Chardonnay and a James Bond film, what more could a girl ask for?'

He touched his glass to hers. She was the perfect antidote to his feelings about Kate. He had no idea where the relationship was going and he was just along for the ride.

After they'd eaten and Wilson had put the dishes into the dishwasher, they took their wine glasses and settled themselves on the couch. Wilson had already put the DVD into the player and he pressed the remote control. As the opening sequence started, Reid lay down on the couch with her head in his lap.

'Will you be staying the night?' he asked as she settled herself.

'Probably.'

There it was, there was no mention of "love" or "commitment". It wasn't in their lexicon. Yet.

CHAPTER TWENTY

1947, Coleville House, Ballymoney

THE FIVE MEN were seated in the dining hall. The doors to the great hall had been closed and the servants warned not to interrupt the meeting for any reason. The scion of the Lattimer family, Sir Jeffrey Lattimer, sat at the top of the table. On his right were his two overseas guests. Directly beside him was Gary Sabulski, a thickset Polish American from Chicago who had served with the Office of Strategic Services during the Second World War and was now employed by the recently established Central Intelligence Agency. Next to Sabulski sat Richard Evershed who had spent his war in the British Special Operation Executive. He, like his American cousin, had gravitated toward the intelligence community after the war and was currently employed by MI6. The two men on the other side of the table were Northern Irish. On Lattimer's left sat George Johnson, the seventh Baron Carncastle. Next to him was the recently demobbed James McCann who at twenty-seven years of age had been one of the youngest lieutenant colonels in the British Army.

'Gentlemen,' Lattimer started after a round of introductions. 'What we will discuss here today is of the highest importance and utmost secrecy. No notes will be taken and nothing that is said in this room will be repeated to another living soul.' He glanced around the group looking for signs of assent. Carncastle and McCann nodded. Sabulski and Evershed remained silent. Secrecy was their stock in trade. 'Mr Sabulski, perhaps you'd like to start.'

Sabulski smiled. 'Gary, please. First, I want to thank Dick here for organising this meeting with you folks. We're all busy people so I'll get right to the point. The geopolitics of the world has changed radically since the end of the war. The Soviets were our allies against the Nazis but they now pose the greatest threat to what we know as democracy. They have a worldview with Communism as the dominant political philosophy. They're already transforming the political landscape of the countries in Eastern Europe that they took over on their way to Berlin. There are active communist cells in Greece and Italy and we in Washington consider it highly likely that a domino effect could take place in Europe with most of the continent falling to the Commies. We've decided that we need to do something to counteract this movement. I've just come from Italy and I can tell you there's a good chance that Italy will go communist unless we do something. We've decided to establish "stay behind" groups in several countries to be ready to fight in case of a Communist take-over. We intend to make sure that these groups will be well funded and well armed with weapons that we will hide in caches. We're calling these groups Gladio. That's where you guys come in.'

James McCann leaned forward. 'Northern Ireland is a long way from Russia.'

'But you do have your subversives,' Evershed said, 'who could be useful to political agitators.'

McCann nodded. 'So, you are proposing to set up one of these "stay behind" groups in Ulster.'

'We don't intend to set up a group,' Evershed said. He looked from Lattimer to the other two men at the table. 'We intend to co-opt your little group for our purpose.'

'Our little group?' Lattimer frowned.

Evershed leaned forward. 'Please do not try to be obtuse. We've been aware of your Circle since its inception and we have no desire to interfere with it. We want to strengthen it and use it. It contains the kind of people we want to deal with, former army officers, the business elite, politicians. It's a ready made organisation.'

'And we are going to fund it,' Sabulski interjected.

'During the war,' Evershed said, 'the MOD hid weapons throughout Britain that could be used by local resistance groups in case of a German invasion. Some of those weapons are cached in Northern Ireland. Should you agree to Gary's proposal we would be prepared to put the weapons buried in Northern Ireland at your disposal.'

'What exactly would be expected of us? McCann said.

'You would have to resist any move toward Communism in Ulster,' Sabulski said.

'Or any other form of subversion,' Evershed added.

'And who would we take orders from?' McCann asked.

'You would have a level of autonomy.' Evershed was now the main interlocutor. 'But, of course, if there were specific tasks to be performed, you might be requested to carry out operations from time to time.'

'And the level of funding?' Lattimer asked.

'I have approval from Washington to offer you an upfront payment of $1.5M.'

Lattimer had difficulty in maintaining a poker face. One and a half million dollars invested in the province would give the Circle unheard of economic power. He looked at Carn-castle and McCann. As usual, the baron had remained silent during the entire meeting. He epitomised the phrase 'a man of few words'. However, he had immense political power. McCann on the other hand was gaining a reputation as one of the most astute legal brains in the province. His impressive war record allied to his double first from Oxford presaged a glittering career. He was the future of the Circle and his opinion would be valued by many of his peers. Carncastle's nod was almost imperceptible, McCann's more definite.

'I think we have an agreement,' Lattimer said. He should have been ecstatic but he felt a level of disquiet. He looked at Sabulski and Evershed. They had self-satisfied looks on their faces. At the back of his mind, he wondered whether they had just made a pact with the Devil.

CHAPTER TWENTY-ONE

E ast Belfast was not only the industrial heartland of the city; it was the industrial heartland of the province. Although the hammers of the great shipbuilders of Harland and Wolff had been long silent, that area still included the iconic industry set up by Short Brothers. East Belfast is famous for the production of the *Titanic* but is equally famous for producing writers, musicians and famous footballers. While many of the iconic industries were no longer present, much of the infrastructure associated with those industries is still there.

Reid was already gone by the time Wilson woke up. He was always astonished at the way she could silently slide from his bed, dress and leave. They had discussed the possibility that she might be part Apache. She concluded that her ability to move silently came from her years living in the northeast of the Congo. As soon as he rose, he put on his running gear for an early morning run. The run was part of his daily routine, a chance for him to psyche himself up mentally for the day ahead and get his blood flowing. The sun was up and shining over Belfast as he took his turn around the Titanic Exhibition building and headed back to Queen's Quay. He had the luxury of a leisurely breakfast since he was already close to the location of Sammy Rice's warehouse. When the intercom sounded, he knew it was Harry Graham. He picked up the phone and said 'I'm on my way.'

Graham was sitting outside in one of the station cars when Wilson exited the apartment building.

'Morning, boss,' Graham said as Wilson slid into the passenger seat. 'Next stop the Upper Newtonards Road.'

'Do we have a set of keys?'

Graham started the car and shook his head. 'I brought along a means of gaining access.' He nodded at the back seat where a set of large bolt cutters lay.

Fifteen minutes later they pulled up outside the two-storey warehouse just off the Newtonards Road. Graham parked beside what looked like the main entrance. Wilson got out of the car and looked at the warehouse. It wasn't what he had envisaged, principally because it looked more like a disused office building than a warehouse. It was solidly constructed of brick and there were windows along the side of both floors. The building was also a lot larger than he'd anticipated. It was at least two hundred feet long and one hundred feet wide giving a total area of forty thousand square feet when both floors were considered. Wilson was sorry that he hadn't organised several uniforms to accompany them. Searching a building of this size could prove to be a time consuming job depending on what they might find inside. Graham was standing at the entrance which had a chain running through the handles of the double doors. He had already inserted the chain into the jaws of the bolt cutters and was awaiting the instruction from Wilson to cut the chain. Wilson was wondering whether they should have gone ahead with a search warrant. The building had the air of being unoccupied so the lack of a search warrant might not prove an impediment. However, there might be an alarm on the inside. He nodded at

Graham who immediately put pressure on the bolt cutters. Graham struggled for a few minutes before the chain snapped.

'Back to the gym, I think, Harry.' Wilson watched Graham pull the chain through the two handles in the double doors and then push the doors in. They entered into the front of the building. It appeared enormous because it was relatively empty. It was apparent that the warehouse hadn't been in use for some time. If there was an alarm, it was a silent one. On the left of the entrance, there was a set of iron stairs leading to the upper floor, which appeared to contain a small number of offices most of which had no doors and whose windows were broken. Wilson nodded at Graham and pointed upstairs. He took out his torch and turned it on. He moved forward into the body of the building turning the beam from the torch on the piles of rubbish that were heaped up at the sides of the building. He moved along the right side of the building poking at the rubbish. It was beginning to look like a wild goose chase. If Sammy Rice had been here, he was no longer in residence. He made his way slowly along the right side of the building and reached the end without discovering anything of interest. The floor of the warehouse was covered in a fine dust. He proceeded back towards the entrance along the left side of the building. He was halfway down the side of the building when Graham appeared from the other end. He shook his head when Wilson looked at him. Wilson continued along the side while Graham started down the centre of the building.

'Boss,' Graham called after he was about twenty feet down the centre of the building.

'What have you got?' Wilson asked.

'Stains.'

'The whole place is covered in stains.'

'Could be blood'

Or engine oil, Wilson thought. He walked over to Graham and looked down. There were definitely some recent dark stains on the floor. He shone the light on the floor and motioned Graham to stand back. There were two very distinct marks. One was larger than the other and had a different pattern. The larger mark looked like the liquid that created it had flowed while the smaller stain was concentrated. He saw the indent of what looked like a chair in the dust close to the stains but there was no chair in evidence. The dust around the area was more disturbed than at the edges of the warehouse. 'Mark out an area around these stains. Then give forensics a call. We need someone here now.' He bent down to examine the marks. Graham might very well be right. He could be looking at blood.

Graham marked out a circular area of five metres around the stains and then placed the call to forensics. 'Possibly half an hour,' he said closing his phone.

'We'll wait outside.' Wilson started toward the entrance.

The forensics team arrived forty minutes later and suited up before entering the building. Wilson and Graham waited at the entrance and watched as the technicians collected samples from the stains that they had identified. When they had finished they assembled outside the warehouse.

'The two stains you identified were blood.' The chief technician pulled off his plastic jumpsuit. 'We tried UV light on the rest of the building but there was no other signs of blood. We collected samples and we'll have them at the lab by this afternoon. Of course, that doesn't mean that they'll be dealt with immediately but that's something I have no control over.'

'Are the stains recent?' Wilson asked.

'Fairly,' the chief technician replied. 'We don't have the equipment with us to check that. The lab will be able to tell.'

'But they're good enough to get DNA from?' Wilson asked.

'I don't think DNA will be a problem.'

The forensics team loaded up their van and left.

'What are you thinking, boss?' Graham asked.

'I'm thinking one of those bloodstains belongs to Sammy Rice. If it's the large one then we're looking for a body. Whatever the outcome, that warehouse is a crime scene. I want it secured.'

CHAPTER TWENTY-TWO

R ichie Simpson spent the morning rambling around the Castlecourt Shopping Centre on Royal Avenue. In his pocket was £100 from the £2,000 that McDevitt had given him. He would have loved to have gone on a splurge with the money but he'd learned his lesson. He had no idea how long the money would last, but he knew that conserving it was a damn sight better than throwing it out the window. However, two grand wasn't going to last forever. He'd been a fool to settle for so little. McDevitt had run with the map and the *Chronicle* had followed up with an article speculating on what options were open to the PSNI. The Justice Minister was already calling for the body to be exhumed. McDevitt had got his money's worth. Simpson had been conned. He'd spent two hours looking around Debenhams and some of the other shops without buying anything. He noticed a Starbucks ahead and decided it was time for a cup of coffee. He joined the queue and was almost at the counter when he felt an arm on his shoulder.

'Mine's a smoked butterscotch latte and Eddie will have a latte macchiato.'

Simpson whirled and found himself looking into Davie

Best's smiling face. A few feet behind Best he saw another of Gerry McGreary's thugs.

Best motioned to his companion and pointed at an empty table. 'There's a table over in the corner that Eddie'll grab. I'll wait with you and give a hand with the coffees.'

Simpson was no longer interested in coffee. In fact, he felt that if he put something into his stomach, it would be instantly rejected. He took a deep breath before speaking. 'Davie, good to see you.'

'Aye,' Best's hand circled Simpson's shoulder. 'Sure, aren't we the best of friends.'

Simpson had reached the counter and gave the order. He removed the roll of tens from his pocket and pulled one off.

'You're in the money,' Best said. 'Happy days are here again, eh! Big win on the gee-gees?'

'Something like that.' Simpson had no desire to go into details. He was too busy wishing himself somewhere else. He watched the server put three Starbucks-decorated cardboard cups on the table before him. The server's mouth moved and he said something but Simpson didn't hear. He handed over the £10 note and held his hand out for the change. Meanwhile the active part of his mind was thinking that he was experiencing his last day on the planet.

Best pushed past him and picked up two of the cups. He stood back and waited for Simpson to pick up the remaining one.

Simpson picked up the cup and followed Best to the table that had been taken by Best's companion. The cups were distributed to the proper recipients and Simpson sat on one of the empty chairs. Best smiled and took a seat across from him.

'Haven't seen you around much lately.' Best took the lid off his cup, poured three sachets of sugar into the coffee and used a small plastic spoon to stir the contents. 'What have you been up to?'

'Nothing much.' Simpson raised the cup to his mouth and

drank. Christ, but it was hot. He looked at Best's companion who was built like a brick shithouse. 'Eddie' appeared to be taking no interest in the proceedings.

'The Peelers have been around asking about Sammy again,' Best said without looking up from his coffee.

'I hadn't heard,' Simpson said. He didn't want to say that he went into a blue funk every time Sammy Rice's name was mentioned. Carlisle had screwed him good and proper. That wasn't exactly true. He was aware that his own greed was the source of his problems.

'We're wondering what sparked their interest again. The search for Sammy had gone cold. Now we have a couple of Peelers goin' around askin' questions. It looks like someone has been opening their big mouth.' Best sipped his coffee.

'You think I'm stupid,' Simpson said. 'You have the Beretta with my fingerprint on it. If they manage to find Sammy, they'll be able to match the bullet to the gun and I'm in prison for the rest of my life.' That was if they ever found Sammy. He had no idea what Best and Ray Wright did with the body. He assumed that Sammy was at the bottom of the Irish Sea, which would mean that they could shove the gun up their proverbial arses. Sammy would have to be found in order for the bullet to be retrieved. He had convinced himself that the threat associated with Best having the murder weapon was negligible. He was hoping that Best would open up on what he'd done with Sammy but there was little or no hope of that happening

McGreary was probably right, Best was thinking. They had taken the opportunity to kill Sammy without having a plan for the future. It was Iraq all over again. You go in, do the business and don't think about the consequences or the exit strategy. Planning on the hoof had been shown not to be the smartest way to go. But it was what it was. Perhaps they had screwed up. If they'd taken him out in the street, there would have been some tit-for-tat. Having him disappear seemed like the best idea at the time. He would dearly like to fit Simpson up for the murder but the arsehole was right, there would have to be a bullet to link the gun to the murder. Sammy was in a hole in Tullymore forest. Bringing him back wasn't an option right now. 'It would be better for all if the Peelers lose interest again,' he said. He had intended to throw the frighteners into Simpson but he knew the bastard had worked things out for himself. Maybe he'd kill Simpson anyway. Plant the gun and point the Peelers in the direction of Sammy's grave. He wasn't about to do anything without thinking on it, and running it past McGreary. He finished his coffee and stood up. 'We'll be seein' you around, Richie.'

Simpson watched the two men leaving the café. His heart, which had been pounding, was gradually slowing down. Best was one of the most dangerous men in Belfast. He was a cold-blooded killer and possibly a psychopath. Simpson knew that in Best's mind he was expendable. If they had Sammy stored somewhere, there was no way he would ever be able to stop looking over his shoulder.

CHAPTER TWENTY-THREE

When Wilson returned to the station he was surprised to find Siobhan O'Neill sitting in the squad room. She stood up as soon as he entered.

'Siobhan,' he said walking towards her. 'I didn't expect you so soon.'

'I turned up for work this morning as usual,' she said. 'At ten o'clock, the boss called me in and handed me my new assignment. It said "with immediate effect". So, here I am.'

Harry Graham came into the room and Wilson made the introductions. 'We have three murder cases on at the moment,' Wilson said to O'Neill. 'Harry will give you the murder books. I want you to get yourself up to speed on all of them. Your initial responsibility will be keeping those books up to date and making sure that the whiteboard reflects the progress on the investigations. '

'Yes, boss. Where do I sit?'

He pointed at Eric Taylor's old desk. 'You can camp there.' He noticed the cardboard box at her feet. 'Your personal stuff?'

She nodded.

'OK, get settled in. Find out where the toilet and cafeteria are located and then get to work.' He turned to Graham. 'The murder books.'

Graham nodded.

Wilson fell into his chair in his office. The small box containing O''Neill's personal effects had at one time held photocopy paper. He wondered what she might have inside; a photograph of her partner, copies of her annual assessments, staples and paper clips, a personalised coffee cup. He looked around his office. When he'd been side-tracked by Campbell, he'd taken nothing with him. There were no personal photographs on his desk, no diplomas on his walls, nothing that he would pack up and bring to his next life. He thought about the two weeks he'd spent in Nova Scotia. It was a different life to the one he had in Belfast. He'd enjoyed the change but deep down he knew that he was where he should be, doing what he should be doing. The *Chronicle*, in the person of McDevitt, had followed up on the Evans theme demanding action from the PSNI. Wilson didn't want to be diverted from the search for Sammy Rice but Nicholson had made it clear that the responsibility for the operation to recover Evans's body would be his. Therefore, he wasn't surprised when he received a call to attend a meeting in Davis' office in the early afternoon.

When he entered Davis's office, he was taken aback to see the visitor's chair was already occupied by a man who was almost as big as he was.

'Superintendent Wilson.' Davis motioned him forward. 'Pull over a chair and meet Detective Chief Inspector Duane from the Garda Siochana.'

Wilson grabbed a chair and walked towards the desk. Duane stood. He was maybe two inches shorter than Wilson but was as broad. His head was completely bald and was as round as a bowling ball. He could see that there was still a growth of hair but the head had been shaven. Duane's face was round and his cheeks were ruddy showing that he spent a good deal of time outside the office. His nose was neither too big nor too small; he had full lips and blue eyes that seemed to bore into Wilson. He extended a large hand as Wilson walked towards him. Wilson placed the chair in front of Davis' desk and took Duane's hand. As they shook hands, he did a double take; Duane's hand was the size of a baseball mitt.

'DCI Duane is here to assist us,' Davis said as soon as they were all seated.

'Jack, please, 'Duane said. 'We're not very formal in the Gardai.'

Davis pursed her lips. 'You can address me as ma'am, Jack.'

'Ian,' Wilson said.

Davis continued. 'Jack has already supervised two exhumations of bodies that were interred in bogs in the South. So he's here to give us the benefit of his experience.'

Duane smiled showing a full set of white teeth. 'It seems that your boss called my boss yesterday. And I was told to get my arse up here double quick. I had a chance to look at the article in the *Chronicle*. To be honest, I never heard of this fella, Evans. What I do know of him after reading the article, he's not the usual candidate for an IRA hit and disappearance. Do you have any further information?'

Davis looked at Wilson.

Wilson sighed. 'We're as much in the dark in terms of motive. Evans doesn't appear to be associated with either the IRA or the UDA. He was some form of communist.'

Duane laughed. 'So you haven't worked out yet whether he was a Catholic Communist or a Protestant Communist.'

Wilson joined in the laughter. Black humour helped most people in Northern Ireland to make sense out of the sectarian situation. 'That's the core of the problem as to who might have planted him in Ballynahone bog. That is if that's where he really is.'

'My boss says you want to get the show on the road right away.' Duane looked at Davis.

'We're under some considerable political pressure,' Davis said. 'The "disappeared" as we call those people we think have been murdered and buried in secret is an emotive issue in this province.' She spoke directly to Duane. 'You've been at the sharp end of the process in the South. Up here we have to deal with the emotional impact.'

'Understood,' Duane said. 'So the search for the body will attract a certain amount of attention.'

'That might turn out to be an understatement,' Davis said. 'You can expect to find yourself in the newspapers and on TV regularly. So, considering the timing to be imperative, how soon can you start?'

'I've already started,' Duane said. 'As I understand it, Ian is in charge of the search. I'm along simply to provide technical support. That being the case, I suggest that you keep quiet about my involvement. Ian can handle the press and TV. I've already contacted the company that leases the ground-penetrating radar and he can have a suitable system up here tomorrow. I'll have a budget for the operation prepared as soon as I've seen the area. Have you restricted access to the area in question?'

'Not yet,' Wilson said.

'Then as soon as we're finished here, I'd like to see the area and we can arrange to restrict access at the same time.' He turned to Davis. 'When I come up with a budget, how soon will you have approval?'

'Assistant Chief Constable Nicholson has already given provisional approval for the ground-penetrating radar. HQ wants to carry out the operation in bite- sized chunks. They don't want to commit until they know what exactly they're committing to.'

'That's reasonable,' Duane said. 'We have to find out whether there's someone there first. But I'll lay out a possible budget so that we can keep going.'

'How long will this take?' Wilson asked.

'How long is a piece of string?' Duane said. 'The ground-penetrating radar will take a couple of days. If we find someone, we can't just dig the area up with a JCB. I suppose this man had a violent death so we'll have to preserve as much of whatever evidence remains. I suppose it might take a week depending on the depth of the grave. How long does it take from here to Ballynahone bog?'

'About an hour,' Wilson answered.

'Then we should be on our way,' Duane said.

Wilson was impressed by the Garda's professionalism. The two police forces on the island often cooperated with each other but there was a history of distrust where political issues were concerned. The RUC and even the newly reformed PSNI were considered to be too close to Protestant military groups. There was considerable proof that the members of the RUC were actively involved in Protestant death squads along with their colleagues from the Ulster Defence Regiment. On the other hand, the Garda Siochana had been accused by their PSNI colleagues of colluding with members of the IRA. There was less evidence for the latter conclusion than for the former.

'Don't let me detain you,' Davis said. 'Superintendent Wilson will drive you.'

Wilson and Duane rose together.

CHAPTER TWENTY-FOUR

Wilson managed to get out of Belfast before the rush hour began. Before leaving, he told Graham to arrange with the local uniforms to restrict access to the area of Ballynahone bog indicated on the map that had appeared in the *Chronicle*. He was more than a little peeved with himself that he hadn't done so already. He might not believe the story of Evans's interment, but there was good reason to close off the area due to rubberneckers, ghouls or possibly even the return of whoever put Evans there. The only reason for his lack of forethought was his almost total concentration on finding Sammy Rice and closing the cases on Grant, Malone and O'Reilly. Wilson commandeered a police Land Rover. He doubted whether he and Duane would have been able to squeeze into the front of a saloon car. He also grabbed a driver.

'I checked you out before coming North,' Duane said as he settled himself in the back of the Land Rover. 'They say that you're good at what you do. They also say that you were pretty good at rugby until you ran into a bomb. What was that about?'

Wilson winced at the memory. 'I was running away at the time. A piece of shrapnel caught me in the thigh.'

'Did you try a comeback?'

'Of sorts, but it didn't work. I'd lost the speed. I walk with a bit of a limp on my bad days.'

'I hadn't noticed. I played a bit of Gaelic football myself, full forward for Galway for more than ten years. Broke my bloody heart when I had to give up.'

Wilson was silent for a moment. He wished he'd had ten years of rugby. He had three years at the top and then the scrapheap.

They left Belfast on the M2 heading in the direction of Newtownabbey. 'What unit of the Garda are you attached to?' Wilson asked.

'Special Branch.'

Wilson's brow furrowed. He looked out the window at the passing countryside. He had recent experience of the duplicity of his Special Branch colleagues.

'I take it that you don't appreciate Special Branch officers,' Duane said.

'You might be right, PSNI Special Branch might be different from down South.'

Duane laughed. 'I doubt it.'

'So why is the Garda Special Branch in charge of exhuming bodies?' They were heading northwest skirting the northern shore of Lough Neagh. The sun was in their faces and they could see the sparkling waters of the lake away to their left.

Duane looked out at the lake. 'You have a spectacular country here, Ian. I'm not an expert on exhuming bodies. I'm an expert on the IRA. The one led me to the other. The IRA had a habit of murdering people in your jurisdiction and burying them in mine. During interrogations, I managed to elicit information on where two bodies were buried. My bosses, in their infinite wisdom, thought it was my case so it was my responsibility to bring up the bodies. But I have my doubts about your Alan Evans. What can you tell me about him?'

Wilson gave Duane a potted history of the man they thought might be buried in Ballynahone.

'It doesn't fit,' Duane said when Wilson had finished.

'What do you mean?' Wilson asked.

'He has no apparent connection with either the IRA, or the UDA. Why would they want to kill him? He wasn't a threat to either of them. So, why would they "disappear" him? That was usually reserved for people considered to be traitors. It was an insult to the person and his family to hide the corpse. One thing I can tell you for sure, it wasn't the IRA. They always bury them in the South.'

'And it's probably not the UDA,' Wilson said, 'because they don't do "disappeared". Where does that leave us?'

'You mean where does that leave you? I'm only here to find and lift the body. If there is a body.'

The Land Rover left the A6 before Maghera and drove to the entrance of the bog. Ballynahone bog is situated in County Derry about three kilometres south of the town of Maghera on low-lying ground immediately north of the Moyola River and about fourteen kilometres from the mouth of Lough Neagh. It is one of the largest lowland-raised bogs in Northern Ireland. Wilson had brought along a GPS (Global Positioning System) with the coordinates of the area closest to the place marked 'X' on the map printed by the *Chronicle* already installed. The Land Rover travelled about two hundred metres into the bog before Wilson gave the driver the instruction to stop.

'We get out here,' Wilson said. 'I hope you're not wearing your best shoes.'

Duane smiled. 'I don't have best shoes.'

They descended from the Land Rover and surveyed the bog. 'Who owns it?' Duane asked.

'It's a natural nature reserve.'

'So the government owns it. What about permission to dig?'

'HQ are organising that. But first we have to have a reason to dig. If they don't think there's a body, no permission to dig.'

'Sensible enough.' Duane started walking across the bog his feet squelching in the water-sodden turf. He noticed a large number of bog holes surrounded by hills or small knolls. He marched on examining the flora and fauna as he went.

Wilson watched Duane bend and examine plants as he made his way through the bog. They both stopped on a small hillock and surveyed the bog.

'Did you ever think of the millions of years it took to create a bog like this?' Duane said. 'We look at historical remains that are five thousand years old and we're amazed. This bog was formed millions of years before man even put his foot on this earth. And we go around digging these places up so that we can burn turf in our fireplaces.'

'I'm sure the people of West Virginia think the same about their vanishing countryside to satisfy the need for coal.'

'You're right. But there's a rare beauty to stand here with the sun setting to the west and the waters of the great lake away to the south. I hope we don't have to screw it up too much.'

'What's the plan?' Wilson asked.

'We'll section off the area of the bog where you think the body is buried. The ground radar people will set up a grid and they'll examine each section of the grid.'

'And that's going to start when?'

'Day after tomorrow. We're done here.'

They moved carefully through the bog back to the Land Rover. 'Have you organised somewhere to stay in Belfast?' Wilson asked when they were settled in the rear.

'I'm in Dublin for the next few days,' Duane said. 'I'll return with the ground radar crew and we'll probably stay somewhere local. I suppose you'll be over here too?'

'There's nothing I can add and I've got an important case on at the moment. I'll come over when I can do something useful.' Wilson eased back into his seat and closed his eyes. He needed the search for Evans's body like he needed a hole in the head. He cursed McDevitt.

CHAPTER TWENTY-FIVE

'Congratulations!' ACC Nicholson looked across his desk into the face of Rory Browne.

'I'm looking forward to the challenge, sir,' Browne said.

'I'm sure you are.' Nicholson had been given the job of ensuring that Browne was the stand-out candidate among those presented to Wilson. 'But the job may present more than one challenge.'

Browne had been around long enough to know when to keep his mouth shut.

'Superintendent Wilson needs careful watching. He has a habit of ignoring the wishes of his superiors while pursuing an investigation. We, at HQ, need someone in the squad who can report back if investigations are going off the rails.' Nicholson didn't read enthusiasm in Browne's face. 'You're an ambitious young officer. It would certainly be in your interest to be seen in a good light by your superiors.'

This was a turn of events that Browne had not anticipated. He actually wanted to work closely with Ian Wilson. The man was a legend in the force and he knew he could learn a lot from him. Now he was being asked to spy on him. It hadn't been couched in those words but that was what Nicholson was asking. If he agreed, and there was very little chance that he would not be able to agree, then his relationship with Wilson would be compromised at the least and poisoned at worst. 'I can't say that I would be happy to spy on my superior.'

'It's not exactly spying.' Nicholson tried a smile. He had been assured that Browne was his man. He decided it was time to appeal to his vanity. 'You're a young man with a glittering career ahead of you. Ian Wilson is yesterday's man. In fact, a few months ago he was almost getting the boot. It's unwise to hitch yourself to a star that's on the wane. All you have to do is to inform me when an investigation is heading in a direction that might be detrimental to the Force.'

Browne knew that resistance was futile. He tried to drum up even a moderate level of enthusiasm. 'As long as I'm not required to subvert my superior.'

'Nothing could be further from our minds.' Nicholson withdrew a paper from his desk and passed it across the desk. 'You are now a member of the new regional murder squad.' He stood up and held out his bony hand. 'I look forward to working with you.'

Browne picked up the paper and stood up. He folded the paper and put it in his inside pocket. Then he took the outstretched hand and shook it. His stomach had suddenly gone a bit queasy. He knew that the next time he looked in a mirror he wasn't going to like what he saw.

CHAPTER TWENTY-SIX

D ublin
It was already dark when Duane arrived at the Dublin Metropolitan Region Headquarters of the Garda Siochana in Harcourt Street that housed the Special Detective Unit (SDU). He made his way directly to the office of Detective Chief Superintendent Bill Nolan, the head of the agency. Although it was after ten o'clock, he knew that Nolan seldom left the office before eleven and was sometimes still at his post at midnight. The SDU was the modern equivalent of the former Special Branch and its principal remit was terrorism. The agency was the most secretive in the Irish Republic and had close connections with military intelligence.

Duane knocked on Nolan's office door and marched in.

'Come right in,' Nolan said looking up from the papers on his desk. 'Never heard of waiting to be invited to enter. I don't suppose you can even spell the word "decorum". Sit down and tell me how things went in Belfast?'

Duane sat in the chair in front of Nolan's desk. 'Interesting. I liked this Wilson guy. But I have no idea what I'm doing there. I don't suppose you'd like to enlighten me.'

Nolan put aside the papers he had been examining. 'We're

giving technical support to our colleagues in the North. Nothing more, nothing less.'

'Bullshit. From what I've seen they're well capable of finding out if there's someone in Ballynahone bog. And if they do find that there's someone there, they're equally capable of digging him up. Why are we interested?'

'The answer to that question is certainly beyond your pay grade and probably beyond mine.'

'This Evans guy was a nobody. Why should anyone have bothered to kill and bury him? Nobody seems clear on that one.'

'So you don't think that any of our usual suspects might be involved?'

'I cannot come up with a single reason as to why the IRA would want to assassinate some low grade would-be politician. My being involved in digging this guy up is not a good use of our resources.'

'Let's just humour our political masters,' Nolan said.

So that's where it's coming from, Duane thought. The people upstairs think that there could be some political fall-out from finding out who murdered Evans, either some fall-out or some advantage. He would have to protect his balls on this one

'Keep me informed,' Nolan said picking up his papers.

CHAPTER TWENTY-SEVEN

Wilson held a morning briefing on the investigation into the disappearance of Sammy Rice as soon as he arrived at the squad room. His newly recruited detective sergeant had shown up and the squad was now complete. As soon as he had brought the team up to date on the examination of the warehouse and the discovery of the bloodstains he motioned for Browne to join him in his office.

'As far as I'm concerned,' Wilson began when they were seated. 'Finding Sammy Rice is the priority. But our friends at HQ have given us the responsibility of looking into the report in the *Chronicle* about Alan Evans being buried in Ballynahone bog. It's a bloody diversion and it threatens to derail the Sammy Rice issue. So, I'm putting you in charge of the search for Sammy. That doesn't mean that I'm to be kept out of the loop. It just means that I'll probably be concentrating on the Evans case. That is if there is an Evans case.'

Browne nodded. 'I'll read up the murder books and get on to the forensics service to speed things up on getting the DNA from the blood samples.'

'The work in Ballynahone probably starts tomorrow. The

powers that be have asked for help from the Garda Siochana and one of their guys, DCI Jack Duane, will be helping to oversee the operation on site. But as far as HQ is concerned we're in charge. I'll be back and forward from Ballynahone during the week. You have Harry and Peter to help you. Get them out on the street. Someone knows what happened to Sammy. On your way!'

Browne left the office and went directly to his desk in the squad room. It was the place that had been occupied by his predecessor, Moira McElvaney. He was still mulling over his conversation with Nicholson. He didn't like the role that Nicholson was asking him to play. It was a huge feather in his cap that he had succeeded in getting a job working with one of the best detectives on the Force. He had no doubt that if Wilson discovered that he had accepted to spy on him, he would be shown the door. He pulled over the murder book of the Grant case and started to read.

WILSON SWITCHED on his computer and settled into the administrative work that he hated so much.

Two hours later he was happy to turn from his computer when his phone rang.

'How's my best friend?' McDevitt's voice was jaunty.

'Piss off,' Wilson said. 'Your quest for the front page has screwed up my investigation into the disappearance of Sammy Rice.'

McDevitt laughed. 'They've given you the job of finding Evans.'

'If Evans isn't in Ballynahone bog at the place you said he is, I suggest you take an extended holiday in Bora Bora.'

'What about lunch in the Crown?'

'I'm not about to let you pump me for the price of a pint and a packet of crisps.

'I was thinking about two pints and a packet of pork scratchings, my treat.'

'You've run out of steam on the story.' Wilson felt sorry for McDevitt. He'd gone with what he had without thinking how he was going to follow up. He knew that McDevitt would give his right arm for an interview with Duane on his plans for Ballynahone. The involvement of the Garda Siochana would be big news.

McDevitt was silent for a moment. 'I need something to continue the story. If there's no follow up, I'll be given two column inches on page five.

Wilson took pity on McDevitt. 'We're sectioning off the area indicated in your story. We'll bring in some ground-pene-trating radar and see what we can find.'

'And you're in charge?'

'So they tell me.' He looked at his watch. It was just coming up to midday. Maybe there was time for a pint after all. 'I might think about that drink.'

McDevitt coughed. 'Something's just come up. We'll have to take a rain check.'

'You little bastard, that's the last time I'm going to give you a lead for your damn front page.'

'I owe you one.' The line went dead.

Wilson was smiling as he put the phone down. He hadn't given McDevitt anything that the press office wouldn't have given him. And he would drag a *quid pro quo* out of the little journalist at some point. In the early afternoon, he received an email from Duane indicating that the ground-penetrating radar crew would be on-site the following morning. He forwarded the email to both Nicholson and Davis. The response from Nicholson was immediate. He was to be at Ballynahone the following morning to supervise the operation. This was a PSNI operation and must be demonstrated to be so. Davis was copied in the correspondence and didn't bother to add anything.

Wilson was contemplating leaving for the evening when Browne knocked on his office door and entered.

'The result of the DNA tests from forensics,' Browne said holding aloft two pieces of paper.

Wilson held out his hand. He scanned the two sheets. The first was the result of the DNA test on the larger bloodstain. The DNA string had been identified but no match had been found. The second sheet was the result of the smaller stain. The DNA string had been identified and a match had been found. The small bloodstain belonged to David Best.

'Who's David Best?' Browne asked when he saw that Wilson had finished reading.

'That would be one Davie Best, the number two man in a criminal gang run by a man called Gerry McGreary.' Wilson knocked on the glass wall of his office and motioned Harry Graham to join them.

'The small patch of blood in the warehouse belongs to Davie Best,' Wilson said as soon as Graham entered the office.

Graham whistled softly. 'And the larger patch of blood?'

'They've got the DNA but no match,' Wilson said.

'No sign of Sammy's blood then,' Graham said.

'That's not what I said. There's no match for the second bloodstain. The question now is, do we have a DNA sample from Sammy?'

Graham took the papers from Wilson and scanned them. 'I can't believe that we don't. Surely to God Sammy has been banged up at some point and a DNA swab taken.'

'That's what we need to find out,' Wilson said. 'Harry get on to records and find out if Sammy was ever lifted. If we don't have his DNA, do we even have his fingerprints?' He tried to remember if Sammy had ever been brought in during his time. He was a "usual suspect". He must have graced the station at some point. 'I'm away to Ballynahone tomorrow morning to start the search for Evans.' He turned to Browne. 'You and Harry pick up Davie Best. Harry knows where he can be found. Bring him here and put him in an interview room. Keep him there until I get back. That should be sometime tomorrow evening. Don't tell him what it's about and if he insists on having a solicitor present, that's not a problem. Don't issue a caution. We can do that when I arrive. Rory, get on to forensics and get a set of the photographs that were taken at the warehouse.'

'Yes, boss,' Browne said.

'Now, off home the pair of you,' Wilson said. 'Tomorrow's going to be a busy day.'

He watched the two men go to their desks before leaving the office. He hadn't noticed much electricity between them. Certainly nothing like the bond that had existed between Harry and Moira. Still, it was early days. He decided that he would have to organise a drink to incorporate the new arrivals into the culture of the squad. Rugby had taught him that a team was only as strong as its weakest member. And he needed a strong team. The old team had its strengths but also some weaknesses. He thought back to his old sergeant, George Whitehouse, who had been a decent copper who had been corrupted by his allegiance to one side of the sectarian divide. The problem was that George wasn't the only copper who had been corrupted in that way. The proof of that corruption lay much closer to home for Wilson. But policemen were people, and in his experience people tended to be flawed. He leaned back in his chair and closed his eyes. Davie Best had been in that warehouse. What was he doing there? Why was his blood on the floor and more importantly whose blood was on the floor close to his? He wanted so much for the larger stain to belong to Sammy Rice. The stain was so large that the person the blood belonged to was either dead or in hospital. They had checked the hospitals when Sammy had disappeared. He was left to draw the obvious conclusion. It was entirely possible that Sammy had joined the ranks of the "disappeared". With that thought, he picked up the papers with the DNA strings and looked at what might be Rice's DNA. Somehow he was going to have to get a sample of Sammy Rice's DNA for a match. But how?

CHAPTER TWENTY-EIGHT

Richie Simpson's good intentions about the preservation of the £2,000 he'd received from McDevitt were in the toilet. He had fallen into bad company early in the day and by six o'clock he had lost count of the number of drinks he had consumed and the amount of bullshit he had talked and listened to. Several times he tried to make an escape but there was always an unfinished drink on the table. He ended up in the corner of the Auld Sash. The company was good and there was a lot of talk about his former, and recently deceased, boss, Jackie Carlisle. The stories about Jackie varied from praise to condemnation giving truth to Oscar Wilde's pronouncement that "the Irish are a fair race, they never say anything good about each other". Simpson had a recollection of buying several rounds and his drinking companions had responded with backslapping and renditions of the *"Protestant Boys"* and *"The Sash My Father Wore"*. By eight o'clock the crowd had dwindled to a couple of hard drinkers. Simpson had never classed himself as a member of the drinking fraternity and somewhere in the recesses of his brain was the knowledge that tomorrow he would wish himself dead. But this evening that knowledge was buried so deep as to be irretrievable. Drink talk about what Simpson and his drinking companions had done for the preservation of Ulster escalated into bragging about the deeds for which they had been responsible. Simpson kept pace but brought his colleague to silence when he asked 'Have any of you killed for Ulster?' He looked around the silent company. The patrons of the Auld Sash were up for a bit of drinking, singing and moderate bragging but no one in his right mind was going to admit to murder. There were far too many loose tongues in Belfast. And right now, one of those loose tongues belonged to Richie Simpson.

JOCK MCDEVITT WAS SLAVING over a hot computer. His publisher was bombarding him with emails asking when she could have the first chapters of his book on Maggie Cummerford. His contract with the publisher committed him to produce a book with a minimum of eighty thousand and a maximum of one hundred thousand words. He was used to hammering out articles of a couple of thousand words, so an average of ninety thousand looked like how the Himalayas might look to a hill walker. His desk was littered with reports on Maggie's mother's death at the hands of a group of women from the Shankill. She had been dropped on her head continually until her skull had cracked open like a coconut. Maggie had sat outside the room while her mother was callously murdered. It was the start of the road that would lead young Maggie to vengeance and the murder of three of her mother's tormentors. He looked at the word count at the bottom of the screen of his computer. He was about to hit the ten thousand-word mark. Only another eighty thousand to go, he thought, and five weeks in which to produce them. The production schedule for the book had been reduced from the usual one year to three months to catch the attention of the fickle public. His mobile phone played the tune from *The Magnificent Seven* indicating that a text message had arrived. Could he afford to look at the message and interrupt the flow of his thoughts? Could he afford not to? He was still a journalist after all. The job at the *Chronicle* was his bread and butter. The book was supposed to be the icing on the cake, if it ever saw the light of day. He picked up the phone and looked at the message. It was from one of his touts. He had informants on both sides of the Peace Wall who fed him information.

Richie Simpson is in the Auld Sash running off at the mouth. Talking about killing people. Could be something useful. Get here quick. Worth £20?

McDevitt typed a quick positive answer, closed his computer and rushed out the door.

Only two men had the staying power to listen to Simpson's ramblings. His diction was almost impossible to follow and his convoluted stories incomprehensible. His companions had long ago given up listening to him and concentrated what energy they had on soaking him of whatever money he had left. McDevitt plonked himself down beside Simpson much to the dismay of the companions who realised pretty quickly that McDevitt was intent on extracting the golden goose from their company. Simpson proved to be a happy drunk rather than an aggressive one. McDevitt had dealt with more than one drunk during his career and he carefully manoeuvred Simpson away from the pub. He had to support him as they walked the short distance to his old Mercedes. He opened the passenger door and shoved Simpson inside praying as he did so that he wouldn't be cleaning a flood of vomit from his prized vehicle before the night was out.

'I'm a bit bolloxed.' Simpson had a stupid smile on his face.

'You don't say.' McDevitt had interpreted drunk-talk before so he made sense of Simpson's slurred speech. 'I hear you've been talking about killing people, Richie.' McDevitt belted Simpson into the passenger seat.

Simpson made a gun out of his hand by pointing his index finger and cocking his thumb. 'Bang, bang, killed both of them.'

He started laughing hysterically then put his index finger to his lips. 'Shhh, nobody knows.'

'Who did you kill, Richie?' McDevitt asked.

Simpson put his face close to McDevitt's. 'Shhhh. Not a word, mind.' Simpson's eyes were blank and staring.

McDevitt knew he was in a race against time. Richie Simpson was minutes if not seconds from oblivion.

"Come on, Richie boy.' McDevitt lifted up Simpson's head. 'Who did you kill?'

Simpson smiled. 'Wouldn't you like to know,' he slurred.

In that moment, McDevitt knew he had lost the race. Simpson's head rolled back against the seat and his mouth hung open. He was dead to the world. McDevitt slapped his face in a vain attempt to bring the comatose man around. 'Fuck you, Richie,' McDevitt shouted. He was now stuck with the drunken man in his car. Simpson was a relatively large man and McDevitt was slight which meant that there was no possibility of getting a dead-weighted Simpson out of the passenger seat. McDevitt closed the passenger door and moved to the other side of the car. He climbed behind the wheel and started the car. He had a mountain of work at home and he had just wasted valuable time on a waste-of-space like Simpson. He would be forced to leave the bastard locked in his car for the night. He was not looking forward to what he might have to clean up in the morning.

CHAPTER TWENTY-NINE

W hen the sun shone on Ireland it was one of the most beautiful countries in the world. Wilson had commandeered a Land Rover for the day and was already skirting the Northern Shore of Lough Neagh when the sun burst through the clouds from the east and turned the lake into a shimmering mass. It was a fine morning to be alive and out of Belfast but Wilson would have preferred if the task of the day didn't have the feeling of a futile exercise. He would have preferred to be awaiting the arrival of Davie Best at the station. He had withdrawn Best's record and had spent the evening reading about the life and times of Davie Best. He was aware that Best was going to be no pushover. Best had been brought up hard on the backstreets of the Shankill. He had been arrested at fifteen for demanding money with menaces but was released when the victim refused to give evidence. There was a catalogue of arrests between the ages of fifteen and eighteen but the salient point was that Best never served a day. He entered the British Army at the age of eighteen and served in both Iraq and Afghanistan. As soon as he left the army, he joined Gerry McGreary's criminal gang and had risen through the ranks to become his McGreary's right-hand man. There were rumours that Best had been involved in beatings and possibly even murder but there was no evidence. One thing was certain. Davie Best was no stranger to killing. It was almost ten o'clock when the Land Rover turned off the A6 and moved along the narrow road that led to Ballynahone bog. A roadblock had been set up on the lane manned by a local uniform. He removed the barrier and allowed the Land Rover through. The area on the *Chronicle's* map was already cordoned off. When the Land Rover arrived at the site, Wilson saw that a considerable number of people were already there and a large van was parked to the side. A group of four men dressed in white overalls with the logo of some company or other on the back were setting up a grid with steel poles connected with yellow tape. Standing beside the parked van was the substantial figure of DCI Jack Duane. Wilson climbed out of the Land Rover and walked over to Duane. 'What time did you people arrive here?'

'We've been on site since seven and I left Dublin at five,' Duane whistled loudly and the four men looked in his direction. One, the smallest member of the crew, walked towards them.

'This is Dr Keane,' Duane said when the small man joined them. 'He's the head honcho of the ground radar crew.' Duane indicated Wilson. 'This is Superintendent Ian Wilson of the PSNI. He's in charge of this operation.'

Keane extended his hand to Wilson who took it. 'Pleased to meet you,' he said.

'Likewise,' Wilson replied. Keane was about thirty-five and Wilson was obliged to look down at least a foot to lock onto his eyes, which were hidden behind glasses that were obviously powerful since they made his eyes look enormous. Keane was bareheaded and his curly hair had already turned grey.

'Dr Keane is a geophysicist,' Duane said. 'It means he's an expert on finding things that are underground.'

'A bit of a simplification,' Keane said. 'Nice to have met

you superintendent, I better get back to the crew.' He turned and headed back towards the other three men.

'Full of chat, that boy. Boring little prick.' Duane opened the side door of the van and took out a thermos. 'Coffee?'

'Why not?' Wilson said.

Duane poured two cups from the thermos and passed one to Wilson. 'We have some chocolate biscuits in there somewhere.'

'I'll pass.' Wilson sipped the coffee. It was surprisingly good and certainly hadn't been made from instant granules. It was almost ten o'clock. The ground radar team had been working for three hours.

'They've nearly finished the grid,' Duane said nodding at the team. 'These guys are the best. If there's someone down there, they'll find him. You really don't need to be here. I'll keep you informed about what's happening.'

Wilson smiled. 'Orders from above, this is a PSNI operation. It's only a matter of time before the media find out that something interesting is going on here. It would be a little embarrassing if the only person they could find to interview was a member of the Garda Siochana.'

'Have you been upfront with me on the significance of this guy, Evans?'

'Absolutely, the guy wasn't connected. Why do you ask?'

'I'm usually around because the IRA are involved. I can't see their hand in this one. And my boss is holding something back.'

'So, what are you thinking?'

Duane didn't answer immediately. Sinn Fein, the political arm of the IRA were becoming a force on the Southern political scene. It would be embarrassing if one of their leaders could be proven to be directly connected to one of the "disappeared". He was sure that was the reason why he was on site but he wasn't sure he should discuss that theory with a PSNI officer that he barely knew. 'They don't pay me to think,' he said.

'I can relate to that.' Wilson was also asking himself why Nicholson had contacted the Garda Siochana. 'What do you and I do now?'

'Did you bring a deck of cards with you?'

Wilson shook his head.

'You're lucky, I did.' Duane produced the cards from his jacket pocket. Before the day was out he and Wilson would know a lot more about each other.

CHAPTER THIRTY

Davie Best was at his usual post, a table in the rear of the Queen's Tavern in the Woodvale Road. His boss, Gerry McGreary sat across from him. Best hated McGreary but he kept that fact to himself. He knew he would make a much better boss of their crew but McGreary had set up the crew from scratch and most of the men owed their allegiance to him. Anyway, Gerry was getting fatter by the day and it was only a matter of time before the Grim Reaper, in the form of a heart attack, stroke or diabetes, came to call. Best had often thought about accelerating the process, but assassinating McGreary while he was still popular with the crew was a high-risk strategy. He contented himself that in time he would become the head of the crew and he must simply bide his time. McGreary and his principal lieutenants were busy discussing the forthcoming war with Willie Rice. Personally, Davie Best couldn't wait for the action. Being at the top of a crime gang wasn't all it was cracked up to be. It was a round of collecting money from brothels, protection from shops and other businesses and counting the proceeds from their drug business. Best often thought that he might as well have gone to college and studied accountancy. It was that bloody boring. Most of the day was spent in a dark corner of the Queen's Tavern bullshitting with other members of the gang. At the moment, it was a talking shop about how they were going to handle what was left of the Rice gang. Best was only half listening when he heard the name 'Richie Simpson' and he immediately sat up. 'What about Simpson?' he said.

One of the men at the table said, 'The arsehole was in the Brown Bear last night pissed as a newt and spoutin' some shite about killin' someone.'

Best was instantly alert. 'And what?'

'And nothing, nobody was takin' a blind bit of notice of the man. He was out of his head and talkin' a load of crap.'

'Who was with him?'

Best's colleague named Simpson's companions and Best relaxed. They were all well known to him and he doubted Simpson's admission was believed.

'Then that wee bastard McDevitt arrived and pulled Simpson out of there.'

'The journalist at the *Chronicle*?' Best asked.

'Aye, a right little arsehole, Simpson was hardly capable of walkin' and McDevitt was makin' a meal of carryin' him out.'

Best slumped back in his chair. Fuck, fuck, fuck. McGreary was right. Simpson was a weak link. He thought he had him in his pocket but in fact he had created his own threat. Word on the street was that the hunt for Sammy Rice was on again. Best prided himself on his ability to read people and he knew that Wilson wouldn't stop looking until he had an answer for Sammy's disappearance. First he would have to deal with Simpson. Dead or alive he was going to end up as the patsy for getting rid of Sammy. As soon as he was through with the day's business with McGreary, he was going to find the fucking wimp and deal with him.

A pall of silence fell over the pub. Best looked up and saw that two men had entered and were looking in his direction. One he recognised as Harry Graham, one of Wilson's men. It was inconceivable that Simpson had already spilled his guts and Wilson had bought the story. One of McGreary's lieutenants stood up and barred the Peelers' path to the rear of the pub. Best watched as Graham leaned forward and spoke into the man's ear. The man glanced over his shoulder at McGreary waiting for a signal. McGreary nodded and the man stood aside.

'Mr McGreary,' Graham said.

'Harry fucking Graham,' McGreary said. 'Who's your pal? Haven't seen him around.'

'Detective Sergeant Browne,' Browne said.

'Where's the wee Fenian bitch with the red hair? We had a plan for her,' one of the men at the table said and the rest laughed.

'State your business or piss off,' McGreary said.

'We need a word with Davie,' Graham said.

Best sat forward. 'What's on your mind?'

'The boss would like to have a word with you in private,' Graham said. 'He was wondering whether you might like to come down to the station with us.'

'Am I being arrested?' Best said.

Graham looked at the group. The faces of the men around the table were no longer smiling. He had pulled most of them, and knew that things could easily turn nasty. 'We hope that won't be necessary,' he said. 'We simply want you to help us with our enquiries.'

'Concerning what?' Best asked.

Graham shrugged his shoulders. 'The boss just told us to bring you in. I think he has a friendly chat in mind.'

Best looked at McGreary. He could almost see the fat man's brain whirling in the centre of his head. It appeared to be moving slowly. The attention of the two Peelers and the group at the table were on McGreary. Finally he nodded.

Best turned to Graham. 'I'll be along when we're finished here.'

'No can do,' Graham said. 'My instructions are to bring you to the station.'

Best looked again at McGreary who nodded. He stood up. He was going to devise something very special for Simpson if he was the reason he was being lifted. Simpson's balls would be well and truly roasted before he was dispatched, Davie Best had already promised himself that pleasure.

Jock McDevitt rose late. He had been struggling with his new role as an author until the wee hours. He was making himself a cup of coffee in his kitchen when he remembered Richie Simpson was in his car outside. He left the coffee, dressed quickly, picked up his keys and went outside. Thankfully, his motor was still where he had left it. But there was no sign of an occupant. He saw that the door was unlocked. The bastard had left his car unlocked on a busy central Belfast street. It was a miracle it was still there. He opened the driver's door. He was immediately assailed by the ammoniacal smell of urine. I am going to kill the bastard, he thought. There was a group of Polish guys who cleaned cars in McCausland's car park in Grosvenor Road. He could drop the car off there. The Poles wouldn't thank him, but there was no way he was going to clean up Richie Simpson's piss. Even getting the car to Grosvenor Road would be a trial. He had one of those masks they used for the SARS (Severe Acute Respiratory Syndrome) virus that he'd picked up in Bangkok. Where the hell might it be? He could kick himself for bothering to reply to his tout's text message. Richie Simpson as a killer didn't compute. However, he was intrigued by the possibility. What if there really was a story there? Somewhere in his mind, he knew that he should pass the information along to Wilson. Maybe he should. Wilson would drag Simpson in and give him the Belfast equivalent of the third degree. That would pay the bastard back for pissing in his car.

CHAPTER THIRTY-ONE

Wilson was digging into his Cajun chicken, chorizo and red pepper linguine in the Maghera Inn. Across from him, Duane had already polished off the full meal version of chowder accompanied by a plate of wheaten bread, and had turned his attention to a main course of pulled bbq brisket and onion rings. They had eschewed wine with their meal and both were on their second pint of Guinness. Their driver had brought his own sandwiches and sat outside in the Land Rover with a flask of tea. Wilson had received two telephone calls just before lunch. The first was from Browne telling him of the events at the Brown Bear and that Best was currently sitting stewing in an interview room. The second call was much more intriguing. He knew it must have hurt McDevitt to give him the news about Richie Simpson. Some of Wilson's best collars had been made because some idiot had sat in a pub bragging about how clever he'd been. McDevitt had been quick to discount Simpson's drunken story. Wilson would have to think on it. During the call with McDevitt, he became aware of the feeling he'd had that Simpson had been involved in something nefarious in the past. The death of Robert Nichol, ostensibly at his own hand, had always bothered him. If he hadn't been so involved in a case of serial murderer at the time, he might have followed up Simpson's involvement more diligently. But it was what it was. It bothered him that he might have missed out on what could have been a murder. But the system was not fail-safe and there was more than one murderer walking free around the streets of Belfast. You could only deal with what you had. And right now, that was the disappearance of Sammy Rice and the hunt for the body of Alan Evans.

Duane looked up from his plate. 'A penny for them.'

Wilson had a flash of *déjà vu*. It was a phrase that he associated with Kate McCann. 'They're not even worth a penny. I've got a missing gang boss who may or may not be dead and I need him to clear up some murders.'

'Terrorist related?' Duane asked.

'No, I don't think so. Most of the old paramilitary gangs have morphed into criminal gangs. It's about money now and corruption, not politics except for some of the diehards on the Republican side.' He pushed his mostly finished plate aside. 'How do you think things are progressing in at the site?'

'The radar guys will let us know when they find something,' Duane stuffed a forkful of pulled pork into his mouth and washed it down with Guinness. 'You married?'

'Widower.'

'How?'

'Cancer, what about you?'

'Divorced Irish style.'

'What does that mean?'

'We signed a separation agreement ten years ago but the knot has never been broken. We've been in a state of war ever since. The breakup was my fault, the late hours, the drinking and the danger. She didn't like the idea that the IRA was threatening my family and me. For me it was part of the job, for her it was mental torture.' He turned again to his plate but didn't eat. 'I don't mean to insult you but sometimes I wish this end of the island had been detached and floated off into the

Atlantic.' He picked up his glass of Guinness. 'We're a sorry lot.'

Wilson didn't join the toast. He noticed that the barman had heard so he nodded in his direction and made the signal for the bill. 'We should get back.' Wilson stood. 'This one is on me.'

'No way.' Duane started to put his hand in his pocket but Wilson stopped him.

'Just this once,' Wilson said. 'You're the visitor.'

Duane smiled. 'My turn in Dublin, OK?'

'OK,' Wilson walked to the bar where the barman was ringing up his bill.

'You the Peelers workin' up at the bog?' The barman put the bill on the counter.

'Why?' Wilson asked.

'You're wastin' your time. There's nothing up there. I've lived here all my life and there's never been any activity around there except for the environmentalists who flood the place.'

Wilson removed some notes from his wallet and laid them on the counter. 'I suppose you'll be happy enough when the journalists and TV crews arrive.'

'To hell with the money,' the barman said. 'We thought that we were finished with that crap. Diggin' up the dead only brings trouble. If that man is up there, he's been at peace for the last thirty years. Why not leave him in peace?'

'Because somebody is responsible for his death and that person should pay.'

The barman scoffed. 'After thirty years, the sod that put him there has probably joined him.'

'That's what we're going to find out.' Wilson turned and found that Duane was standing directly behind him. 'We're off.'

They walked to the door together. 'You're a little too good to be true,' Duane said as he opened the door. 'Either that or you were wanking that man.' A broad smile creased his face. 'I've been on to the crew, nothing so far. If you have business in Belfast, now would be the time to tackle it. Things could get hectic if we find a body.'

Wilson opened his mouth to protest.

'Don't worry,' Duane said. 'If we find someone, you'll be the first to know.'

They walked towards the Land Rover. 'I'll drop you back at the site,' Wilson said.

CHAPTER THIRTY-TWO

Davie Best was getting testy. According to his watch, he'd been sitting in the interview room for more than three hours. In that time, his only diversion was drinking two cups of tea and eating a canteen ham and cheese sandwich that contained little or no ham or cheese. Over the past hour, he had risen several times to bang on the door but with little effect. He'd been mulling over in his mind what reason Wilson could have for pulling him in. It had to be Sammy. Maybe Wilson had already got to Richie Simpson and the arsehole had spilled his guts. If that were the case, Ray Wright, the other man who had been present when Sammy was dispatched would be sitting in the room next to his. He was about to start breaking up the furniture when the door opened and Wilson entered closely followed by the new detective sergeant. They didn't speak but sat on the two chairs at the other side of the table.

'About bloody time,' Best said.

Wilson laid a file on the table and nodded at the tape recorder. 'Do the necessary, Sergeant Browne, please.'

Browne turned on the tape and when it was running stated the time and those present.

Wilson opened the file and took out a photograph of the warehouse where they had found the bloodstains. He turned it to face Best. 'Sorry for the delay. Do you recognise this building?'

Best made a drama out of picking up the photo and examining it. 'Looks familiar, but then again one warehouse looks like another.'

'I'll ask the question again,' Wilson said. 'Do you recognise this building?'

'I think I was there once,' Best said.

'Do you know that this warehouse is the property of Sammy Rice?'

So it was about Sammy. Best decided he would have to tread carefully. He wasn't at the "no comment" stage yet. 'Yes.'

'And under what conditions did you visit this warehouse?'

'I was a guest of Mr Rice.'

'When did you visit the warehouse?'

'Just after the death of Mr Rice's mother.'

'When you went missing?'

'Yes.'

Wilson withdrew a second photo from the file and presented it to Best. 'I am showing Mr Best a photo of some bloodstains on the ground of Mr Rice's warehouse. What can you tell me about these bloodstains?'

Best examined the photos. They should have cleaned up after killing Sammy. He should have known the pedantic Peelers would eventually find the warehouse. 'Nothing.'

'What would you say if I told you that the bloodstain on the right has been identified as yours?'

'I had a nosebleed when I was there. I bled like a stuck pig.'

'Was the bloodstain on the left present when you visited the warehouse?'

Best handed back the photo. 'I'm not sure. I was too busy bleeding all over the place.'

'What would you say if I told you that the bloodstain on the left belongs to Sammy Rice who is currently missing?'

'Nothing.'

'Is that a "no comment"?' Browne asked.

'No, I never saw that bloodstain before. As far as I'm concerned it could belong to anyone.'

'So,' Wilson said. 'You haven't visited the warehouse since you were invited by Mr Rice and where you had a substantial nose bleed.'

'No, I haven't visited the warehouse since I had the nose bleed.'

Wilson put the photos back into the file. 'Thank you, Mr Best. And please accept my apology for detaining you for an extended period.' He nodded at Browne who declared the interview terminated and turned off the tape. Wilson watched as Best stood and went to the door. 'We may need to speak to you again soon,' he said as Best put his hand on the handle.

Best turned and looked at him.

Wilson smiled. If looks could kill, he thought. He took the file from the table and he and Browne walked to the squad room. Harry Graham joined them at the whiteboard. 'Best was involved in Sammy's disappearance,' Wilson said as they entered the room. 'He might not have pulled the trigger but he was there. Sammy's crew worked Best over in the warehouse. People like Best live on their reputations. He would never have forgiven Sammy. I don't know how he got Sammy to that warehouse on his own. But he did. Harry, go through every frame of CCTV from the area of the warehouse for the day Sammy disappeared. Find me something that shows Davie Best or someone from McGreary's gang in the vicinity.'

'OK, boss.' Graham started to move away.

'And Harry, find Richie Simpson and bring him in. Apparently, he was in the Brown Bear last night talking about having killed someone. I don't think in his wildest drunken dreams he could have killed Sammy. But I want to know whether it was drink-talk or if there was something behind it. Any news on Sammy's or Willie Rice's DNA?'

'You're not going to believe this, boss,' Graham said. 'We don't have a DNA sample for either man. Strange that, eh!'

'Very strange,' said Wilson.

'Rory, get Siobhan to put Davie Best's mugshot on the whiteboard. He's my number one suspect for Sammy Rice's disappearance.'

CHAPTER THIRTY-THREE

Richie Simpson was no longer in Belfast, and he felt the better because of it. That morning he woke and realised that he was belted into the passenger seat of an old Mercedes. There was an overpowering smell of stale urine and it took several minutes, and the examination of the wet patch on the groin of his jeans, to realise that he was the source of the smell. Although his head was pounding, he used what little willpower he had to think back on the past twenty-four hours. The events came to him in flashes and as they accelerated so did his sense of disquiet. He had broken with the habits of a lifetime. At the orphanage, he was taught to speak only when he had been spoken to. Listening was a virtue and as a good Protestant he should try to be as virtuous as possible. His two mentors, Jackie Carlisle and MI5, reinforced the message he received as a small boy. Jackie's mantra was simple: you already knew what you thought, the object of the exercise was to find out what everybody else thought. MI5 was like a giant vacuum cleaner pulling in information from hundreds, maybe thousands of touts like him. In his case, if he didn't have anything solid to report, his imagination was active enough to produce something credible. His memory of the Brown Bear was sketchy but one thing was certain. He had shot his mouth off. He felt his stomach heave when he realised what he might have said. In the pantheon of arseholes he would rank as one of the highest. His big fucking mouth had probably succeeded in getting him killed. He couldn't be that stupid. It had been an attempt at death wish. He climbed out of the car and stood on the footpath. Someone had driven him home. Slowly, the memory of the driver formed a picture on his brain. It couldn't have been, not Jock McDevitt. Davie Best wasn't going to just kill him. That would have been far too easy. He was going to suffer before he went. He rushed home, had a shower, put on new clothes and collected his money. Then he packed a bag. He went to Belfast Central train station and looked at the board indicating departures. The train for Derry would leave in thirty minutes. He bought a ticket and went to the cafeteria. He bought two cups of black coffee and a full Irish breakfast. When he looked at the plate of food swimming in grease his stomach heaved again, but he tore into it with gusto. He needed to think and he wouldn't be able to while his brain was still addled. People in Ulster held that the best cure for a hangover was a plate of fried sausages, black pudding and bacon. He hoped that they were right. The train from Belfast to Derry has only two sections that one could consider to be of interest. The first is as it passes through Antrim town and runs along the northeast corner of Lough Neagh. The second is where the train line reaches the northern coast at Portstewart and then hugs the coast on its way to Derry. However, scenery had little effect on Simpson. He spent the one and a half hour trip trying to devise a strategy that might keep him alive. When he arrived in Derry, he examined a map of the North West of Ireland. He needed a location where he could lie low. Maybe in a week or two his comments in the Brown Bear would be forgotten. He smiled. That genie was out of the bottle. He had been present in the warehouse when Sammy Rice had been murdered. He had pulled the trigger even though Best and

Ray Wright forced him. His evidence would certainly put both men in jail. But he would go there too. At least he would be alive. His best chance of survival had been to keep his mouth shut and he had blown that. As he examined the map on the wall of the station, his eyes fell on the small seaside town of Bundoran in the south west of Donegal. He went to the Ulsterbus depot in Foyle Street and bought a ticket. As he sat in the bus waiting for it to pull out of the depot, he wondered whether Davie Best's arm could reach into the Irish Republic. He was still suffering the effects of the hangover and slept fitfully during the two-hour trip traversing the county of Donegal. It was early evening when he finally came fully awake and saw that he was arriving at his destination. He took his bag and descended from the bus. He walked the short distance from the station to a street called Atlantic Way. The first building he came to was an imposing residence with a large sign offering bed and breakfast for the princely sum of thirty-five Euros. It looked ideal. Ten minutes later he dropped his bag on the floor of a small room on the second floor. He flopped down on the bed. He was four hours away from Belfast. It didn't sound like a lot but it was enough to convince him that he was safe ... for the moment.

CHAPTER THIRTY-FOUR

As soon as Davie Best was released, he picked up two gang members, both of whom he had recruited, and went looking for Richie Simpson. His interview with Wilson had convinced him that the Peelers weren't about to drop Sammy's disappearance. McGreary and he had developed the plan to get rid of Sammy on the hoof and that had been the cardinal mistake. If he had learned one thing during his army career, it was that planning trumped action every time. McGreary's desire to avoid an all-out war with the Rice faction meant that there had to be some ambiguity about Sammy's disappearance. If the body didn't turn up, who could say that Sammy was dead? That would be Wilson's problem. He had no idea where the body was and since Best and Wright were the only ones who knew, he would never find out. The weak link was Simpson. He could kick himself for not taking care of him right away. If the Peelers had found Simpson's and Sammy's bodies in the warehouse, hot guns in hand, maybe this shit-storm might have been avoided. Best spent half an hour on the phone putting the word out that a reward was available for the man who indicated the current whereabouts of Richie Simpson. The two men he sent to Simpson's address had torn the place apart but there was no sign of their quarry, nor any indication as to where he might be. There was no point in freaking out. Simpson would surface somewhere and when he did Best would be waiting for him, and one loose end would be eliminated.

Gerry McGreary was still sitting at the table in the back corner of the Queen's Tavern when Best entered. It was most unusual to find the head of the gang still holding court so late in the afternoon. McGreary was a morning person and by early afternoon he had already handled the day's work and was relaxing at home.

'Davie, boy.' McGreary nodded at one of his men to make room for Best at the table. 'Good to see you out so soon.'

'No problem, Gerry.' Best took the proffered seat and nodded at the barman for a drink.

McGreary smiled exposing a set of tobacco-stained teeth. 'You were a long time. We were gettin' worried.'

The barman put a pint of lager on the table in front of Best and he drank half the glass in one swallow. 'They kept me sitting in an interview room for three bloody hours. That arsehole Wilson was off supervising digging up that guy who's buried up in Antrim somewhere.'

Gerry McGreary hadn't survived the "Troubles" and the ensuing chaos in which he had established one of the most effective criminal gangs in the province by trusting even his closest comrades. Too many men were languishing in jail on evidence provided by a "trusted" colleague. So, when Davie Best had spent most of the day being "interviewed", McGreary's well-attuned antennae had begun to twitch. 'So when Wilson arrived what did you discuss?'

Best looked into McGreary's eyes. They were slightly hooded and Best had been around his chief for long enough to recognise the look. He took a long breath. He decided that full disclosure was in order. 'Wilson found the warehouse where we killed Sammy. There were two bloodstains on the ground close to each other. The smaller stain belonged to me from the time Sammy's guys lifted me and beat the shit out of me. The bigger bloodstain belongs to Sammy.' He put up his hand. 'I know, I know. We should have cleaned up. But everything was done without a plan. It was eighty per cent execution and twenty per cent planning instead of the other way around.'

'Wilson has marked you for eliminating Sammy?' McGreary asked.

'Maybe.' Best knew there was danger in agreeing the possibility. They had been whittling away at the Rice empire but Willie still had enough firepower to make a decent fight of a turf war. If Best were to be arrested for Sammy's murder, there would certainly be a reaction from old Willie. Best was beginning to find himself between a rock and a hard place. 'They haven't a shred of evidence. We have the gun. Only Ray and me know where the body is. They have a bloodstain on the floor of a warehouse indicating I was there. So what, they can't prove that I was there when the second bloodstain was made. If we keep a tight arsehole, there's nothing that Wilson can do.'

Gerry McGreary had been known as "Slim Ger" when he had played for Linfield. As soon as he stopped training, his body had blown up like a balloon. He shifted uneasily in his chair and ran his fingers through his mane of steel-grey hair. Best was right. Eliminating Sammy had been opportunistic rather than planned. That meant that all eventualities had not been covered. The Devil was always in the detail. The man that believed that he had committed the perfect crime was a deluded fool. He was aware that Best had ignored the biggest loose end. McGreary prided himself on the fact that he knew if a flea farted in Belfast. He had heard about Richie Simpson shooting off his mouth the previous evening. He didn't give a shit about Davie Best and Ray Wright going down for Sammy's murder. Davie was a good boy but good boys were a dime a dozen. However, he had been in the warehouse just before Sammy was dispatched. Conspiracy to murder was still on the statute books so he risked going down along with the other two idiots. 'What about Simpson?'

Best now knew that McGreary had the same information he had about the drinking bout in the Brown Bear. He had carefully ignored Simpson in his analysis of their situation. Now it was time to come clean. 'I'm on it. On the surface it looks like Simpson has done a flit. I sent a few men around to his place but there was no sign of the bastard. I've put the word out in Belfast and if he surfaces, I'll be there. As soon as I find him, he's dead.'

'And if you don't find him?' McGreary asked.

'I'll find him.'

McGreary stood up. 'I'm off home. I won't sleep sound in my bed until Simpson is in the ground. And neither should you, Davie.'

CHAPTER THIRTY-FIVE
_____

Wilson held a briefing at the whiteboard. Davie Best's photo had been affixed to the board directly under a photo of Sammy Rice and a line drawn between the two. The annotation "prime suspect" had been added beside Best's photo. Wilson had decided to concentrate the efforts of the team on finding Rice. There may, or may not, be a body buried in Ballynahone so there would only be an investigation when one was discovered. He was sure that they had a lead. There wasn't any evidence yet but every solution to a crime begins with a hypothesis. Testing that hypothesis turns up evidence that either confirms or rejects the premise. The main problem at the moment was establishing the larger bloodstain as belonging to Sammy Rice. 'Rory, would you brief the team on the interview with Best?'

Browne coughed to clear his throat. He proceeded to give a fairly clear exposition of the interview.

Wilson turned to Harry Graham. 'Have you put in a request for the CCTV footage?'

'Yes, boss. The disks should be here tomorrow.'

'As soon as they arrive, I want you to go through them. If there's a lot of footage, Siobhan will help.'

The new recruit nodded vigorously.

'Where can Willie be found these days?'

'During the day,' Peter Davidson said. 'He's in the back bar of the Brown Bear. He's moved into Sammy's house in Bally-gomartin Road. It's a far cry from his own two-up two-down in Malvern Street. Sammy's missus is barred from Belfast at the moment. She shacked up with some Dago golf professional in the Costa. Willie has a few old friends living down there that keep an eye on her.'

'I need to talk to him,' Wilson said. 'And I don't want to spend the evening searching Belfast for him.'

Davidson took out his mobile phone. 'I'll make a call.' He walked to the other end of the squad room.

Wilson and the rest of the team watched Davidson talking animatedly on the phone.

'Willie's in Ballygomartin Road,' Davidson said when he re-joined the group. 'I have a number so we can call ahead.'

Wilson turned to Browne. 'Rory, you're getting to meet all the bad guys in one day. Call the number, Peter. Rory and I will be there in fifteen minutes.'

WILLIE RICE WAS TOO old to lead a gang of young men. But what could he do? In the absence of his son, someone had to take the reins. Also, he'd been obliged to give up the drink temporarily. That sat badly with him. His wife had been murdered, his son had disappeared probably for good and he had very little to live for. He would gladly have handed the crew over to the next generation. But he didn't like any of them. They weren't the same kind as Willie and his mates who had started the crew. The people Sammy brought in were a ruthless bunch of bastards. He stared over at the man sitting across from him. He was ostensibly his minder but Willie could see that if it were required his minder would put a bullet in his skull. He wanted out. If it was proven that McGreary had killed his son, he was prepared to go out in style and take McGreary with him. There was a ring at the door and Rice motioned to his minder to answer it. Peter Davidson had called ahead and he knew it was Wilson. He wondered whether there was anything new on the search for his son. The minder returned to the living room closely followed by Wilson and a young peeler who Rice didn't recognise. He muted the television as they entered. 'What's the problem?'

'Good evening to you too,' Wilson said. He stood aside. 'This is Detective Sergeant Rory Browne.'

Browne nodded.

Rice looked at the young man. 'Are you a fuckin' Taig?'

Browne didn't answer.

The name was Protestant, but you never could be sure. 'Where are you from?' Rice asked.

'DS Browne joined us from Coleraine,' Wilson said. He removed a series of A4 pictures from his inside pocket. He selected a picture of the warehouse and handed it to Rice. 'Do you know this building?'

Rice took a cursory look at the picture. 'Never seen it.'

'It belongs to one of Sammy's companies,' Wilson said. He took a second photo and passed it to Rice. 'We found those bloodstains on the floor of the warehouse. We've identified the smaller stain but we haven't been able to identify the bigger one. Somebody bled profusely on that floor. There's a good chance that the person who produced that stain is dead.'

Rice handed back the photo. 'And where do I come into all this?'

'The bigger stain might belong to Sammy,' Wilson said.

'And it might not,' Rice said.

'We need Sammy's DNA to check it out,' Wilson said.

Willie Rice left school at fourteen. In the past fifty years, he hadn't read a single book. If a documentary programme came on TV, Willie's first reaction was to switch channel. His knowledge of DNA and how it worked was almost non-existent. However, he did know one fact. The Peelers could use DNA to put you at the scene of a crime. Willie and his son, Sammy, had used their friends in high places to avoid having to give blood samples and DNA to the Peelers. But this was a dilemma. Rice wanted to find out what happened to his son. Maybe giving DNA would advance that process.

'Can I use the toilet?' Browne said.

Rice was still considering the DNA issue. 'OK,' he said without thinking.

Browne immediately left the room. He had no idea where the toilet was but he headed directly for the stairs. At the top of the stairs there were a series of bedrooms. He chose the largest, entered quickly and found an en-suite bathroom to the side. This was certainly the main bedroom. He entered the bathroom and saw a hairbrush and comb on the side of the washbasin. He removed a plastic evidence bag from his pocket and carefully pulled all the hair from the brush and comb before placing it in the plastic bag. Then he flushed the toilet.

Willie Rice had made up his mind, there'd be no DNA. He looked around the room. 'Where the fuck did that muppet go?'

'The toilet,' the minder said.

'Find him,' Rice shouted. 'Now. I don't want him wandering around the house.'

The minder rushed outside and almost ran into Browne. They re-entered the living room together.

'We're done here,' Rice said. 'Get the fuck out, the pair of you and don't come back.'

'So, no DNA,' Wilson said.

'Find my Sammy, that's what you get paid for.'

Wilson turned and nodded to Browne. They both left the house. As they sat into the car, Browne took the plastic evidence bag from his pocket and handed it to Wilson.

'Good man.' Wilson looked at the hair inside the bag. 'There's got to be at least one sample of Rice DNA here.' Willie was still a cute old bastard, Wilson thought. But he was going to find out whose blood was in that warehouse.

CHAPTER THIRTY-SIX

The ground radar crew knocked off work at exactly five-thirty, much to the chagrin of Jack Duane. There was still plenty of light and the quicker the search area was covered the sooner that Duane would be back where he belonged. He phoned Wilson and gave him the news that the search had so far proved fruitless and that the crew would be back at work early the next morning. Duane had decided that Maghera was not exciting enough to spend an evening. He had booked a hotel in central Belfast and had imposed on Wilson to 'show him the town' as he put it. Although Wilson was reluctant initially, he could see the sense in extending the arm of friend-ship to a colleague who was as pissed off with the search for Alan Evans as he was. At eight o'clock, Wilson was sitting in his snug at the Crown enjoying his first pint of the evening when Duane pushed in the door and plonked himself in one of the chairs which complained by creaking loudly under his weight.

'Mine's a pint,' Duane said as soon as he was settled. 'And by God I feel I've earned it.'

Wilson pushed the bell and ordered the drink. 'No luck today then?'

'Depends what you call luck. We didn't find anything, and I suppose it would be best for the both of us if nothing were to be found. '

'How much of the area have they surveyed?' Wilson asked.

'A little less than half.' The barman opened the hatch in the snug and handed a pint of Guinness through. Duane took the glass and immediately downed a half. 'At this rate they might be through by tomorrow or the next day at the worst.'

'Then you'll be back in Dublin. This must be flat beer for an experienced professional like you.'

'You can speak. A chief inspector and a superintendent screwing around in the middle of a bog, they must have money to burn. Either that, or this fellow Evans is a lot more important than you and I have been led to believe.' Duane finished his Guinness and pushed the button summoning the barman.

'I hope it's not going to be one of those nights.' Wilson drained his own glass.

'Did you ever make any money out of the rugby?'

Wilson shook his head. 'They went professional as soon as I decided it was time to retire. How about you?' Wilson passed the two glasses to the barman and nodded.

'Never made a penny. A hundred thousand people in Croke Park on All-Ireland final day and the players don't take away a cent. Amateurs and proud of it, others would call it exploitation.'

Two fresh pints of Guinness were passed through the hatch. This time they clinked glasses before drinking.

'How did it end?' Wilson asked.

'Not exactly in tears, when I started playing the manager said I wasn't much for speed but he wouldn't like to run into me. By the time I finished, I was so slow I was almost static but anyone who ran into me still knew all about it.'

The snug opened and Jock McDevitt stuck his head around it. 'If it isn't Burke and Hare.' He pushed into the snug and slipped past Duane onto the bench Wilson was sitting on.

'Who's the leprechaun?' Duane asked.

Wilson laughed. 'Jock McDevitt, crime reporter at the *Chronicle*. Jock is known for his ability to get blood from a stone so no work talk.'

'And Superintendent Wilson's best friend.' McDevitt stuck out his hand in Duane's direction and pulled it back when he saw the look on Duane's face.

'What's with the Burke and Hare thing?' Duane asked. He was impressed that Wilson hadn't introduced him by name.

'You never heard of Burke and Hare,' McDevitt said. 'They were two famous grave robbers in Edinburgh in the 18th century. I hear a little rumour that's what you two are up to.'

Wilson ordered a Guinness for McDevitt. 'What Jock neglected to say was that Burke and Hare weren't just grave robbers, they murdered most of the people they subsequently dug up.'

'If the cap fits.' McDevitt smiled. 'I hope I haven't interrupted an important conversation.' He was aware that Wilson hadn't introduced his drinking companion. That only meant one thing; his companion did the kind of work that required him to remain anonymous. McDevitt guessed he might be a spook, but a southern spook. The question was, what was a southern spook doing digging up a minor northern politician?

'We were talking sport,' Duane said. 'What sport did you play?'

'Chasing women.' McDevitt took a pint of Guinness from the barman's extended hand. 'But my luck ran out when I caught one of them. I'm a bit of an expert on Irish accents. I bet you're from Galway.'

Duane was surprised. He'd been in Dublin for a long time and his Galway accent had been modulated. 'Close.' Too bloody close, he thought. He hadn't counted on spending the evening with a journalist. Perhaps he'd have to develop an alternative plan.

'Any news from the front?' McDevitt asked.

'Why don't you check with the PSNI press office?' Wilson said.

McDevitt sipped his drink and smiled. 'When you arrive in Ballynahone tomorrow morning prepare for the gathering of journalists who have nothing better to do.'

'So, you won't be there?' Wilson noted that Duane was sitting glumly. He guessed that journalists were not among his favourite people.

'I'll be sending an intern.' McDevitt was aware of a certain coldness from the direction of Wilson's companion. It didn't bother him in the least.

'How's the book going?' Wilson asked.

'Don't mention the war.' McDevitt took another sip of his drink. 'I'm a two thousand words maximum man. Nobody told me how hard it is to write sixty thousand words on one subject.'

'Have you been in to see Cummerford?' Wilson saw that Duane had finished his drink. 'Another?'

'Pint of Guinness and double Jameson, then it's an early night.' Duane didn't look too happy at the prospect of an early night.

Wilson gave the order.

'Cummerford won't see me.' McDevitt continued the conversation. 'I've even begged. Maybe you can intervene for me. She seems to have a fancy for you. Speaking of fancies, any news of Kate McCann, QC?'

Wilson saw the interest spring into Duane's eyes. 'That particular ship has sailed.'

The three men drank in silence for a few minutes.

'Did you get my message about Richie Simpson?' McDevitt broke the silence.

Wilson had put Simpson out of his mind. 'Yes, something about admitting to a killing.'

McDevitt explained the message from his tout and his excursion to the Brown Bear. He didn't stint on the details of the condition of his car or the curses of the Polish car cleaners.

'Drink talk,' Wilson said when he'd finished.

'Maybe,' McDevitt said. 'I went looking for him to present him with the bill for cleaning the car. He's nowhere to be found. And I wasn't the only person looking for him.'

Wilson sat up straight. 'Tell me.'

McDevitt had almost finished his pint. 'I heard that a couple of heavies from McGreary's crew were around his place and they're asking questions around town about where he might be. There's even talk of money being in it for the person who indicates his whereabouts.'

Wilson took out his mobile phone and contacted his new sergeant. The phone went immediately to voicemail. 'Tomorrow I want to talk to Richie Simpson. Find him.'

McDevitt put down his glass. 'I'm off. My publisher is going to squeeze my balls until I produce this bloody book. You two boys can continue talking about, eh, what was it? Oh yes, sport.' He stood up laughing and walked out.

'You have very peculiar friends,' Duane said. He picked up his double Jameson and downed it. 'I thought he'd never leave. Now let's see what your capacity for drink is.'

Wilson had stopped listening. His mind was on Richie Simpson. What had Richie done to make him run away? And why did McGreary want him so badly?

CHAPTER THIRTY-SEVEN

Helen McCann sat in the Great Room of Coleville House. She could never be in this room without remembering her husband. James McCann had been a giant. She sometimes wondered what he could have achieved if he had entered politics instead of the law. It was inevitable that he would become the highest law officer in the land. He was by far the most intellectually gifted man she had ever met. He was more than thirty years her senior when she had met him as a fresh faced just-out-of-college financial analyst of twenty-two. She had followed up a first-class honours degree in economics at Oxford University with a master degree from Harvard as a Rhodes scholar. From the moment she clapped eyes on him, she decided that she would marry him. The Circle was his legacy and she would maintain it until her last breath. However, she could not dispel the feeling that she was trying to support a structure that was already collapsing. The man who sat at the table with her, Sir Philip Lattimer, was a pygmy in comparison to her husband. The men who had created and sustained the Circle were gone. Lattimer represented the new generation and she was aware that he saw her as an anachronism. Nothing would please him more than to pack her off to her villa in Antibes. All he needed was a reason.

'They began looking for Evans at Ballynahone today.' Lattimer was cradling a brandy in his hand. He had the ruddy look of a country squire. But although his day job was running an estate of more than five thousand acres, he was also an astute businessman who sat on the boards of more than a dozen publicly listed companies.

McCann smiled. Did Lattimer think that Evans might be the straw that would break her back? 'Carlisle was a fool to keep a map of his final resting place. That piece of paper should have been incinerated immediately.

'They'll find him eventually.' Lattimer sipped his brandy. Helen McCann was one of the best-preserved women he had seen. He had no idea whether nature or the plastic surgeon's scalpel was responsible but, if required, he would guess her age to be fifteen years less than what he knew it was.

'And?'

'It was a decision of my father and your husband that put him in the ground.'

'And both of them are dead.'

'The police will still investigate.'

'Let them. They'll find nothing. All the principals are dead.'

'Rice is still alive.'

'He could give them Carlisle but no one else. And Carlisle is dead, so the trail ends there. But you have something in mind?'

'We may be required to give an explanation that will close the case completely.'

'Yes.'

'Our Italian friends have ensured that the details of Gladio are well known. You can go on Wikipedia and discover that there was a branch of Gladio established in Northern Ireland. But you cannot find the names of the individuals who belonged to that branch of the organisation.' He paused waiting for an answer.

'Continue,' McCann said.

'Gladio is defunct. The weapons the Americans left behind are rusted antiques. The couple of million dollars they contributed to our coffers have been written off. I think we should already prepare a story that will put the murder of Evans to bed without exposing the fact that the money from Gladio helped to maintain and expand the Circle.'

'And how will we do that?'

'A document could be discovered here at Coleville Hall which would explain my father's and your husband's involvement in Gladio and their decision to assassinate a dangerous communist at the behest of their American masters.'

'The CIA would issue a disclaimer.'

'It's the shadow world. Nothing is what it seems. Nobody would believe them.'

'You want to hand them your father and James McCann on a platter. You want them to be labelled murderers.' McCann's voice was strident.

'I want to separate the present from the past.'

McCann had always hoped that her daughter, Kate, would take over the mantle from her but she accepted that that hope was lost. 'I won't countenance such an idea.'

'We need to have something in hand which explains Evans's death.'

'Well think of something that doesn't sully my husband's name.'

'I have no intention of sullying anyone's name. They will be presented as patriots who signed on to protect the free world from Communism. They were men of their time. It was the forties and fifties. It was the Cold War, and Evans was the only out-and-out communist we had.'

'I'm not sure about this course of action. I'll think about it.'

Lattimer finished his brandy. 'The decision has already been taken. I just wanted to keep you in the loop.'

McCann was too old to register the shock she felt. In her mind she was the Circle. No decision could be taken without her accord. She smiled. It was not a pleasant smile. 'I see. Perhaps you would have someone call my driver.'

'Of course.' Lattimer put his Waterford brandy snifter on the table and stood.

McCann waited until he had left the room to stand. She wasn't sure that she wouldn't stumble when her legs took her weight. It was the first shot in what might prove a short war. She walked slowly and deliberately towards the door through which Lattimer had disappeared. On the way she passed a mirror and glanced into it. She didn't recognise the woman reflected in the glass. It could have been her mother. She immediately straightened her back. The reflection wasn't the real Helen McCann. She still had control over the money and whoever controlled the purse strings controlled the Circle. She may have lost round one but the fight was not yet lost.

CHAPTER THIRTY-EIGHT

Richie Simpson slept fitfully. At some point in the middle of the night he had awoken to the fact that he was a dead man. He hadn't become a dead man when he shot off his mouth in the Brown Bear. Neither had he become a dead man when Davie Best had forced him to put a bullet into Sammy Rice's head. He had signed his own death warrant when he had accepted £5,000 from Jackie Carlisle to arrange the death of Sammy Rice. It was strange but he felt a certain peace when he realised that he was dead. It was something akin to the peace a suicide feels when they have made the decision to end it all. He had played every possible scenario over in his mind. The result of every one had him in a coffin at the conclusion, except for one. He could go to Ian Wilson and spill every detail of Rice's death. After all, he had been forced to fire the fatal shot. He had no intention of following through when he had accepted the money from Carlisle. Wilson was a sensible man. He wasn't sure that the PSNI had a witness protection programme but if they had Wilson would surely put him on it. He would have to become a bottle-washer in a restaurant somewhere in Cornwall but at least he would be

still alive. And if his evidence managed to put Best and Ray
Wright in jail, he wouldn't have to look over his shoulder. But
what if they got off? Then he would be toast. There wasn't a
witness protection programme in existence that would keep
him safe from the McGreary mob. But it was his only chance.
He didn't need to make up his mind now. He would sleep on
it. If only he could sleep.

Davie Best rolled away from the woman he had been
attempting to have sex with.

'It's alright darlin',' the woman said lighting a cigarette. 'It
happens to everyone. They say it's stress.'

Best turned and punched the woman in the face sending
the cigarette flying across the room. The woman tumbled off
the edge of the bed and started crying. They were in a private
room in one of the crew's brothels. 'Get your fucking clothes
on and get out,' Best said, 'and keep your fucking mouth shut.'
Right now, he needed a good fuck not pop psychology from a
prostitute. Davie Best had never failed to perform. He wasn't
supposed to feel stress. He had tramped across the Iraqi desert,
and gone hand to hand with the Taliban in Afghanistan. He
was as tough as they come. And yet, his erection had let him
down. Richie fucking Simpson. He scarcely noticed the
woman putting on her clothes and rushing from the room. He
lit a cigarette and lay back on the bed. He pulled hard on it
drawing the smoke deep into his lungs. You can run but you
can't hide, he thought. Simpson didn't have much money so he
wouldn't run far. Ulster was a big province but he had connections everywhere. Sooner or later Simpson would stick his ugly
mug above the parapet and when he did, Best would be there.
'You're fucking dead,' he shouted.

Ian Wilson had just finished a Skype call with his

mother. Because of the time difference she had been in the middle of making dinner and had continued the conversation while she chopped vegetables and prepared fish. It all seemed so normal. When she asked about what he was up to in Belfast he talked about drinking with friends in the Crown. He tried to reflect her normality but he didn't have a normal life. It wasn't normal to be involved in digging up a body that had been laid in a bog thirty years before. It wasn't normal to be searching for the body of a ruthless gangster who had disappeared off the face of the earth. His life was just about as far from that of his mother's as you could get. Somewhere in the past he had friends. But they had normal lives. They married, bought a house, had two point four children and a humdrum job that paid the bills and the golf club membership. As time went on, the people he called friends fell by the wayside. Policemen don't have friends. Just like policemen don't have families. He'd already had enough to drink, but he poured himself a Jameson as a nightcap. He sat back and watched the lights of the city away to the west. It looked so peaceful. But looks were deceiving. Beneath the light was the darkness. Somewhere out there a woman was being raped. She probably wouldn't report it because unless there was brutality involved it was a normal occurrence. In another part of town a group of nascent criminals were beating up some old drunk for the few pounds in his pocket. And somewhere else someone was thinking about murder. There were more than three thousand unsolved murders in the province most dating from the "Troubles" but some were in the recent past. It seemed in Ulster old habits died hard. He sipped his whiskey and like clockwork Kate McCann came into his mind. He wondered what she might be up to. Perhaps she spent the evening at the theatre or the opera, clinging to the arm of someone with a normal job and a normal life. Kate was gone and while somewhere in his mind he hadn't yet fully accepted that as fact, he knew that the daily flagellation associated with thinking of her would have to stop. He would have to move on. He drank his whiskey and looked out at the city. If you could forget about the darkness beneath, it looked beautiful.

RORY BROWNE TURNED in the bed and lay on his back. The young man he just had sex with was fast asleep beside him. Browne was castigating himself for being so stupid. On the surface, the PSNI was one of the most politically correct employers in the province. But the rank and file didn't exactly share the opinion of the Policing Board and the hierarchy. So it was better to keep the question of one's sexuality to one's self. He had picked up his companion in a gay bar in Donegall Street. It was his first foray into the gay scene in his new home. There was one gay bar in Coleraine and out of necessity he had resisted the temptation to become a patron. He had known he was gay since his mid teens. Although he made several efforts to follow the path of his school friends, his dates with girls generally ended in disaster. He threw himself into his schoolwork. It was preferable to be known as a swot than gay. By the time he went to university he was ready for his first sexual experience. One of his classmates picked up on his vibe and invited him back to his rooms for a drink. One thing led to another and his cherry had been well and truly popped by the time he staggered back to his digs in the morning. He was promiscuous at college but as soon as he joined the police he put his sexuality aside. It wasn't unusual for policemen to have failed marriages or failed affairs. He joined the usual locker room banter but he kept his sexual life for his holidays and breaks away. He was sure that no one at the Coleraine station knew of his sexual orientation. That's what made his interview with Nicholson so strange. He lay staring at the ceiling. Being a gay policeman was not an oxymoron. There were plenty of policemen who had come out. There were even a couple who got married. He wondered whether Wilson had sussed him out. He didn't seem to be the sort who cared. Browne had heard of Wilson's reputation as a lothario but it didn't seem to fit. He rose quietly, put on his clothes and slipped out of the room.

CHAPTER THIRTY-NINE

W ilson passed by the station before heading for Ballynahone to hold a quick briefing with his team. There were three orders of business. He needed to know whether the blood at the warehouse belonged to Sammy Rice, the CCTV from the warehouse area would have to be collected and reviewed and Richie Simpson was to be located. He left it to DS Browne to hand the jobs out since he intended to spend the day at Ballynahone. According to Duane, this could be a make-or-break day in the search. Castlereagh had approved only a search of the immediate area indicated on the map. Once that was completed, Bally-nahone would be left with whatever secrets it contained. The ground radar crew were already at work when Wilson arrived. After listening to McDevitt the previous evening, he was not surprised to find a couple of people wandering around in waxed jackets. A van with the UTV logo on the side was parked on the edge of the crime scene tape but there was no camera in evidence. Someone with half a brain had organised for a couple of local uniforms to stand guard at the crime scene tape blocking the entrance to the bog. It was a beautiful summer day with just a few puffs of white clouds

floating across a perfectly blue sky. It was Wilson's experience that death and the burying bodies was generally associated with rain. He had been drenched at more than one
funeral. He descended from the police Land Rover and
immediately there was a flutter of activity among the four
journalists standing by the roadblock. Wilson brushed past
them without responding to their shouted questions. The
radar crew were at work about a kilometre into the bog and he
could see the X-ray machine being manhandled over the
rough ground.

'Fantastic day.' Duane was sitting on a camp chair
watching the crew.

Wilson was astonished. If he'd drunk as much as Duane,
he would still have been in his bed. He certainly wouldn't have
been sitting in the middle of a bog enjoying the already hot
sunshine. 'How long have you been here?'

'We started at seven,' Duane said. 'You Northerners aren't
the only ones with the work ethic.' He produced his flask and
two cups. "Ready for a cup of coffee? It was made on a real
coffee machine at the hotel this morning.'

Wilson nodded. He obviously needed more practice at
drinking. 'No progress?'

'Not so far.' Duane handed across a cup of steaming coffee.
'Probably another day in the can, at least the lunch at the
Maghera Inn is up to scratch. On my last dig in County Louth,
the food in the local hostelry wasn't fit for human consump-
tion. There's another chair in the crew's van. Pull up a pew. It
could be a long day.'

Wilson didn't need another day in the can. Every day was
vital in the hunt for Sammy Rice, whether he turned out to be
alive or dead.

'You don't look too happy at spending another day in my
sparkling company.' Duane sipped the hot liquid.

'Things to do, places to go,' Wilson said. He walked to the
van, removed a camp chair and placed it beside Duane's.

'I see the vultures are circling.' Duane nodded towards the roadblock.

'Aye, and it can only get worse.' Wilson sat down and sipped his coffee.

'I hope you brought your sun tan lotion,' Duane laughed.

'No cards today?'

Duane finished his coffee and tilted his head back. 'No, today we enjoy the sun. God only knows when we'll see it again.'

Wilson finished his coffee and followed Duane's example. He leaned back and allowed the sun to warm him. He spent ten minutes thinking about what might be happening in Belfast before the heat lulled him into sleep. It was over an hour later when he felt Duane's hand shake him awake.

'We're needed,' Duane said simply. 'No show of excitement, mind, but we might have something. We don't want the journalists alerted. We're just going to have a quiet word with the crew.' He stood up and motioned for Wilson to follow. They walked the hundred or so metres to where the crew had stopped working.

'What have you got, Keano?' Duane asked.

The chief of the radar crew looked harshly at Duane. 'I don't appreciate the Keano crap,' he said. 'You can call me Dr Keane or Tom, but not Keano.'

'Ok, Keano,' Duane said. 'Sorry Dr Keane. So what have you got?'

'An anomaly.' Keane pointed to a fuzzy image on the screen.

'Umm!' Duane stared at the screen. 'You'll need to up the magnitude of the rays.'

Wilson looked at the screen. It was a mass of swirling clouds as far as he could see. If there was an anomaly there, he was damned if he could see it.

Keane fiddled with a few knobs on the machine and turned to look at Duane, who nodded.

The machine made a loud whirring noise. 'It's not dangerous to stand near the machine?' Wilson asked.

'Afraid for your jewels, are you?' Duane laughed. 'The rays penetrate the ground. They're directional and the sides of the machine are lead-lined so that none of the operatives have problems producing children. Well, not caused by the machine anyway.'

The machine stopped and Keane started to turn dials and check levels. Eventually there was a picture on the screen.

'No excitement now, lads.' Duane peered at the image.

Wilson followed his gaze but saw only another pattern of fuzzy lines.

'Bingo,' Duane said.

Keane looked at the two policemen and smiled.

'We have something?' Wilson asked.

'We certainly have something,' Duane looked at the screen again. 'No jumping in the air while we're being watched. What do you think, Kean... Dr Keane?'

'I'm not sure but it looks like two bodies buried in the same grave.' Keane moved his finger over one of the fuzzy marks.

'Two bodies.' Wilson followed Keane's finger. He'd expected to see skeletons but saw nothing that he could identify as a body.

'Looks that way,' Keane said. 'Of course, it could be a man and a dog. We'll only know when they're dug up. But right now it looks like two bodies.'

'What's next?' Wilson asked.

'That's up to you,' Keane said. 'We've a half day to finish the marked out area. We can pull out now or finish the job.'

'Can I make a suggestion?' Duane said.

'You're the expert,' Wilson said.

Duane bent forward toward his companions. 'We're being watched and we don't want to give away what we've found. So, we mark this spot with a GPS and we let Dr Keane and the boys survey the rest of the area. That way we won't alert the journalists. Our bosses will have to consider the impact of what we might find down there.'

'You're sure there are two bodies?' Wilson asked.

'That's what it looks like,' Keane said. 'But we won't know for sure until your forensic people organise the dig.'

Wilson was ready to accept that one of the bodies was Alan Evans, but who the hell did the second body belong to? 'OK, let's go with Jack's suggestion. I've got to inform my boss.' He started walking back towards the van.

Duane fell into step beside him. 'If you intend to call your boss immediately, I suggest that we take a little walk until we're out of sight of the journalists.'

They started walking away from the roadblock and further into the bog. As soon as they were out of sight of the journalists, both men took out their mobile phones and moved away from each other.

'Yes,' Davis's voice was business-like.

'It's your favourite superintendent,' Wilson said.

'Cut the bullshit. Do you have news?'

The effects of the drink had obviously worn off. 'The ground radar crew think they've located what looks like two bodies.'

'Think, two bodies.' Davis's voice was strident. 'What do you think?'

'As far as I'm concerned looking at those pictures is like looking into a bush. The chief of the crew is pretty sure there are two bodies in one grave.'

'Shit, it might not be Evans after all. What's next?'

'There are a group of journalists staking out the site. Duane and I made it all look natural and the radar crew are continuing with the operation. We don't want news leaking out before we've had time to consider future actions. We've marked the spot with a GPS marker.'

'Well done.' Davis's voice was calmer now. 'I'll pass the word along to Nicholson. You stay on-site until the radar crew are through. I'll get on to the local police and make sure that the site is cordoned off. In fact I think we should block all access to the bog. It won't take the media long to sniff out that we're on to something. This second body bothers me.'

'It bothers me too. Unfortunately the only way we're going to find out who exactly is down there is to dig them up. You better get on to Castlereagh and get budget approval for the next phase of this operation.'

'I'm not going to be very popular with HQ.'

'Nothing to do with you, I'm more worried about what's going to happen when we dig them up. What I don't need at the moment is spending resources investigating a thirty-year-old murder or murders.' Wilson had been down that road and he didn't want to go there again.

'Keep me informed.' The line went dead.

Wilson looked over and saw that Duane was still talking on the phone. He started to move toward Duane but the Garda officer moved in the opposite direction. Wilson got the impression that Duane didn't want his conversation overheard. He wondered why.

Duane cut his conversation and re-joined Wilson. 'You get a reaction?'

'There doesn't appear to be much joy in PSNI circles at the news. How about you?'

'Same story, the people who count south of the border don't want the past raked up. Some of the people who might be involved are now politicians in our jurisdiction.'

They walked slowly back towards the site where the radar crew were working. 'How do we organise the dig?' Wilson asked.

'Remove the scragh with a JCB, and then your forensic pathology team will have to do their job. The people down below were most probably murdered. Bogs are good for preserving organic material. That's why bogs all over Europe have yielded up bodies with pretty good skin and hair condition. The down side is that the flow of water through the bog isn't very good for the preservation of DNA. In other words, you may not have much evidence concerning who put the bodies in the bog.'

They came over a small hillock and started to walk back towards the radar crew's van. As soon as they came into sight, Keane started in their direction. He was walking slowly and methodically.

'Oh! Oh!' Duane said. 'I don't like the way Keane is moving towards us.'

The two men stopped where they were and awaited Keane's approach.

'You're not going to believe this,' Keane said when he joined them. 'We started a new pass and lo and behold I think we've located another one.'

'What!' The word exploded from Wilson's lips.

'Shush,' Duane said. 'Speak normally.'

"There's another one down there for sure,' Keane said. 'It looks like someone was using this spot as their private burial ground.'

'Mark it and keep going,' Wilson said. 'God only knows how many more bodies you're going to find.'

Duane smiled. 'Looks like we need to retrace our steps and get back on the phones.'

'Lots of people are going to be very unhappy at this particular piece of news.' Wilson turned and started walking back the way they came. Three bodies might be just enough to put the search for Sammy Rice on the back burner.

CHAPTER FORTY

The meeting took place in the conference room of PSNI HQ in Castlereagh. The chief constable was on business in London, so Nicholson took the chair and sat at the head of the table. To his right was Chief Superintendent Bill Nolan of the Garda Siochana Special Branch and on his left was a department head from the Forensic Service of Northern Ireland. Ranged around the table were Davis, Wilson, Duane, Dr Keane and Professor Stephanie Reid. After Nicholson had welcomed the colleagues from the south, he invited Dr Keane to outline his findings.

Keane tapped a few keys on his laptop and turned it to face the assembly. 'What you're looking at is the image from the first grave site.' He could see from the faces around the table that he was going to have to get basic. 'Ground penetrating radar, or GPR as we call it, is a geophysical tool for finding bodies which have been clandestinely buried. It is one of a series of tools that have been used by law enforcement agencies to locate bodies but over time it has proven to be one of the most effective. There are situations where it is less effective than some of the other geophysical tools for example when a body is buried in very dry soil. However, in the present case where there has been a lot of fluid movement it is perhaps the ideal tool.' He looked around and saw six sets of eyes staring intently at him. The seventh set of eyes, which belonged to Jack Duane, was staring intently at the lady who had been introduced as the pathologist. Keane ignored Duane. He was now in full pedagogic mode. 'GPR systems work by sending a tiny pulse of energy into a material via an antenna. An integrated computer records the strength and time required for the return of any reflected signals. Subsurface variations will create reflections that are picked up by the system and stored on digital media. These reflections are produced by a variety of material such as geological structure differences and man-made objects like pipes and wire. Depth of GPR penetration depends on the material being surveyed and also upon the antenna frequency being used. For instance, GPR will penetrate ice, rock, soil and asphalt differently due to each material's unique electrical properties. Lower frequency antennas will generally penetrate deeper, but there is a loss in resolution with the drop in frequency. Soil conditions can vary greatly, which in turn affects GPR penetration. In general, dry sandy soils with little salt content return excellent survey resolution, but heavy clay-based soils are difficult to penetrate with GPR. In some situations, penetration depth may be limited to a few feet or less within clays, whereas pipes residing in sandy soils could be detected at depths up to 30 feet.' Keane stopped and looked around the table. 'Any questions?'

'I think that we're clear on the purpose and how the technology operates,' Nicholson said. 'Perhaps we should get on to the meat of the presentation, if you'll excuse the pun.' He smiled in a self-satisfied manner.

'So this is the rough image from the first site.' Keane pushed his glasses up on his nose. He didn't appreciate Nicholson's discounting of the technological complexity of his work. 'The images can, of course, be improved by a propriety computer programme which we have back at the office. These are what we call "field images". On this one you can quite clearly see that two bodies have been buried at this location' He removed a pen from his top pocket and traced the anomaly on the screen.

'You obviously have much more experience interpreting these images,' Nicholson said. 'But I have to confess that all I can see is a rather fuzzy cloud.'

'That is the anomaly,' Keane said. 'And I can assure you that when you dig at the location you are going to find two bodies.'

'And how can you assure us of that?' Nicholson asked.

'You can take it as gospel,' Nolan said. 'We've worked with Dr Keane before and he's never been proved wrong.'

Keane preened. 'Shall I continue?'

'Please do,' Nicholson said.

Keane tapped some keys on the laptop. 'This is the image from the second site.' He used the pen to show the fuzzy image. 'This is a single body.' He looked around the table. 'We've finished surveying the area and we have left the site.'

'Do you have any idea when the bodies might have been buried?' Davis asked.

'That is not the purpose of the GPR,' Keane replied. 'They could have been buried last week or twenty years ago.' He looked over at Stephanie Reid. 'Your pathologist might be able to answer that question when she has the subjects on her table.'

'Thank you, Dr Keane,' Nicholson said. 'I don't think that we need to detain you any longer. Perhaps you'd be so kind to furnish us with a report detailing your findings?'

Keane closed the laptop and put it into a messenger bag. 'That is part of our brief.' He stood up, bowed slightly to the assembly and left.

As soon as the door closed Nicholson turned to Nolan. 'Where do we go from here?'

'You dig,' Nolan said simply.

'And who will enlighten us on the procedure for that?' Nicholson looked around the table.

'Jack,' Nolan said looking at Duane.

'We'll need a JCB to dig down close to the bodies,' Duane said concentrating his gaze on Stephanie Reid who he noted with dismay was continually staring at Wilson. 'It's not exactly an archaeological dig. Those bodies have been down there for thirty years. It's been our experience that the flow of water in a bog and its acidic nature is very detrimental to the preservation of DNA evidence. So I wouldn't hold out much hope there. Professor Reid probably knows better than me but the bodies will be pretty well preserved. The water inhibits decomposition so there'll probably still be skin and hair. We should be able to have the bodies on the surface in reasonably complete condition in two days, maximum. The collection of whatever evidence is in the area of the grave could take longer. You might want to sieve the earth that's removed.' He looked at Nicholson. 'The options are yours. I assume JCBs are readily available?'

Nicholson looked at Davis.

'We'll have one on site tomorrow morning,' she said.

'So,' Nicholson said. 'Do I take it from what you said that we have very little chance of recovering evidence as to who might have put these people in the ground?'

'That's the gist of it,' Duane said.

'Three more murders to add to the three thousand or so on the unsolved list,' Wilson murmured.

'You said something, superintendent?' Nicholson said.

'Just reflecting on the difficulty of solving thirty year old crimes, sir.' Wilson added a sigh to show his frustration.

Reid smiled from across the table.

'Professor,' Nicholson said. 'Do you have anything to add?'

'I tend to concur with DCI Duane,' she said. 'As soon as the bodies are exposed our friends from FSNI will have to do their collection of the evidence. I'd like to visit the site as soon

as possible after the disinterment but I have no desire to conta-
minate a site which may produce so little direct evidence.'

'In summary,' Nicholson said. 'We will proceed with the
disinterment of these three bodies starting tomorrow morning.
Present will be Superintendent Wilson who will be in charge
assisted by DCI Duane. A team from FSNI will be present
and will begin work as soon as the bodies are disinterred.
Professor Reid will be kept informed and will decide when she
wishes to visit the site. Until the work is completed the whole
of the Ballynahone bog is off limits to the public. No statement
will be made to the press until the bodies have been disinterred. Are we all agreed?' He looked around the table and
registered the nodding of heads. 'Chief Superintendent
Nolan, if you would remain behind. I'd like a word.'

Wilson and Duane were the first to stand followed by Reid
and the man from the FSNI. Wilson stood close to the door
and Reid brushed him as he allowed her to pass.

'You busy,' she whispered.

He slipped out directly behind her. 'You obviously have
been.'

She smiled. 'Conference in Oslo, boring as hell but one
must keep the side up. I need a drink.'

'A woman after my own heart,' Duane chimed in from
behind them. 'I'd love to invite.' He paused for a second and
smiled. 'The two of you.'

Wilson saw that they weren't getting rid of Duane. 'I need
to check in back at the station. Let's meet at the Crown in an
hour.'

'Perfect,' Duane said leaning to take Reid's right hand and
kissing it.

CHAPTER FORTY-ONE

The murder squad room was a hive of activity when Wilson arrived. He had phoned ahead from Castlereagh to ensure that all the staff would be present for a briefing. He stood at the whiteboards with the team in a half-circle around him.

'I'm not going to go into details of the operation at Ballynahone,' Wilson said, 'except to say that it looks like we have three bodies.'

'Bloody hell,' Graham said.

'Exactly,' Wilson continued. 'Just what we don't need at the moment. I don't have much time. Bring me up to date on the Sammy Rice situation and the whereabouts of Richie Simpson.'

'I spent most of the day harassing FSNI to do the DNA testing on the hair from Rice's house,' Browne said. 'There's a backlog and we're not a priority. I'm hoping that we have something early tomorrow morning.'

Harry Graham took over. 'I've been trawling through the CCTV from the area around the warehouse from the day we think Sammy disappeared. There's a hell of a lot of it, boss.

And not a lot of it is relevant to the warehouse. Could take bloody days before I locate something.'

'I've been out and about,' Peter Davidson said. 'There's no word on the street about Sammy but the McGreary crew are getting frantic about the search for Simpson. Someone wants him, and they want him bad. I think Siobhan has come up with something.'

They all turned to face the new female member of the team. She blushed. 'I decided to review the CCTV from Belfast Central Station. I only had a photo of Simpson to go on but Harry helped me out.' She nodded towards her colleague and pinned an A4 photo print to the whiteboard. 'This is an image of Simpson standing on a platform at Belfast Central. You can see from the panel above his head that the next train due in is heading for Derry.' She pinned a second print to the white-board. 'This shows Simpson boarding the train. I've requested CCTV from Derry train station and from the Ulsterbus Terminal on Foyle Street. It should be here by tomorrow.'

'Good work, Siobhan,' Wilson said. 'We're more than a few steps ahead of McGreary on finding Simpson.'

'Don't bet on it, boss,' Davidson said. 'McGreary has put the word out province-wide. He has connections all over, especially in Londonderry.'

'I'm off to Ballynahone first thing tomorrow morning,' Wilson said. He was sorry that he had agreed to the drink. Work was piling up and he couldn't really afford to socialise until his plate became a little emptier. On the other hand, he wasn't about to deliver Reid into Duane's waiting arms. He wondered whether he was feeling jealous. Part of his agreement with Reid was that there was to be no possessiveness. That was fine in theory but difficult in practice. He wanted the briefing over so he could get to the Crown. 'In the meantime Rory will manage things here and I'm always reachable on the mobile.'

'I'm sorry, boss,' Browne said. 'We don't have the resources to follow all the lines of enquiry. How long will the Ballyna-hone business go on?'

'The bodies should be up in a day or two,' Wilson said. 'But that may only be the start of our troubles. We have to assume that the three people were murdered before they were interred. That means we could be launching an investigation.'

'Into a thirty-year-old murder,' Graham said. 'Surely that's the business of the Historical Investigations Team.'

Wilson winced inside every time he thought of his brush with historical crimes. 'They'll only review a previous investi-gation. If the people in the bog were murdered, there'll certainly be an investigation and that means us.' He glanced at his watch. It was an hour and fifteen minutes since he left Castlereagh. He knew he was being irrational but he needed to get to the Crown. 'Rory, you're in charge. I'll contact you from Ballynahone.'

CHAPTER FORTY-TWO

Gerry McGreary was also looking at his watch. It was four hours beyond the time he normally quit the Queen's Tavern but he was still seated at his corner table talking bullshit with members of his gang. He knew that his presence was creating a level of tension but that wasn't a bad thing. Somewhere out there was a man who presented an existential threat to McGreary. His extended presence in the Queen's was intended to show his crew just how seriously he took that threat. The reports coming in during the day made it clear that Simpson had run. The question was, where had the little bastard run to. He certainly wasn't in Belfast. He tried to put himself in Simpson's shoes. Mainland Britain was a big place. It would be easy to hide there. He could have caught the boat at Larne and been in Stranraer in a couple of hours. A few hours later he'd be lost in the Highlands. But would he feel safe? There would always be the chance that someone would recognise him. He would still be Richie Simpson and his name could appear in a local newspaper. He would constantly have to look over his shoulder. If he were Simpson, he would be looking for a solution to the problem that would include an element of safety. That meant that Simpson was holed up somewhere formulating a plan. They would have to find him before he was able to put that plan into action. One of McGreary's contacts in the PSNI had informed him that Ian Wilson was also looking for Simpson. That increased the threat that Simpson posed by a factor of ten. His contact also informed him that Wilson was sure he had found the site of Sammy Rice's murder. Simpson could place McGreary at that site. McGreary had spent no little time formulating a plan for his own safety. He could throw Davie Best and Ray Wright under a bus by pinning Sammy's murder on them. Unfortunately, while he had a certain amount of trust in his crew, Ulster had a habit of throwing up "supergrasses" who would spray shit over everyone they knew. Whoever said, *"dead men tell no tales"* had got it right. He glanced again at his watch. There was no point in hanging on here. Best knew that his skin depended on finding Simpson, so there was nothing McGreary could do for the moment. He envisioned that little rat Simpson in his little hidey hole. What morsel could he put on the table to attract that rat out of its hole?

CHAPTER FORTY-THREE

By the time Wilson arrived, Jack Duane had Reid squeezed into a corner of "his" snug. The Garda officer was so close to Reid that he was almost sitting in her lap. He didn't try to hide his disappointment when Wilson pushed in the door and sat down on the opposite side of the table. Wilson could see the look of relief in Reid's eyes.

'I thought you'd forgotten all about us,' Duane said.

'Hardly,' said Wilson giving Reid a reassuring smile. He wasn't about to leave her defenceless against Duane's charms. On his way from the station to the Crown, he had been reassessing his feelings towards Reid. He wasn't sure that the "adult" approach to their relationship suited him. He wasn't so out of touch with popular culture that he'd never heard of "friends with benefits". He just wasn't sure that it was part of his make-up. One thing was for sure, he'd been more nervous about Reid being with someone else than he would like to admit. He knew he was being stupid. Reid was her own woman. She had been to a conference in Oslo where men probably dominated. She would be drinking in the bar and it was inconceivable to him that men wouldn't try to hit on her. He had begun to feel those first pangs from the fork of the green-eyed monster. Was he really so shallow that he'd already moved on from Kate? She was supposedly the love of his life. She had carried his child. But Kate was gone, for good. He looked across at Reid. He knew that he wanted to be more than a "friend with benefits". The barman stuck his head through the hatch and Wilson ordered a round of drinks.

Duane finished his pint of Guinness. 'I wish to God that there was a pathologist as attractive as Steph in Dublin. Most of the people who do the cutting for us are old farts who smell of stale tobacco and alcohol.'

'A girl could get a swollen head from Jack,' Reid said. 'I don't think there's any doubt that he has kissed the Blarney Stone.'

'That's only for tourists,' Duane said. 'I always tell it as I see it.'

'Special Branch in the south must be different from Special Branch up here,' Wilson said. 'Our crowd are a bunch of liars.'

Duane feigned being hurt. "And here was I thinking we were getting along so well.' He put his arm around Reid. 'Aren't we just the perfect happy band to be disinterring bodies?'

Wilson and Reid both smiled. The drinks arrived and Wilson paid.

Duane lifted his drink with his free hand. 'To the happy band.'

Wilson and Reid joined the toast. Reid sipped her drink and then manoeuvred herself out of Duane's arm. 'You guys will have to excuse me. I need to powder my nose as the Americans say.' She slid along the seat away from Duane who was preparing to move to allow her to pass. Instead she moved in Wilson's direction and brushed past him on her way out of the snug.

'You lucky bastard,' Duane said as soon as the snug door closed.

'How so?'

Duane winked. 'There's something going on between you and the good professor.'

'I don't know what you mean,' Wilson said defensively.

'I mean you're screwing her.'

'How did you work that out?'

Duane smiled. 'I'm a detective.'

Wilson picked up his drink and took a deep swallow. If Duane had noticed the chemistry between him and Reid, others would too. That was the kind of rumour that could easily gain traction, so it wouldn't be long before Kate heard it. Why did it always come back to Kate? Why should he care if Kate knew about him and Reid? Kate was the one who finished with him. God only knew what Kate was up to. Maybe she had already found someone new. This train of thought was toxic. It would have to stop. But how could he stop it?

Reid returned to the snug and made a point of sitting beside Wilson.

Duane finished up his drink. 'I'm off,' he said. 'Tomorrow's a big day and I've intruded enough into your evening.' He bent down, kissed Reid on the cheek and extended his hand to Wilson. 'You make a fine pair.'

Reid was about to react but Wilson squeezed her arm. Instead she smiled. 'You're quite a character, Jack.'

'You're quite a character yourself, Steph. I'm going to enjoy working with you,' Duane said as he left the snug.

Reid waited until Duane would be out of earshot. 'Thank God you arrived when you did. That man has more arms than an octopus.'

Wilson smiled. 'I have a feeling that Jack's bark is worse than his bite.'

'I don't know about that but I was beginning to wonder whether I was going to be obliged to protect my virtue.'

'How was Oslo?'

'Oslo was boring. Conferences have two purposes, network and ass-kissing. Neither is of interest to me. Why do you ask?'

'Because you never said you were going.'

'My God, it's true.'

'What's true?'

'As soon as an alpha male comes sniffing around, the incumbent starts getting twitchy. You're jealous.'

'I am not.' Wilson insisted.

Reid leaned forward and kissed him lightly. 'You have nothing to worry about. Nobody has interfered with your property.'

Wilson finished his drink. 'This conversation is getting out of hand. I'm ravenous, how about dinner.'

She finished her drink. 'Lead on, alpha male.'

CHAPTER FORTY-FOUR

There were more than twenty people stationed at the now permanent roadblock into Ballynahone bog. The sunny weather had broken and the sky was full of threateningly dark clouds. The small Ulster Television van of the previous day had been replaced by its larger brother with a tripod and camera already perched on the roof. The BBC News had also sent a van, an indication of public interest into the "disappeared". Davis, who wanted to see the dig site for herself, had joined Wilson on the trip to Ballynahone. Cameras flashed at them as they stopped at the barrier and reporters shouted inaudible questions while shoving out recording devices. It was only the beginning. The media would have a feeding frenzy when the bodies were finally exposed. Wilson noticed McDevitt at the back of the bunch and when their eyes met the journalist winked. The story had obviously become important enough for McDevitt to cover in person. The uniform manning the roadblock raised the barrier to permit them entry. They drove the fifteen hundred metres or so to where a JCB stood with a group of people surrounding it. Wilson and Davis descended from the police Land Rover and joined the group. Jack Duane stood in the centre of the gathering giving orders to the machine operator. Listening on was the FSNI team already suited up in their plastic jumpsuits.

'Are we ready to start?' Wilson asked as he and Davis joined the group.

Duane looked in their direction. 'Just making sure that this boy doesn't rip up half the bog getting the bodies out of there.' He bowed to Davis. 'Chief Superintendent, you honour us with your presence.'

'You're so full of it, Jack,' Davis said. 'Show me the sites.'

They walked over to the area that had been marked out for digging. The two gravesites were fifty metres apart. The area was relatively flat and covered with moss and various types of grass. In the distance there was a fen and a stand of birch trees.

'We'll get the bodies up in reasonable condition?' she asked.

'As long as that arsehole on the JCB follows my instructions,' Duane said.

Davis removed a handkerchief from her pocket and blew her nose.

'You alright,' Wilson noticed that her eyes were reddening.

'I'm allergic to pollen,' she said. 'I took an antihistamine before we set out but the pollen count here must be off the charts.'

'It's a feature of the raised bog,' Duane said. 'We need to get you out of here before it gets worse.'

'Anyway,' Davis turned and started to walk back towards the Land Rover. 'I've put my hand in the wound. If Nicholson asks, I can say I was here for the start of the digging.' She turned to Wilson. 'I'll take the car to the station and send it back for you.' She had quickened her pace and they were already at the Land Rover. The driver opened the door for her and she climbed in gratefully.

The noise of the JCB starting up caused the two policemen to turn together in its direction. It moved slowly towards the first gravesite containing the two bodies.

'How long do you think it'll take?'

Duane nodded towards the forensic team. They were busy constructing the frames for two plastic canopies that would be erected over the gravesites when the holes had been dug. 'If the operator knows his job, those guys will be at work before the morning is out. We've done our bit, let's have a coffee.'

'What were Nicholson and your boss meeting about last night?' Wilson asked.

'Damned if I know.' Duane went back to where the forensics team's van was parked. 'These "disappeared" cases are very sensitive. They bring back the whole horror of what was done during the "Troubles". It's *let bygones be bygones* time. It's quite possible that there are people who might have been involved in disappearing people who have morphed into politicians.' He removed a flask from the van, poured two cups of coffee and handed one to Wilson.

'Politics and justice don't mix.' Wilson took the coffee and sipped it. 'This is so good.'

Duane walked towards the first site and watched the JCB operator at work. 'He knows his job,' he said to no one in particular.

'I don't like it when we're excluded from conversations.' Wilson joined him and saw that the hole was already opening. 'What's your guy Nolan like?'

'The same as your guy Nicholson, they don't get there without the help of friends and by having a conscience. You and I are expendable. We're the fall guys whichever way this ball bounces.' Duane started to walk away. 'Just as well they're makin' the canopies. I wouldn't be surprised if we were heading for a downpour.'

An hour later the heavens opened and the rain came down so solidly that it resembled stair-rods falling from the sky. After all, this was Ireland where you could have all four seasons in one day. The forensics team had already moved their canopy to the sites in order to put it over the holes as soon as the JCB was finished. Wilson and Duane watched the proceedings from the forensics team van since the Land Rover hadn't yet returned from Belfast. Just before midday, they saw the JCB move back and the forensics team move forward with their canopy. As soon as the canopy was in place, they exited the van and made their way to the first site. As they passed the JCB, the driver alighted.

'Something's there,' he said as they passed. 'I'm off for a fag and a cup of tea.'

'Half an hour,' Duane said. 'I want the other site opened as soon as possible.'

By the time they got to the canopy they were drenched. They entered the white plastic sheeting which covered not only the hole but also the area around it. Rain beat against the roof and sides of the makeshift tent. One of the forensics team was busy making a video recording of the scene while a second was shooting still photographs. They walked forward and looked into the hole. It looked like there was a bundle of filthy rags at the bottom in a pool of mucky water. There was no discernible body shapes just muck-covered lumps. Wilson thought he got a glimpse of very tanned skin sticking out from among the clothes but he couldn't be sure.

'You can bet your house on that little bugger Keane,' Duane said. 'There are two of them alright.'

'How the hell can you tell?' Wilson asked.

'This isn't my first dance,' Duane replied. 'It's not going to be pretty when they come up.'

'We need you guys out of here.' The head of the forensics team was a small middle-aged woman who looked like she could chew nails.

'How soon will you have them up?' Wilson asked.

'We'll try to finish before this evening,' she said. 'We too have homes to go to. However, we were thoughtful enough to bring arc lights in the van. If we need to work on, we've got the gear. But we'll be trying to avoid it.'

'So we can order a meat wagon for this evening,' Wilson said.

'It wouldn't be a bad idea to have one on site.' She made a pushing movement with her hands. 'Now, how about getting out of here and letting us do our work?'

CHAPTER FORTY-FIVE

W ork began on opening the second gravesite as soon as the JCB operator refreshed himself. The forensics team was working steadily on the first site. Nobody stopped for lunch. Cups of tea were passed around at one o'clock but weren't allowed to impede progress.

At two o'clock, the head of the forensics team motioned Wilson and Duane to approach. 'It's a man and a woman,' she said. The rain had abated temporarily and they stood just outside the plastic sheeting. 'We had to drain off quite a bit of the water to fully expose them. We have cleaned the muck off the bodies. We're preserving the earth that was around them for examination. Apparently the priority is preparing the bodies for removal. What we want to do is use the JCB to lift the bodies out of the hole. We have stretchers that we can get underneath the bodies but in an effort to preserve as much as possible of whatever evidence there is, we should take them out as gently as possible. How's progress on the second site?'

Duane walked across to the second site and motioned the JCB operator to stop. He looked into the hole. It was almost three feet deep. He signalled the JCB operator to continue.

'We're about three feet down,' he said when he re-joined Wilson and the head of the forensics team. 'It won't take much longer.'

'OK,' she said. 'As soon as he's through we should be ready to bring the bodies up. We'll keep them under the canopy until the transport arrives.' She nodded in the direction of the road-block. 'Our friends over there will be anxious to get some shots so we'll be as discreet as possible. They'll still be covered in mud so don't expect to identify them. There's a woman's handbag as well. We've already bagged it and we'll take that away with us. Are we clear?'

Wilson and Duane looked at each other and then nodded.

Half an hour later the JCB operator moved back from the second site and the forensics team moved forward with the second canopy. The operator walked away in the direction of the forensics van lighting a cigarette as he went.

'We'll give the poor bastard a break,' Duane said. 'He's done a hell of a job.'

'Let's take a look in the hole.' Wilson started walking toward the recently set up canopy.

Earth had been piled up in a large mound just outside the canopy. They entered through a gap in the sheeting. The second hole was almost the same size as the first. Wilson looked over the edge and saw the lump of mud at the bottom with pieces of clothing material visible at intervals. He thought he could see a shoulder and the top of an arm but decided that he was making something out of the lump that may not have been there. He looked over at Duane who was examining the hole from the opposite side. "What do you think?"

'It's a body.'

This was bizarre. McDevitt's article had set them off on the search for the body of Alan Evans and so far they had located three bodies. On the one hand, three families would now find closure and the ability to lay their loved ones to rest.

On the other, three bodies meant three murder investigations with, if Keane could be believed, very little forensic evidence. A thirty-year-old crime with little or no forensic evidence was not a scenario that he was happy with.

The transport, in the shape of two ambulances, had arrived and was stationed beside the forensics van. As they had anticipated, the arrival of the ambulances had caused a flurry of activity from the journalistic community. A camera was now mounted on the roof of the BBC van and figures could be seen manning both the UTV and BBC cameras. There would be a shot of Wilson and Duane on the TV news programmes that evening.

The JCB had been repositioned to assist in bringing up the bodies from the first burial site. As soon as they were up, the head of the forensics team approached Wilson and Duane. She looked at her watch. 'I think that we've made excellent progress but, if you agree, we'd like to continue until we have all the bodies above ground and shipped back to the Royal Infirmary. We'll be back here tomorrow to go over the site and see if there's any evidence that might help you find the people that did this.'

'We'll be here as long as you are,' Wilson said.

'Then I suggest that we get an ambulance down here to remove the first two bodies.'

Duane let out a loud whistle and the driver of one the ambulances climbed into his vehicle. He started his engine and rolled slowly over the bog in the direction of the first burial site. Duane indicated that he should park on the side of the canopy out of sight of the journalists. The driver removed two body bags from the rear of his vehicle and handed them to the head of the forensics team who took the bags and disappeared under the canopy. She reappeared ten minutes later and called the driver who opened the rear hatch. Wilson and Duane watched as two members of the forensics team carefully carried the body bags from the canopy and loaded them gently into the rear of the ambulance. Wilson was sure that the TV cameras would have captured at least part of the scene. It would have quite an impact on those who would watch it. It was easy for people to forget the violence, which had been perpetrated in their name, but scenes showing body bags being loaded into ambulances brought a sense of immediacy to events that had been dismissed as mere historical footnotes. The people in the body bags were real and possibly had paid no part in the violence that had marked more than thirty years of the history of the province. They were as innocent as the family sitting in their living rooms before being brutally murdered by a death squad made up of their neighbours. They were as innocent as the bystanders torn to pieces by a bomb. They were the innocent and the dead. And people like him were entrusted with obtaining justice for them. Sometimes it felt like a heavy burden.

The ambulance pulled away moving slowly over the bog until it reached the road into the bog. It stopped briefly at the roadblock and there was an avalanche of flashes as the photographers tried to get a picture of the contents of the ambulance. The driver increased speed when the barrier was lifted and managed to knock one of the photographers to the ground as it skidded onto the main road.

The forensics team moved to the second site while Wilson and Duane went back to the van. It was near seven o'clock in the evening when the head of the team exited from the canopy and motioned to them to come forward.

'We've cleared away most of the muck,' she said when they arrived outside the canopy. 'It looks like a woman but the pathologist will have to confirm. We'll have the body ready for transport in ten minutes.'

Duane whistled up the driver of the second ambulance and repeated his instruction to park on the side away from the journalists. Ten minutes later the third body had been loaded into the ambulance and it was on its way out of the bog.

'Good job,' Wilson said to the head of the forensics team.

'Thanks,' she said. 'But we're only beginning. We'll be here all tomorrow and maybe part of the next day depending on what we find. There's a lot of ground to be gone over.' She handed Wilson a large plastic evidence bag containing a muddy woman's satchel. 'This is the bag we found in the first grave. It might help identify the victim.'

Wilson took the bag. 'Additional uniforms are arriving soon to keep the vultures away from the site. Are we done for today?'

'I don't know about the rest of the team,' she said. 'But I'm bone tired. I need a hot bath, a glass of wine and a massage from my auld man.'

'I can relate to that,' Duane said. 'We've been drenched and dried out. It'll be a miracle if we don't catch our death of cold.'

Wilson and Duane watched the ambulance go through the same gauntlet of photographers as its predecessor. 'Three bodies,' Wilson said as they began to walk back towards where their cars were parked. 'We came here to find Alan Evans and we end up with one male and two female bodies. It looks like we've stumbled on someone's private burial ground.'

'Your problem, my friend.'

'You mean this is the end of our beautiful friendship?'

Duane smiled. 'I certainly hope so. But that might not be the opinion of my boss. Nicholson seemed to have something on his mind when he asked Nolan to stay behind. And I don't think it involved sharing a glass of something or other. I'm going back to Dublin this evening but there's an even money chance I might be back in some capacity.'

'So you get to spend an evening with the family.'

Duane took his car keys from his pocket and opened the driver's side of the car. 'To do that, I'd have to take a plane for more than twenty-four hours. The former Mrs Duane and my kids currently reside in Auckland.' He extended his hand. 'It's been a pleasure working with you. I hope you find the bastard who put these people in the ground.

Wilson shook Duane's hand. 'It's not over until it's over. Safe journey.'

CHAPTER FORTY-SIX

Richie Simpson was sitting in the Waves Surf Café on Main Street in Bundoran. On the table in front of him was the detritus of a meal that might be loosely described as dinner. He had spent the day wandering around the small seaside town looking like any other early summer tourist. Bundoran is a holiday town and one of the top centres in the world for surfing. The problem was that Simpson had never spent time as a tourist and he definitely had no interest in surfing. Was this really going to be his future? Pissing around some out-of-the-way hole praying that when he turned a corner or looked behind him he wouldn't see Davie Best's ugly mug. He looked at the table with the remains of his meal. This was money out and the only money he had coming in was the dole, and to collect that he would have to go back to Belfast. He took up his bill and went to the cash register. He carefully counted out the exact amount. The girl at the register took the money and glanced at the bowl in front of her that contained the tips for the staff. Simpson saw the look but ignored the bowl. There would be no tipping until his finances were in better shape. That thought caused him to smile. The chances of his financial situation improving were as slim as his chances of staying alive.

He was tempted to call the Queen's Tavern and speak directly to McGreary. Maybe he could convince him that what had happened was an aberration. There was no way he was going to blab to the Peelers. Who was he kidding? McGreary might agree to let him live today, but might wake up one morning and decide that he had made a mistake. Safety in general might be an illusion, but his safety in particular was too important to be left to the whims of people like McGreary and Best. They didn't like loose ends and that was exactly what he was. He ignored the harsh look of the waitress and left the café. He walked along Main Street in the direction of his digs in Atlantic Way. He turned left onto Promenade Road and bypassed the street containing his B and B. The Atlantic Ocean was directly in front of him. How he wished he could just fly across that ocean and put three thousand miles between him and his current predicament. He sat down on a bench facing the ocean and removed a folded sheet of paper from his inside pocket. He unfolded it and looked at the pros and cons he had developed concerning his situation. He knew that sooner or later he was going to have to make a decision and whatever that would be, he would have to live with the consequences. Ever since his father had died and his mother had consigned him and his sister to Social Services, he had been alone. When Robert Nichol and his friends abused him, there had been no one to turn to. Jackie Carlisle had used him for his own benefit and when he was through had discarded him like a used handkerchief. His handlers in British Intelligence had no use for him now that he no longer had access to Carlisle's secrets. He had a valuable secret but it was valuable only if he could trade it for his safety. He looked again at the paper in his hands. A gust of wind pulled it from his grasp and it hovered in the air before rushing out to sea. Tomorrow morning he would call Superintendent Wilson. It was his only chance of survival.

CHAPTER FORTY-SEVEN

Wilson was having a quiet evening in. He thought about calling Reid but he discarded the idea. If forced, he might admit that there had been a subtle change in his relationship with his "friend with benefits". Perhaps Reid was right and the sight of another alpha male sniffing around had exposed his growing feelings for the pathologist. In any event, he decided that it would be better to leave well enough alone and continue their relationship as it was. And yet, when he entered the apartment the first person he thought of calling was Reid. He opened the fridge and saw that she had thoughtfully included an additional steak in the purchases she had deposited on her last visit. Again, he felt the inclination to call and ask her to come over. Neither Duane nor he had taken lunch and his stomach was beginning to rumble. He tossed the steak on the ridge pan and found the remnants of a salad, which was just about edible. He was about to sit down at his small dining table when the buzzer went. His heart jumped when he thought that it could be Reid. He picked up the handset of the intercom.

'It's your new best friend bearing gifts.' McDevitt's voice was unmistakable.

'Piss off, I'm tired and hungry and if you come up here you might add irritable to an already long list of negative emotions.'

'That's no way to speak to a friend who has helped you break cases.'

McDevitt was like one of those flies that you swat and swat but always comes back for more. Wilson pushed the button on the intercom that opened the hall door. He opened his apartment door and returned to his seat at the table. There was no way McDevitt was going to interfere with his need to put food into his stomach. He heard the door close behind his back and looked up as McDevitt sat in the other chair at the dining table. He placed a six-pack of Guinness in front of Wilson and three black Moleskine notebooks in front of himself. 'Where do I find the glasses?'

Wilson's mouth was full so he didn't bother to answer and simply nodded at the press to the right of the cooker.

McDevitt took two glasses and opened a can of Guinness, which he poured carefully into one of the glasses before leaving it in front of Wilson. He repeated the process for himself. 'Cheers,' he said raising his glass.

Wilson ignored him and continued eating.

'Tough day at the office, I see.' McDevitt sipped his drink.

'If you've come here to get a story for tomorrow's paper, you are sadly mistaken.' Wilson's stomach was no longer rumbling. The steak had disappeared as had most of the droopy salad. He stood up and put his plate, knife and fork in the dishwasher. He picked up his glass as he passed the table and sat down on his couch facing the window that looked out on the city.

'Tomorrow's *Chronicle* has already been put to bed.' McDevitt joined him bringing along his glass and the notebooks, which he laid on the coffee table. 'You're in piss poor form. Although, I suppose spending the day digging up dead bodies is not conducive to good humour. I hear from the Royal that they received three bodies.'

'You have touts everywhere.' Wilson sipped the Guinness. It tasted good, like mother's milk.

McDevitt smiled. 'Sources, I have sources everywhere. There's a lot of nervousness in town about who might be put in the frame for planting three bodies in a bog.'

'I can imagine.' Wilson looked across the city. The murder of the three people they had dug up happened more than thirty years previously. It was even money as to whether the perpetrator was sitting out there somewhere or under six feet of earth in Milltown or Dundonald Cemeteries.

'Assuming that one of the bodies is Evans, any idea who the other two are?' McDevitt asked.

'Not a clue, if they've been down there for thirty years we may never know. Starting tomorrow we're going to make a damn good effort to find their identities.' Wilson finished his Guinness, rose, went to the table and returned with two cans. He handed one to McDevitt and opened the other for himself. "What sort of arsehole kills three people and buries them in a bog?"

'The kind of arsehole that Jackie Carlisle knew.' McDevitt pulled the tag at the top of the can.

Wilson sat up straight. 'Spit it out.'

McDevitt carefully poured the contents of the can into his glass. 'You remember those journalistic ethics we talked about some time back. Well, sometimes we have to put those ethical considerations to one side. Mind you, I'd never hand a source over on a court order.'

'I know you're too much of a professional for that. If you've come here to tell me where you got the map, get on with it, man.'

'I got the map from Richie Simpson.'

'That's a name that's been cropping up a lot lately in dispatches. And where did Simpson say he got the map?'

'When Carlisle retired he took all his papers from the office of the UDU away with him. It appears that the remover left at least one box of goodies behind and Simpson took it away with his stuff when the party went belly up. He was going through some of Carlisle's papers when the map fell out.'

'So, somehow Carlisle knew where Evans was buried.'

'And had known for years, maybe even since the day that Evans was murdered.'

'Carlisle was involved in the murder?'

'Thirty years ago, Jackie Carlisle was involved with some pretty unscrupulous characters. He changed his spots around the time all the others recanted and apologised for murdering people. Then he morphed into the glad-handing politician we all knew and loved. Have you ever seen his house in Hillsborough?'

Wilson shook his head.

'Let's just say that politics has been good to Jackie Carlisle.'

'I don't take Carlisle for a trigger man,' Wilson said.

'Neither do I. But I bet he knew plenty of people who'd put a bullet in you as quick as look at you.'

'But why Evans?'

'Damned if I know. I heard somewhere that you're a detective.'

'It could hardly be politics. Could it be money or, God forbid, women?'

McDevitt shrugged. 'All Carlisle's papers went up in smoke as soon as he died. It was the dying man's last request apparently. I would have given a pretty penny to have had the opportunity to examine those papers before his widow incinerated them.' He picked up the notebooks from the coffee table. 'Simpson also found these notebooks in the box that he took in error. There were others but he claims they contained nothing of interest.'

'Where are they?'

'Destroyed. These are the only written words left by Carlisle. He wife didn't leave as much as a postage stamp.'

'Which seems to indicate that Mr Carlisle had a lot to hide.'

'There are quite a few men and women in this province in a similar position.'

'Do you think that Simpson has any idea about what Carlisle might have been up to?'

'Simpson was Carlisle's boy. He was on the lowest rung of the food chain. That's why the UDU folded when Carlisle retired. Everybody knew where Simpson stood in the pecking order.'

Wilson held out his hand. 'Show me the notebooks.'

McDevitt passed them across. 'Half is in English, the other half is some kind of code he appears to have made up for himself.'

Wilson flipped through one of the notebooks. The hand-writing was small but clear. 'Carlisle was no brainbox. I can't imagine that a code he dreamt up is unbreakable. Can I hold on to these?'

'One condition.'

'What is it?'

'You find something interesting, I'm the first to know.' He could see doubt on Wilson's face. 'After all, I bought those notebooks with my own money. I own them.' McDevitt went to the table and retrieved the last two cans of Guinness. 'Deal?' He handed a can to Wilson.

'Deal,' Wilson said reluctantly. He took the final can from McDevitt.

'Good.' McDevitt pulled the tab on his can and filled his glass. 'Now that I've proved myself to be your best new friend yet again, tell me what you found today and who the hell is that joker from the south?'

Wilson slowly poured the can into his glass. 'I know I've said this before, you are incorrigible.'

CHAPTER FORTY-EIGHT

Wilson stood before the whiteboards in the murder squad room. The other members of the team stood in a semi-circle around him. 'We have three bodies from Ballynahone bog, one man and two women. The man and one of the women were in one grave, and the second woman was buried alone. For the moment, we have no identification on any of the corpses but we must assume that the man will turn out to be Alan Evans. So our first task is to identify the female bodies.'

'Does this mean the Sammy Rice investigation is put on hold?' Browne asked.

Wilson had spent a large part of the night thinking about the disposition of his limited resources. 'The short answer is no. Sammy has been missing for more than two months. Every day that passes makes it less likely that we're going to be able to come up with his body or any evidence as to who might have killed him.' He looked at Browne. 'Is there any news about the hair you took from Ballygomartin?'

Browne shook his head. 'We might hear something today.'

'You and Peter will continue with the Sammy Rice investigation,' Wilson said. 'For the moment Harry and I will deal with the bodies from Ballynahone bog and we'll share Siobhan.' It was the best he could do. Browne was new to Belfast and Peter was an old hand. So they should make a solid team. 'I'm going to be in and out so if anyone needs me I'm on the mobile. As soon as we identify the bodies and have a cause of death, I'll discuss the situation with the higher ups and we'll decide where the investigation will go. We're going to have a lot of balls in the air and it's important that we don't drop any of them. We'll try to have a daily briefing and Siobhan will keep the whiteboards and the books up to date. Anything else?' No one responded. 'OK, Harry my office now.'

As soon as Graham entered, Wilson instructed him to close the door. He brought him up to date on his conversation of the previous evening with McDevitt. The three Moleskine notebooks were on his desk. 'What do you think?' he asked.

'I don't like it,' Graham said. 'Carlisle's political. I could never see a reason why either side of the sectarian divide would want to get rid of Evans. He was just a communist with a small following. Carlisle was connected to the Loyalist community and there's no apparent reason why they would want Evans dead. He wasn't advocating a split from Britain.'

'And Simpson?'

'He would have been a young boy when all this happened. He stumbled upon Carlisle's involvement and made himself a few pounds. That his style.'

'Then why has he disappeared?'

'The word on the street is that shooting his mouth off in a pub has made some people very nervous. You know what they say 'three people can keep a secret as long as two of them are dead', and Belfast is a city full of secrets that more than three people know.'

'Simpson is a person of interest. Maybe not for the bodies in the bog but he wouldn't have skipped town if there wasn't a good reason.'

Wilson's phone rang and he picked it up.

'How are you this morning?' Reid's voice came over the line.

He wanted to say all the better for hearing your voice but he said. 'Fine, how are things your side?' He pushed the speaker button on the phone. 'You're on speaker phone.'

'You and your friend Duane have furnished me with plenty of work. I have three bodies for the table. Do you have any preference about the order in which I should process them?'

'Do the male first,' Wilson said. 'We need to establish his identity. What's the chance of recovering DNA?'

'I won't know until I get the bodies cleaned up. There's one of your forensic people here to gather up the mud we're going to clean off the bodies and collect up the bits of garments that are left. If there's any useful evidence to be collected, your forensic people are doing you proud. Are you sending anyone over?'

Wilson looked across at Graham. 'Harry Graham will be with you within the hour.'

'Pity, I was hoping you'd come yourself.'

Wilson turned the speaker off. 'I'll call back this afternoon for an update.'

'See you soon...' She cut the line.

'You heard, 'Wilson said.

'On my way.'

Wilson looked at the three Moleskine notebooks. He had examined all three after McDevitt left his apartment. They were, indeed, written in a mixture of English and Carlisle's own code that involved letters, numbers and symbols. There was no way he was a code breaker and to his knowledge PSNI did not employ one either. He had racked his brain but so far he had come up with no one who was a recognised code breaker. He was about to fire up his computer to check his emails when his phone rang.

'Superintendent Wilson?'

'Yes.' Wilson didn't recognise the voice.

'George Tunney from FSNI, I did some work for you on the case of the elderly ladies being murdered.'

Wilson remembered Tunney from his last visit to FSNI. 'Yes, George, what can I do for you?'

'My colleagues from Ballynahone sent me over the handbag that was recovered from one of the graves. I've cleaned it off and examined the contents. There was nothing much of interest. The purse contained about fifteen pounds but there was also a student's card from Queen's University with a picture of a very pretty girl on it.'

'Is there a name on it?' Tunney had a habit of beating around the bush.

'Yes, it's laminated so it's quiet easy to read. The young lady's name is Jennifer Bowe. I'll be making a full report of the forensic examination but I thought that you might like to know her name.'

'Thank you, George. You've been a great help.' Wilson was about to ring off when he stopped. 'Maybe you can help me with something else. You don't happen to have someone over there who can break codes.'

Tunney laughed. 'Not exactly in our remit. But there is a guy in Queen's University that might be able to help. I don't know whether he considers himself a code breaker but he's certainly interested in puzzles.'

Wilson picked up a pen. 'Name?'

'Professor Michael Gowan, he's a philosopher I think.'

Wilson wrote the name. 'Thanks George, you've been a major help. You'll email the report on the contents of the bag as soon as it's ready?'

'Of course, nice talking to you.'

Wilson looked up the number for Queen's University and phoned. He asked for Professor Gowan and ended up speaking to a secretary. Professor Gowan had a full morning of lectures and tutorials. He could meet Wilson at three o'clock that afternoon at the philosophy department office at 25 University Square. Wilson wrote the appointment into his agenda. He tapped on the glass window of his office and pointed at Siobhan O'Neill. When she responded he crooked his finger and motioned her to his office. She arrived with a pen and pad in hand.

'Jennifer Bowe,' he said as soon as she entered. 'That's spelled B-O-W-E. She was a student at Queen's University in 1983. FSNI found a student's card with that name in a handbag we retrieved from the first grave at Ballynahone. I want you to look up missing persons for 1983. Pull me the record for the disappearance of this Jennifer Bowe. Contact Queen's and ask for a transcript of her studies. Get on to Social Welfare and any other government department that might have information on her. Unfortunately, I don't have a birth date for her but she must have been born in the early sixties or possibly late fifties. By close of play this evening, I want to know everything there is to know about Jennifer Bowe. Got it?'

She finished writing on her pad. 'Got it, boss.'

Wilson leaned back in his chair. Where did the student fit into this? Evans had nothing to do with Queen's University. Why was Jennifer Bowe buried along with Evans? They'd been working on the hypothesis that some paramilitary group had murdered Evans. There was really no basis for such a hypothesis other than the *modus operandi*. Harry was right, why should either side have wanted to get rid of Alan Evans? What if the motive wasn't politics but sex? Evans was a forty-year -old man and Jennifer Bowe was probably somewhere in her twenties and they had been buried together. Perhaps it was time to pay another visit to Karin Faulkner. He was about to pick up his phone to call her when it started to ring.

'Superintendent Wilson?' The voice was a man's.

'Speaking.'

'This is Richie Simpson.'

Wilson could hear the stress in the voice.

'What can I do for you, Richie?'

'I hear that you've been looking for me.'

'Yes, it seems you were making some pretty outlandish claims in the Brown Bear a few days ago.'

"Who told you that?'

'We had Jock McDevitt in. He pulled you out of the Bear before you managed to get yourself into deeper trouble than you're already in. We're not the only ones looking for you. McGreary and Best are tearing the city apart. You're in a very tight spot, Richie. Where are you?'

'Somewhere safe.'

'With McGreary and Best on your tail, nowhere is safe. Tell me where you are and we'll bring you in.'

'I wouldn't last a day. McGreary has people everywhere.'

'OK, so why are you calling me?'

'I have information for you but I don't want to give it in Belfast. I want you to get me to the mainland. It has to be somewhere safe and then I'll talk to you.'

'You must have something very important to trade with.'

'I can tell you what happened to Sammy Rice.'

Wilson decided to take a chance. 'We already know that he was shot and killed in a warehouse in East Belfast.' He could hear the sharp intake of breath on the other side of the line. 'And we know that Davie Best was there.'

'Oh Christ,' Simpson's voice was cracking. 'They'll think I squealed for sure.'

'So, you were there too?'

'I'm not saying anymore. You fix it for me to be safe on the mainland and I'll tell you everything. I'll call the day after tomorrow. Jackie always said you were the most honest copper on the force. If you tell me that you've arranged what I've asked, I'm going to trust you.'

'Give me your number?'

Simpson laughed. 'I'll call the day after tomorrow.'

Wilson said. 'If I'm not in the office, here's my mobile number.' He called out his number. As soon as he'd finished, the line went dead. Simpson was in the wind again. It would be a race as to who found him first. Right now, Wilson was in the lead in that race. He'd had contact with Simpson but that lead could be easily cut and McGreary and Best could over- take him if they located the whereabouts of Simpson. Going dark takes money and skills that few people have. He had no idea how much money Simpson had but he assumed he was of limited means. Working as an assistant to a politician doesn't normally develop the skills that are required to go on the run successfully although being an assistant to a politician in Belfast would certainly develop some evasive skills. McGreary had Loyalist contacts throughout the province. He might also be able to plug into Republican circles. Simpson would give him McGreary and Best. He would have preferred Rice but he was pretty sure that Sammy would not appear. He picked up the phone and dialled. 'Is she available?' he said as soon as the phone was answered. 'Tell her I need to see her now.'

CHAPTER FORTY-NINE

Yvonne Davis was a thirty-year veteran of the PSNI. She had come up the hard way. After police college, she had spent ten years on the beat before being promoted to sergeant. It took another seven years to make inspector, then five more for chief inspector and finally eight more to arrive at the exalted rank of Chief Superintendent. She had survived years of sexual remarks and stopped counting the number of times her arse and breasts were touched, accidentally, of course. She had made a million cups of tea and suffered a thousand indignities. Along the way, she had lost her marriage and her husband, and if she was forced to admit it she had also lost her family. Her two sons and daughter rarely contacted her and she could understand why. She had never been there for them. They resented her not only for neglecting her role as a mother but also for neglecting it for something as pointless as breaking the glass ceiling. Her pursuit of the brass ring had cost her everything and as a prize she had been given charge of one of the most difficult stations in the most difficult city in the province. She was seeing a psychotherapist and she knew that she was drinking too much. Some days she broke into crying fits that left her feeling exhausted. She had hoped to ease herself into her new job but that had been a pipe dream. The common perception was that crime in the province was decreasing. That might be true for violent crime but her patch was replete with other crimes: burglary was rampant, drugs were everywhere, public order offences relating to alcohol, sexual offences and the ever-present hate crimes. She had come to the conclusion that someone at HQ hated her. And now Wilson wanted to see her urgently. She'd heard that Wilson attracted trouble the way shit attracted flies. And trouble was something that she certainly didn't need at the moment. So it was with a deep sigh of resignation that when she heard the knock on her door she uttered the words 'Come in.'

Wilson entered Davis's office. His new boss looked tired. Running a station could do that to you. He had never harboured a desire to sit at the top of the tree and he never envied those that did. He could see by her face that his visit was an unwelcome one.

'Sit!' She pushed some paper aside and nodded at her visitor's chair. "What's the matter?'

Wilson gave her a condensed version of his conversation with Richie Simpson. 'He won't come in unless we can assure him of his safety. Quite honestly I don't blame him. He can probably put two of the most dangerous men in Belfast behind bars. They've been scouring the city for him over the past few days and by now they've extended their search province-wide. We have the march on them at the moment but that might not last long. So the question is, are we going to comply with his conditions?'

'Are we going to have to?' She was contemplating another trip to Castlereagh and another discussion with Nicholson about budgets.

'He won't come in otherwise. And if you want an educated guess, the longer we wait the more chance there is that when he does come in, it'll be in a pine box.'

'And without his evidence?'

'Without his evidence we have nothing. We can place Best in the warehouse where we believe Sammy Rice was murdered but we have no evidence linking him with the murder.'

'How much time do we have?' She was thinking about the decision making process in HQ.

'We don't have any. Simpson is here today. Tomorrow who knows where he'll be. You'll need to go to the Chief Constable.'

'I'll call Castlereagh.'

'You want me along?'

'No, I'll go myself. When do you expect a call from Simpson?'

'I don't know. He'll probably give us a day to get organised. Don't accept a move to Scotland. McGreary will have contacts there.'

'What about Ballynahone?'

'Reid is doing the autopsies at the Royal. I sent DC Graham to attend. We have a name for the woman who was found in the communal grave. I'm having her checked out at the moment. We're really stretched.'

'Aren't we all? Keep me informed and I'll let you know how the Simpson business goes.'

'Sorry for dropping all this in your lap.' He stood up.

'It comes with the territory I suppose.' There was a tone of resignation in her voice.

'It gets easier with time.' He half-smiled. It was a lie but it was what she needed to hear. The truth would send her rushing through an open window.

CHAPTER FIFTY

H arry Graham hated autopsies. He had seen dozens of dead bodies during his career and corpses didn't freak him out. It was all the messy things that were inside and had to be taken out, weighed, examined and put back in. He was already gowned up and standing to the side of the table that contained what was left of the corpse of the man taken from the grave in Ballynahone. It didn't look like any corpse that Graham had ever seen. It was more like a large lump of brown mud with tattered bits of clothing. Professor Reid was busy hosing down the corpse with water. The mud and bits of earth were sluiced into the channels that normally drained away blood. The third occupant of the autopsy room, a female technician from FSNI, had fitted a fine mesh over the drain to catch any particles that might be washed away. Graham watched as the body gradually took on a shape that resembled a human being. Gradually bones, bits of skin and some hair appeared out of the mud. The bits of clothing that were freed by the action of the water were collected and bagged by the technician. After an hour of careful cleaning, the body of a man was exposed. Graham was amazed by the state of preservation. The skin was stained dark brown but the features were recognisable. 'Amazing,' he said when Reid had finished.

'Not really,' Reid said. 'Bodies buried in bogs a lot longer than this one have been preserved. Bogs consist primarily of decayed vegetal materials that inhibits decomposition in organic material due to constant wetness, acidic makeup and anaerobic conditions. The presence of mosses in the bogs further aid in preservation, as they act as an anti-bacterial. When a body is buried in a bog the cold water prevents putrefaction, the conditions of the bog prevent decomposition of proteins and tissue in the body, and further the lack of oxygen inhibits insect activity.'

Graham and Reid watched as the FSNI technician took photographs of the body from every angle. When she was finished, Reid pulled down the microphone and took up a scalpel. 'The body is that of a male of somewhere between thirty and forty years of age,' Reid said. The scalpel cut though the skin with the sound of a knife cutting through leather. An hour later, she switched off the microphone. 'I need a coffee,' she said to Graham. 'And I'm sure your boss is anxious to hear from you.' She strode off in the direction of her office.

Graham went out into the corridor, pulled out his mobile and hit the contact for Wilson.

'Harry' Wilson said when he answered. 'What news?'

'Professor Reid has finished the autopsy on the man.'

'And?'

'He was shot in the face. She recovered a .22 bullet from the skull. It would have made a right mess of his brain pinging around in there.'

'What about the DNA?'

'She thinks she has enough material to get a DNA sample. There was a FSNI technician here who bagged everything. We should have a ballistics report and a DNA analysis in a couple of days.'

'Good man, stay where you are until the other two bodies are autopsied.'

'What are you up to, boss?'

'I'm off to Queen's University to see a man about breaking a code.'

CHAPTER FIFTY-ONE

The office of the Queen's University Philosophy Department is located at twenty-six University Way. The row of three-storey Georgian red-bricked houses that were taken over by the university would once have been one of the most imposing and elegant addresses in Belfast. Wilson considered himself lucky to find parking on the street at the end furthest away from the official university parking. He placed his "Police officer on duty" card in the window before making his way to number twenty-six. All the houses in the row were associated with some department or other of the university. Number twenty-six had a series of stone steps leading though a small garden to a stout pink door. A brass plaque on the wall to the right of the door identified the building as the School of Politics, International Studies and Philosophy. Wilson pushed open the front door, entered and found that reception was in the first floor room directly inside the door. There were two ladies in the front room both sitting in front of twenty-three-inch computer screens. They looked up when he entered.

'Superintendent Wilson.' He stood in the doorway. 'I have a meeting with Professor Gowan.'

'First floor,' the nearest woman said. 'Up the stairs and end of the corridor. I think he's in.'

'Thanks,' Wilson smiled. He made his way up the stairs to the first floor and located the room at the end of the corridor bearing the legend "Professor Michael Gowan". He knocked and pushed the door open.

The room looked like a bomb had hit it. Papers and books were strewn on a bookcase, the desk and even the chairs. Queen's University professors certainly hadn't heard about the paperless office. A small man sat behind a desk that was so laden with papers and books that he was almost completely hidden.

'Professor Gowan?' Wilson asked.

'Yes,' Gowan stood. He was a slight man of advanced middle age. He was bald but had allowed the little hair he had to grow long at the back where it almost touched his collar. His eyes were a clear blue and his nose prominent. 'I suppose you're Superintendent Wilson.' The accent was more English than Northern Irish.

'Ian Wilson.' He entered the room and closed the door behind him. 'I got your name from George Tunney at FSNI.'

'Yes,' Gowan extended his hand and Wilson took it. 'Please sit down, superintendent.' He noticed that both his visitors' chairs were in use. 'Hand me that stack of papers.'

Wilson picked up the papers and handed them over. Then he sat on the chair.

Gowan took the papers and deposited them on a clear corner of his desk. 'George and I play a game of chess every couple of weeks or so. How can I help you?' Gowan was certainly English. Wilson thought the accent was Yorkshire.

'George tells me that you're something of a code breaker,' Wilson began.

Gowan laughed. 'I would consider myself more of a puzzler than a code breaker.'

Wilson took one of the black Moleskine notebooks from

his pocket. 'This notebook belonged to Jackie Carlisle. You may have heard of him, he was a local politician.'

'This is the School of Politics, International Relations and Philosophy, superintendent. You don't have to explain anything about politics to me. I am well aware as to who Jackie Carlisle was.'

'I'm sorry. It's a habit to think I have to explain everything. As I was saying, this is one of Carlisle's notebooks. He's been mentioned in a case and a lot of this book is in code. We don't have code breakers in the PSNI so that's why I've come to you. But as you might be aware the situation is sensitive. There may be issues of confidentiality.'

'I understand, show me the notebook.'

Wilson handed it across and watched while Gowan flicked through the pages.

'Interesting,' Gowan said. 'I'm intrigued. What's the case you're investigating?'

'I'm not at liberty to say.'

'I'll draw my own conclusions. The code associated with the letters is probably breakable. The symbols are quite another matter. I'd like to give it a crack. It all depends whether you're ready to trust me when I say that what I find will stay between you and I.'

'I need to find out what's in that book and two others that I have in my possession. Right now you're my only hope of accomplishing that. So, I have to trust you. How long do you think it'll take you to crack the code?'

'I have no idea. I'm not a professional code breaker. I'll contact you when I have something. It might be tomorrow or it might be in six months. It depends how obtuse Mr Carlisle was.'

Wilson took a card from his pocket and handed it to Gowan. 'My mobile number is there. Call me anytime, day or night.'

CHAPTER FIFTY-TWO

Wilson decided to make a detour on his way back to the station. As he was leaving University Way, he telephoned Karin Faulkner and asked whether he could drop around. He was half-surprised when she said yes. Twenty minutes later, he pulled up outside the imposing Faulkner residence in Stormont Wood. There was a vintage red Mercedes 280 SL parked in the drive. Before he could knock, the door opened and Karin Faulkner invited him in.

'Thanks for seeing me,' Wilson said. 'As I'm sure you've heard, your ex-husband's case is progressing.'

'I read the papers.' She led the way into the living room. 'Has Alan been identified?' She motioned for Wilson to sit down.

'We've recovered the body of a man along with the bodies of two women. One of the women was in the same grave as the man. And I hasten to add that the man is as yet unidentified.'

'I see.' She sat opposite him. She was wearing a white silk blouse matched with a pair of black silk harem trousers. 'It'll turn out to be Alan. So one of the women was with him when he was killed.'

'It looks that way. Did you ever hear your husband speak about a student called Jennifer Bowe?'

She paused for a second. 'No.'

'Are you sure? It was a long time ago.'

'I'm quite certain. Alan and I never spoke of other women.'

'Was he attracted to other women?'

She laughed. 'He was a man. Aren't they all?'

'We've been struggling with a motive for killing your husband. We can't think of any reason why either the IRA or the UDA might want him dead.'

'So,' she said. 'In the absence of a political motive you've come to ask whether Alan might have been killed because he was having an affair with this student.'

'That thought had crossed my mind.'

'Have you decided whether it was the student's former boyfriend or me who's responsible for the killing?'

'It's like Sherlock Holmes said, *"When you eliminate the impossible whatever remains, however improbable, must be the truth"*. 'We're not quite there yet. However, we are having difficulty formulating a hypothesis for murdering your husband and disappearing both him and this young lady.'

'And a crime of passion would be a convenient motive,' she said calmly. 'I understand it's a line of enquiry you have to follow but I assure you I had no part in my ex-husband's death. He may have wandered but by the time he disappeared I wouldn't really have cared less. Even then I was getting ready to divorce him. So be my guest. Look into my past. Do your job. Is that it?'

Wilson stood. She was a formidable woman and he had a feeling that she was telling the truth. That didn't mean that he wouldn't put it past her to commit murder. However, he could well imagine if she wanted rid of her husband she would go the legal route. 'For the moment. The male was autopsied this morning and a DNA sample taken. I hope we'll have a positive identification in the next day or so. We may need you to make a formal identification.'

'He has a brother.' She led him towards the door.

'I've met him.' Wilson followed behind.

'I'd prefer if you asked him.'

'I'll see what we can do.'

She opened the front door and made way for him to leave.

He stood in the open doorway and turned back to face her. 'One final question, did you know Jackie Carlisle?'

'What a peculiar question. How is that relevant?'

"Did you know him?'

'I met him once or twice. My current husband did some work for him at some point. '

'So your husband and he were friends?'

'That's not what I said. They did some business together.'

'Thank you.' Wilson turned to go. 'Please call me if you think of anything else, especially relating to Jennifer Bowe.'

The door shut in his face.

CHAPTER FIFTY-THREE

Wilson was suddenly very hungry. He'd had enough of the food in the cafeteria and he wanted to go somewhere where he could have a decent lunch in peace. He needed time to think. It was a fine day, warm but with more than a few puffs of cloud hiding the sun and creating patches of blue sky. He sat in his car, turned on the engine and moved off. Twenty-five minutes later, he arrived outside the Yellow Door Deli on the Lisburn Road. He hadn't been to the Yellow Door in ages and the decision to go there had been made more by his car than by himself. Or that's the way it seemed. It was quiet and he found a table outside. He treated himself to a sandwich box and a cup of coffee and thought himself a civilian as he watched the ordinary people of Belfast going about their business. He was almost through his sandwich box and on his second cup of coffee before he allowed himself to reflect on his interview with Karin Faulkner. She had swopped a two-up two-down in central Belfast for a future that included a mansion in an exclusive enclave, a Mercedes 280SL and a wardrobe to match. Not a bad deal! The only bugbear was her former husband. He wasn't about to change his mind about her potential as a murderer. It was a stretch to think that she could have intercepted her husband on his way back from Down-patrick in an era before mobile phones. Then she would have to shoot him and Bowe before transporting them to Ballyna-hone, digging a grave, burying them and disposing of the car. It could have happened that way but she would have needed help. Enter Jackie Carlisle. He knew the kind of men who would do a murder like that. Maybe she was simply the paymaster. He was sipping his coffee when his phone rang. He took a quick look at the caller ID. 'Harry, tell me.'

'Reid has just finished the autopsy on the young woman.'

'She was shot in the face with a .22,' Wilson said.

'How did you know, boss?'

'I'm psychic. What about the second woman?'

'Reid has a lecture so the second woman will be done tomorrow morning.'

'You know what that means.'

'I'm back here tomorrow.'

'Now you're psychic. I'm heading back to the station. We'll have a briefing at eighteen hundred. Siobhan should have something on Jennifer Bowe by then.'

CHAPTER FIFTY-FOUR

It was always evident when an investigation was going well. There was a buzz in the murder squad room when Wilson arrived and he decided to hold the briefing immediately. Otherwise, all information would be circulated before the briefing and the freshness of the responses would be lost.

'Let's start with Sammy.' He looked at Browne.

'The DNA has been confirmed as a match for the hair I took from Ballygomartin. So, the blood in the warehouse belongs to the same person as the hair. The problem is that we have no direct evidence that the hair is Rice's.'

'I think we can conclude that the blood at the warehouse is indeed Sammy's and that he's no longer in the land of the living. We have to turn our attention to the CCTV. We need to place McGreary and Best at the warehouse or in its vicinity around the time Sammy disappeared.'

'Peter and I have been going through the CCTV from the area of the warehouse,' Browne said. 'The problem is that there's a hell of a lot of it. Most of the buildings in the area are industrial so they have all provided footage. That's good on one side, we have plenty of footage but bad on the other side, we have too much to go through.'

'Find me McGreary and Best,' Wilson said. 'Now for a piece of important, and highly confidential news. I was contacted by Richie Simpson this morning.' He gave a short briefing on the content of his conversation with Simpson. 'The Chief Super is presenting the case to the hierarchy in Castlereagh. Richie Simpson in a witness protection programme is going to be a stretch for the powers-that-be.'

'If I know Richie,' Peter Davidson said, 'he's picturing a witness protection solution that has him sitting by a pool somewhere sipping on a Pina Colada. The truth is that he'll probably spend the rest of his life roasting his nuts off on a sheep farm somewhere in the middle of Australia.'

They all laughed.

'Simpson has information that could put McGreary and Best behind bars for a long time,' Wilson said. 'If I was about to grass those guys up, I would seriously consider a sheep farm in the centre of Australia as the safest place to be. Simpson is holed up somewhere he considers safe. But he's not dumb. So he knows nowhere is safe from characters like McGreary and Best. I just hope the Chief Constable has the balls to spend the money. We might be able to place McGreary and Best in the area but Simpson can give us them murdering Rice.' He turned towards Graham. 'Harry, the autopsies.'

Graham gave a briefing on his day at the Royal watching Reid working on the man and woman from the first grave. He had handed over the .22 shells taken from the two bodies to FSNI and a ballistics check was being run.

'Thanks, Harry,' Wilson said. 'Siobhan, what do we know about Jennifer Bowe?'

O'Neill's face reddened as four sets of male eyes stared at her. 'Absolutely nothing,' she said simply. 'She never attended Queen's University. The student's card is a fake. I found four Jennifer Bowes with National Insurance numbers but none of them fit our Jennifer Bowe. She was never listed as a missing person. I found a birth certificate for someone who could have been her but it was matched with a death certificate. Jennifer Bowe died aged five in south Armagh.' Her face reddened further. 'I'm sorry, boss. I really tried every database.'

There was silence in the room as each member of the team assimilated Siobhan O'Neill's information.

'I don't like it, boss.' Harry Graham was the first to speak.

'I know, Harry,' Wilson said. 'I'm not too happy myself.'

Browne looked from one to the other. 'What's the problem?'

Wilson wrote a question mark after Jennifer Bowe's name on the whiteboard. 'Tell him what we don't like, Harry.'

'There are several things we don't like,' Graham said. 'Firstly, people with fake identities, especially people with fake identities that have never been on any grid. We also don't like people who disappear and nobody lists them as missing. And the reason we don't like any of these things is that they smell like spooks. And where there are spooks investigations can get messed up. You think we have a spook here, boss?'

'I certainly do, Harry. And I'm worried. When I heard that there was a woman in the car with Evans, if it is Evans, I thought that maybe there might be a sexual motive for their deaths. If the woman was a spook, that theory is out the window. We don't think the IRA or the UDA were involved and the crime of passion theory is dead. That leaves us with one major question; why the hell did someone put a bullet into the heads of a third division political wannabee and a spook?'

CHAPTER FIFTY-FIVE

Wilson sat alone in the snug at the Crown. There was a pint of Guinness on the table before him but it was almost untouched. He wasn't there for the alcohol or the company. He wanted to be alone to think. It was clear that Sammy Rice was dead and that he had been sent on his way by either McGreary or Best, or a combination of both. That meant that the man responsible for the murders of Grant, Malone and O'Reilly would never stand trial. Rice may have been behind the killings but there was no way that he had the nous to set up the operation that had milked government funds. It was somewhat of a consolation that Rice had paid a much higher price for his misdeed than would have been extracted by a court of law. The men who actually did the killing would eventually be brought to book. Big George Carroll would be the star witness against them. Despite some level of justice being achieved, Wilson was left with the feeling that something wasn't quite right about the whole affair. He had passed the information on Carson Nominees to his colleagues in the Fraud Squad but even the computer geeks there had hit a brick wall in trying to untangle the web that had been created to protect those ultimately behind the corruption. It was the problem with white-collar crime; the criminals weren't the usual dopes. He preferred dealing with the likes of Rice and McGreary. They were honest to God criminals. They didn't hide behind dummy corporations and offshore accounts. Dragging Baxter and Weir before the courts would see that justice was served. But knowing that the real culprits had escaped would leave him with a bad taste in his mouth. He picked up his pint of Guinness and took a big swallow. He thought about calling Reid. Her lecture would be over by now but she would be tired after a day of cutting and sewing. She would be better left alone. Maybe it was better if he were left alone too. Then there was the Ballynahone business, another multi-dimensional crime. Why couldn't murder be straightforward? Who was he kidding? Without the challenge of peeling back the layers of the onion he would have given up policing years ago. That was the problem with his crime-of-passion theory for Evans. If Karin Faulkner wanted her husband dead, she would probably have shot him herself. Men and women did it all the time. Burying him and his supposed mistress in Ballynahone bog was a layer of complication that probably wouldn't have occurred to her. If she'd been the culprit, he would have been planted in a back yard in Belfast. But the real fly in the ointment was Jennifer Bowe, or whatever her name was. Harry was right. Everything pointed to her being some kind of intelligence agent. He'd been a child in the Eighties but he'd read all the books. During the 1970s and Eighties, Northern Ireland had been crawling with British agents from every branch of the security services. Agents from MI5 and MI6 were banging into each other as they tried to recruit operatives from the ranks of the IRA and the UDA. Then there were the covert operations involving assassination and bombing. It was field training for British agents. He could imagine a sort of sub *Le Carre* world were sophisticated Russian agents were replaced by murderous operatives with code names like "Steak-knife". Someone had dropped Jennifer

Bowe into that world and it had led to her receiving a .22 bullet in the face. He wondered what her parents had been told. Whatever it was, it had been pure bullshit. He looked up as the door of the snug was pushed in and Jack Duane's face came around the corner.

'I thought I might find you here.' Duane sat across from Wilson.

'Goodbye really is the hardest word to say where you're concerned.' Wilson smiled and pressed the button for service.

'Don't worry there are many places I'd prefer to be other than here.'

'That begs the question; Why are you here?' The barman stuck his head through the hatch and Wilson ordered two pints of Guinness.

'Orders from the big boss: *Stay close to this one, Jack. Might involve important people, Jack. Get up the nose of that poor fucker in Belfast, Jack.*'

'You know what they say, if you're not part of the solution, you're part of the problem. Are you part of the solution, Jack?'

Duane rubbed his forehead. 'I'd like to think so. What's been happening since I left?'

The drinks arrived and Wilson paid the barman. He pushed one drink across the table towards Duane. Nicholson and Nolan had buddied up but what did that mean for him? And Duane? He hadn't yet briefed Davis on the Jennifer Bowe issue so he wasn't about to give Duane advance information. The autopsies appeared to be safe ground. 'Reid carried out autopsies on the man and woman from grave one. They were both shot in the face with a .22.'

'Slainte!' Duane sipped his drink. 'So you're dealing with someone who had been there before. A .22 in the face probably from close range doesn't leave any doubt about the outcome. We were hoping that it might not involve the paramilitaries but I think that hope is out the window.'

'So, Jack, you know what we know. Where do we go from here?'

'I think we both might have a problem.'

'How so?' Wilson sipped his drink.

'Even if it was thirty years ago, my bosses would like to know who might have been involved in murdering Evans. Anything from forensics?'

'Not yet, looks like you've made a trip for nothing.'

'I wouldn't say that. I get to spend another evening in your scintillating company.'

'Are you sure that you're not part of the intelligence community?'

'Using intelligence and Garda Siochana in the same phrase is what they call an oxymoron.'

'You haven't answered the question.' Wilson's face was serious.

'Come on, Ian. I'm a policeman just like you. OK, my police world is a little more cloak and dagger than yours but we're both on the side of the angels.'

Wilson finished his drink and stood up. 'Its been a long day.'

Duane put his hand on Wilson's arm. 'Just one for the road, eh!'

'Not tonight, Jack. I'm sure I'll see you around.'

Wilson walked through the crowd in the Crown. As he passed, he stared at the faces of the patrons. Were they what they seemed? Was he becoming paranoid? Ninety-nine per cent of people wanted a happy life, a job, a house and a wife and two point four children. It was strange that the other one per cent spent their time looking for ways to screw it up for them?

CHAPTER FIFTY-SIX

K arin Faulkner pushed her plate away and looked into her husband's face. They were sitting in the dining room of their house in Stormont Wood. They were eating off Limoges porcelain and their cutlery had the mark of the St. Medard factory on it. The carpet beneath their feet was a Persian Isfahan that had cost Karin £10,000. 'He thinks one of us or both might have killed Alan.'

Robert Faulkner pushed his plate away. Although he hadn't finished, he suddenly didn't feel hungry.

'Did you?' she asked.

'Don't be ridiculous. I had nothing to do with it. It was a time when it was dangerous to be involved in politics. Alan should have kept his big mouth shut and he would probably still be around today.'

'That policeman, Wilson, asked me whether we knew Jackie Carlisle. You were friendly with him at one point.'

'At one point yes.' He and Carlisle had discussed Alan Evans but only in terms of what an arsehole he was spouting that communist shit.

'So we have nothing to worry about.'

'Not from my side.'

She smiled. 'So, you thought that I might have had something to do with Alan's disappearance?'

'The thought crossed my mind.'

The smile turned into a laugh. 'Where did you think I'd buried him? The back garden?'

'I didn't care as long as I had you.'

'For the past thirty-three years you've been thinking that you were living with a murderess. You are a silly man. Why didn't you ask me if I'd killed Alan?'

'It didn't matter.'

'What did you think when the piece appeared in the *Chronicle*?'

'I was worried for you.'

She stood and walked behind him. She bent down and kissed him. They hadn't been intimate for some time and she had wondered whether they still cared for each other. 'I love you. Not just because you thought I might have murdered to get you but because you're ten times the man Alan was.'

He stood up, turned and kissed her hard on the lips. 'Let's leave the dishes for tomorrow.'

THE CLEANING LADY pushed the steel bucket containing the mop and water into the murder squad room at the station. The room was empty and she switched on the light. She looked around furtively before starting to mop the floor. She worked her way slowly towards the top of the room mopping the floor and squeezing out the mop into the bucket as she went. Her objective was just ahead of her. When she reached the top of the room she dumped the mop into the bucket and removed a mobile phone from her pocket. She looked around one last time. She was alone. She selected the camera icon on her phone and quickly photographed the whiteboards. She smiled as she slipped the phone back into the pocket of her jeans. It hadn't been as difficult as she thought.

CHAPTER FIFTY-SEVEN

'Oh Jesus!' Chief Superintendent Yvonne Davis held her head in her hands. She had listened with growing apprehension as Wilson briefed her on the autopsies of the previous day and on the situation with regard to Jennifer Bowe. 'Is there any possibility that Siobhan messed up?'

'She's a very competent lady,' said Wilson leaning back in his chair.

'I've got to go upstairs with this right away.' She ran her hand through her hair. Her management of the station was already getting too much exposure. Some people like to have their heads up the Chief Constable's bum but she preferred to beaver away quietly. Since taking over, it seemed like she was running to Castlereagh every second day. She was worried that it would be looked on as the inability to control her environment. 'If it turns out that you're wrong and this Jennifer Bowe was simply a student, I can pack my few pictures and start looking for another job.'

'They'll find something for you but it won't be as cushy as managing people like me.'

'This is a major complication, Ian. Are you doubly sure?'

'She was never at Queen's, the only birth record for a

Jennifer Bowe is a child who died aged five, she doesn't appear on a government database and the clincher is that nobody reported her missing. She was a spook either for the British or the Irish. Evans was espousing Communism that would have interested our friends across the water. It was a twitchy time and the Cold War was still a reality. It's entirely conceivable that they would put someone close to him.'

'But could that be the reason that Evans and her were murdered?'

'I doubt it.'

'Then how is it relevant?'

'I don't know. We have two dead bodies, both shot in the face with a .22. There's no apparent motive and we have no idea who was involved. And to cap it all we have very little or no forensic evidence and the crime occurred thirty-three years ago. Finding the answer to the motive, and who pulled the trigger is called police work. Only in this case the police work might require some divine intervention. Any news on the Simpson situation?'

'Oh God! This Jennifer Bowe business put Simpson out of my mind.' She wondered whether it wouldn't be such a bad idea to be told to pack up her pictures and head for the hills. 'They're thinking about it. It's a question of budgets. Protective custody costs money, witness protection costs money.'

'Someone should tell them that you can't catch criminals without spending money. I need Simpson to put McGreary and Best in the warehouse when Rice was murdered. We'll eventually get CCTV that puts them in the area but Simpson was there. He saw who pulled the trigger. And hopefully he saw what happened to the body. Whatever he costs, he's worth it. They need to get that message.'

'Don't worry that's the message I passed. I should hear the result later today.'

Wilson stood. 'I'm more than a little pissed that I didn't get Rice myself. He was responsible for the deaths of at least three men.' He was thinking of the parents of Brian Malone standing tear-faced in the morgue at the Royal Infirmary examining the body of their dead son. It wasn't justice for them that Rice was murdered for some gangland feud. They deserved their day in court. So did he.

CHAPTER FIFTY-EIGHT

Richie Simpson was bored with Bundoran. He had walked the town from end to end and sat for hours looking out at the blue of the Atlantic. He thought back to the halcyon days when he joined the Ulster Democratic Union. Jackie Carlisle was already a political figure and somehow he picked Simpson out of the crowd and made him his contact with the paramilitaries. Simpson had traded on his leader's power. He was somebody in Loyalist circles as long as the UDU existed and Carlisle was at its head. All that was gone now. Every time he thought about the future all he saw in front of him was bleakness. He was thirty-five, unmarried, no trade to speak of bar a couple of years as a labourer on a building site and skint. The best he could do was to fill his pockets with stones and walk into the Atlantic but that would take a certain amount of desperation and he was not there yet. He had played the only card in his hand and it was either shit or bust. Either Wilson would come through for him and he would have some kind of future, or maybe he would fill his pockets full of stones. There was no way he was going to let Best get him. He knew a psychopath when he saw one and he was aware of what Best would do if he ever laid hands on him. He looked at his watch. It was almost twenty-four hours since he had phoned Wilson. He had waited long enough. He took out his mobile phone and made the call.

Wilson didn't recognise the caller ID on his mobile but answered anyway.

'Any news?'

He recognised Simpson's voice. There was more than a little fear in it. He pressed the record button on his phone. 'We're working on it.'

'The hell you're working on it. I'm sittin' here with my arse hanging out and you're working on it. I'm the only one that can give you Rice's murderers and time is running out for both of us. You know that it's only a matter of time before McGreary or Best finds me. Either you come through for me or I have to run again and I won't be calling from the next place I run to.'

'Patience, Richie. These things can't be arranged in a day. You come in to us and we'll make sure that you're safe. '

'Bollocks to that.' Simpson's voice raised an octave. 'I go to Belfast without a copper-fastened arrangement and I'm a dead man. There isn't a station in Ulster that McGreary can't get to me. I want to be on the mainland.'

Wilson was going to tell him that they would need at least twenty-four hours in Belfast to interrogate him but Simpson was already freaked out enough. 'Call me this evening at about six o'clock.'

'Fuck you.'

The line went dead in Wilson's hand.

Simpson sat with his head in his hands. The stones in the pockets were one step closer.

CHAPTER FIFTY-NINE

Wilson sat in his office. Facing him across his desk was Rory Browne and Peter Davidson. Wilson's mobile phone was on the desk replaying his conversation with Simpson.

'I've never heard Richie so twitchy,' Davidson said when the conversation ended. 'The guy is on the edge. It could go either way. We need to bring him in asap.'

Wilson valued Davidson's advice. He had been born and raised in the Shankill and he was personally acquainted with every "character" in the area. He'd known Simpson since the time he'd become prominent as Carlisle's bagman.

Wilson switched off the phone. 'They're making their minds up in Castlereagh. We should have the result of their collective reflections by this evening.'

Davidson shook his head. 'That's thirty-six hours since the first call. From the sound of it, Richie already has his fingers bitten to the quick. He's not a million miles from doing something crazy.'

'Like what?' Wilson asked.

'Like topping himself,' Davidson said. 'If I had McGreary and Best on my tail, and if it was a question of them going to prison for a long stretch, then I would surely be crapping myself that they'd catch up with me. That's particularly true of Best. I know hard men who wet themselves every time that they have to deal with that guy. He's a right nasty piece of work.'

'So what should I do?' Wilson asked.

'Lie to him.' Browne spoke for the first time. 'Call him back and tell him everything has been arranged and Peter and I will pick him up from wherever he is.'

Wilson looked at his new sergeant. He felt he had just learned something about him. 'That lie could get him killed. If he's right and McGreary can get to him if we put him in protective custody, we lose our chance to nail McGreary and Best for Rice's murder. I prefer to bring him in when we have an agreed plan of action. The two of you should be ready to travel as soon as we have word from Castlereagh.'

'I don't want to add fuel to the fire,' Davidson said, 'but Best is no longer in Belfast. They don't have the same resources as us but they have other channels. You can bet that they've traced him as far as Londonderry. Let's hope they lose the trail there.'

Wilson's mobile rang. He picked it up looked at the caller ID and pressed the green button. 'Harry, speak to me.'

Graham's voice was breathless. 'Boss, get your arse down here pronto.'

'What's up?'

'Not on the phone. Just get down to the Royal immediately. You got to see this for yourself.' The line went dead.

CHAPTER SIXTY

It wasn't like Harry, Wilson was thinking as he parked his car in a free parking spot outside the mortuary of the Royal. He made his way as fast as he could to the autopsy room. Harry was standing beside Reid at the autopsy table. Both were fully gowned. Wilson assumed that the gowned figure on the far side of the table was a forensic technician.

Reid turned as Wilson entered. 'Put a gown on first.'

Reid's assistant appeared from the office at the corner of the autopsy room carrying a gown.

Wilson slipped the gown on. He was also handed a pair of overshoes and a plastic hat. When he was fully covered he made his way to the table. The figure Reid was examining wasn't the skeleton he had expected. There were still strands of hair visible at the head and the skin was still there although it was tobacco coloured. 'What's the problem?' Wilson asked.

Reid turned the head of the figure around. 'Cause of death, multiple blows to the top of the head.'

'And that's interesting because?' Wilson stared at the head. The crown was totally caved in.

Reid turned to face him. 'It's consistent with the victim being dropped on her head multiple times.'

'Are you telling me that this woman could be Francis McComber?' Wilson was staggered.

Reid turned her gaze back to the table. 'We'll have to try to scrape enough DNA together to do a match with the Cummerford woman but I'd say there's a pretty good chance that it's her. The damage to the head is consistent with the supposed method of death. I still have a lot of work to do. Cummerford said that she was pregnant. I'll have to check that out.'

Wilson motioned the technician to join them. He addressed her directly. 'If there is one scrap of evidence on this woman, I want you to find it.'

'I've sieved all the water that was used to clean her,' the technician said. 'If there was anything on the body, I'll have it. I was super careful when I bagged the clothes. We'll examine them back at FSNI.'

'Good girl,' Wilson said. 'As soon as you know something, I want to be contacted. Immediately. Got it?'

The technician nodded.

Wilson turned to Reid. 'When will you be finished?'

'There's not much work on her. There's a lot of degradation on the organs. I suppose I'll be through in a half hour or so.'

'OK, I'll wait.'

'You're really so busy?' she asked smiling.

'Three bodies in a bog in Ballynahone and a missing, presumed dead crime boss, I'd call that a full house.'

'Then I should crack on.' She pulled down the microphone and began her examination.

Almost an hour later, Wilson, Reid and Graham sat in Reid's small office. They were each cradling a cup of coffee. 'So,' Wilson said. 'What do you think?'

Reid sipped her coffee. 'Like I said, the wounds are consistent with the woman being dropped on her head. Given that people don't get dropped on their heads until their heads crack open every day of the week, I'd say there's a damn good chance that the woman on the slab is Francis McComber.'

'Holy God!' Graham said to himself

'I wonder what else there is in Ballynahone bog,' Wilson said. 'It was obviously somebody's own private burial ground.'

'You're talking about a serial killer,' Reid said.

Wilson blew on his coffee. The words "serial killer" were ones he didn't like hearing. 'I hope to God we're not. Two issues bother me. Firstly, the IRA were the main force behind the "disappeared" and most of the people they did disappear were buried in locations down south. Secondly, we've already established that Francis McComber met her end in the romper room operated by the Loyalists. Both of these factors lead me to believe that we're looking at a Loyalist burial ground.'

'It's not their style,' Graham said. 'There have never been the witch-hunts among the Loyalist paramilitaries that took place among the Republicans. They weren't so paranoid because the security services were assumed to be on their side. When the Loyalists killed they wanted people to know about it. I can understand the need to get rid of McComber's body but what's behind Evans and the Bowe woman?'

Wilson took a slug of his coffee. 'That's a question we're going to have to answer. For the moment we're only assuming that we have McComber's body.'

'It's her,' Reid said. 'Forensics will get some DNA and you'll be able to confirm her identity but you can take my word for it now.'

'That screws things up a bit.' Wilson finished his coffee. 'We know McComber was killed by Loyalists and they buried her in Ballynahone. We can hypothesise that Loyalists also killed Evans and Bowe. The question is why?'

CHAPTER SIXTY-ONE

Gerry McGreary went over the figures for the past month. Revenues were up substantially since Sammy had gone missing. The McGreary gang's drug business was gradually expanding its reach and if it kept going at this pace he would soon be the biggest drug dealer in Northern Ireland. The news was good on every front except one; they hadn't yet found Richie Simpson. McGreary's gang was in fact two gangs. The men who habitually sat with McGreary in the back corner of the Queen's Tavern were the old crew. They were men that McGreary had grown up with and who he trusted completely. Times had been good for them and they had done well from their association with him. But they were getting old and tired. The second part of McGreary's gang was the younger guys on the way up and they were centred on Davie Best. A lot of the younger crowd had served in the British Army and had seen action in Iraq and Afghanistan. They were tough, aggressive and vicious. McGreary would never admit it but he was scared of the guys on the way up. He wasn't dumb and he realised that sooner or later he would be pushed out. Like his old crew he was tired and he had no desire to meet his Maker prematurely. But realistically, that was a distinct possibility. He wondered whether getting rid of Best would dampen the enthusiasm of the young men around him. It might delay the inevitable challenge to his leadership but the train was coming and there was very little he could do about it. Simpson might present him with a heaven-sent opportunity to get rid of Best. But Simpson would place him in the warehouse just before Sammy Rice was murdered. The Crown Prosecution Service would not need doctorates to join that particular set of dots. If Best went down, he would drag McGreary with him. He had contemplated killing Best both to protect his arse and to send a message to the up-and-comers. But he had been forced to accept the fact that Simpson held the key. First Simpson and then Best, he thought to himself. He looked up as the front door of the Tavern opened and Best entered. He had two of his ex-army mates with him. 'Speak of the devil.' McGreary watched as Best pulled up a chair and sat at the table. He noticed the old crew's nervousness at Best's arrival. He realised that he wasn't the only one who saw the train coming. 'I was just thinking about you.'

'I'll bet you were.' Best knew that he was an existential threat to McGreary. The only advantage he had was the fact that Simpson was an existential threat to both of them. 'I've tracked Simpson as far as Londonderry. Our best guess is that he took a bus from the Ulsterbus station in Foyle Street. We've canvassed the Ulsterbus guys but nobody remembers seeing an inconsequential fucking pipsqueak.'

'Is it so bad if he disappears?' McGreary asked. 'As long as he stays away, he's no threat.'

'I don't intend to spend the rest of my days looking over my shoulder,' Best said. 'I'm only going to feel right when Simpson is planted in the ground.'

McGreary folded the paper with the month's revenue figures on it. 'Simpson is becoming a diversion. We have a business to run.'

Best had known Gerry McGreary since he was a child.

McGreary was famous in the Shankill as 'Slim Ger', probably the best midfield player Linfield ever had. McGreary had been a skilful player but he was also a vicious bastard. It was the latter quality that propelled him through the ranks of the para-militaries when his playing days were over. McGreary was no longer slim but he was still venomous. Best glanced around the table. They were all yesterday's men, grown fat and compla-cent. Best knew that his turn was coming and when it did every man at this table would be on his knees begging for his life. For only one man that would be a forlorn hope. Gerry McGreary was going to have to die.

McGreary watched Best as his eyes scanned the men at the table. *I know what you're thinking,* McGreary said in his mind. He looked at the men behind Best. Their eyes looked vacant. They were trained killers. Maybe it would be better if Wilson found Simpson first. Best would go down for killing Rice and he might just squirm clear. Maybe.

CHAPTER SIXTY-TWO

Stephanie Reid took a light lunch in the cafeteria of the Royal. She wanted to have a word with Wilson but saw that the discovery of what would surely turn out to be Francis McComber had set his mind working in that direction. She wished that he'd accepted her invitation to stay for lunch but he was like a hound after a rabbit. He was as obsessed with his job as she was with hers. They were a fine pair. Both were weighed down with a mass of baggage. She had no illusions as to how their affair, if that's what it was, would end up. They both valued their space but she was beginning to want more time with him. This was unusual for her. She'd tried the cohabiting route before and it had ended in a nasty break-up. Perhaps it had something to do with the years she had spent in Africa working for Doctors Without Borders. When you've spent two years living in a cramped tent with three other women, you get an appreciation for living on your own. But her emotions were mixed. She loved waking up in his bed in the morning but at the same time she loved going home to her own place where she could do what she wanted. Sometimes she wondered what he thought about their arrangement but she didn't want to ask in case there would be a change. At this point of their relationship, she didn't want to talk about commitment. Like most women of her age she wanted it all: the fantastic job, the stunning house, the hunk of a husband and two beautiful children. But it was a fantasy and she wasn't buying into it. Most of the female hospital consultants that she knew had miserable lives trying to juggle the fantastic job, the housework, the always-on-the-prowl hunk and the needy children. She was happy with what she had. Things might change but that was the future. Three years in the Kivus in the Congo in constant fear for her life had convinced her that the only important time was now. She finished her salad, nodded to a few of her colleagues and headed back to her office at the mortuary. She was in the middle of her reports on the autopsies she had performed over the past few days when her assistant rushed into her office.

'Professor, please come quick!'

She looked up from her computer. 'Can't you see that I'm busy?'

The young man was breathless. 'We need you. One of the corpses has disappeared.'

'Corpses don't disappear.' Her new assistant wasn't a patch on his predecessor. She wondered where the hospital was finding these people. 'You've probably put it in the wrong compartment.'

'I've checked and double-checked. One of the corpses is missing.'

Reid sighed and stood up. She hated writing the reports and would usually take any opportunity to take a break but this was ridiculous. She followed the assistant into the morgue where the bodies were stored. The assistant withdrew corpse after corpse. One of the compartments was tagged but empty. Reid walked along the line of corpses. One of the bog corpses was missing. She examined the tags of the other two. It was the woman from the first grave. She took her mobile from the pocket of her white coat and called Wilson.

'Stephanie.' He hadn't expected a call from her so soon.

'Where are you?'

'Back at the office, is there a problem?'

'You could say that. You should get over here as soon as you can. We've lost one of your corpses.'

'Which one?'

'The woman from grave one.'

'I was afraid that might happen. I'll be right over.'

Wilson was back at the Royal Victoria twenty minutes later. During the trip from the station, he had given himself half a dozen metaphorical kicks in the arse. As soon as he had guessed that Jennifer Bowe was a spook, he should have put a guard on the morgue. Now she was gone. When he arrived, he went immediately to Reid's office.

She was sitting white-faced behind her desk when he walked into the room. 'How am I going to explain this?'

He remained standing. 'It's not your fault. I'm to blame. We held a briefing yesterday evening and I learned that Jennifer Bowe didn't exist. Her student card for Queen's University was a fake. She didn't appear on any database. It was clear that she was a spook. I should have immediately placed a guard on the morgue. You've got lots of CCTV around the place.'

'It seems to be everywhere.'

'Where's the security office?'

'In the main building.'

'Call them and tell them that we're on our way.'

'I've already reported that we'd lost a body. They said that they'd send someone over.'

'Forget it. This is a police matter. We go there. Make the call.'

She picked up the phone and did as he said. 'The head of the security team will meet us at the control room.'

The control room was locked and they pressed the button requesting entrance. The door swung open when they identified themselves. The control room was exactly what it said on the tin. A security guard sat before a bank of screens showing different areas of the hospital. The control panel in front of him allowed him to change the views and to control the individual cameras. As soon as they entered, a man dressed in black trousers and a black windcheater with the logo of the hospital on the front came towards them. He held out his hand. 'Mal Donaghy, chief of security.'

Wilson took his hand. 'Detective Superintendent Wilson and this is Professor Reid.'

Donaghy took Reid's hand. 'We haven't met but I've seen you around. So you're missing a corpse?'

'That's the nub of it,' Wilson said. 'But not just any corpse, you've heard about the bodies recovered from Ballynahone bog.'

Donaghy nodded. 'Aye, I saw a piece on the television news. There were three bodies recovered.'

'Well, now there are only two,' Reid said. 'I have never lost a body before.'

'It wasn't lost,' Wilson said. 'Someone took it.' He turned to Donaghy. 'That's why we've come to you.'

'When was it taken?' Donaghy asked.

'We locked up as usual about six o'clock last night,' Reid said. 'We only noticed it was missing this afternoon. '

'We need to look at the overnight footage from the cameras at the morgue,' Wilson said.

Donaghy spoke to the man at the controls.

They watched as the controller played with buttons and levers. 'Let's start at six o'clock and move forward,' Wilson said. 'Let's have the main camera at the entrance.'

The screen in the centre of the panel came to life and they saw the area in front of the morgue. 'You're sure everything was secure when you left?' Donaghy asked.

Reid didn't bother to answer and Donaghy understood the message from her silence. The picture on the screen moved forward quickly and Reid and her assistant could be seen leaving the building after everyone else had departed. The picture gradually darkened as night fell. The time clock in the corner of the picture raced ahead. It was showing just after four o'clock when a black SUV pulled up in front of the building. A man wearing a hoodie and a pair of dark glasses exited from the rear and took something from his pocket and pointed it at the camera. The screen suddenly went green.

'What the...' Wilson said.

'It's a laser,' Donaghy said. 'He's pointing a bloody laser at the camera.'

Wilson cursed under his breath. 'He knew exactly where it was located. Switch to the cameras inside the morgue. Move the time along to four ten in the morning.'

The camera was focussed on the front door, which swung open within a minute of the SUV's arrival.

'So much for locking up securely.' Reid watched as a man in a hoodie with dark glasses entered the morgue. He was holding a small contraption in his hand. Suddenly the picture on the screen disappeared and was replaced with a series of horizontal lines.

'Electronic jammer,' Donaghy said quietly. 'It'll take out every camera in the morgue.' He tapped the controller on the shoulder. 'Try the camera in the storage area.'

A picture of the area where the bodies were stored appeared on the screen. As the time advanced it too descended into a series of horizontal lines.

'Back to the outside camera,' Wilson said. The screen went green. 'Move it ahead.'

The timer in the corner moved forward. After three minutes, the picture cleared and the SUV was seen speeding away.

'Shit,' Wilson said. Although he was annoyed, he was forced to appreciate the professionalism of the crew who'd taken the body. Three minutes in and out. 'Can you make me a copy of the arrival and departure of the SUV? And I want a picture of the guy with the jammer in his hand.' He knew he was whistling in the wind. They would never identify or find the SUV. If he had to guess, he would say that the SUV was already somewhere in England. And so were the crew who'd removed the body. They would never see Jennifer Bowe, or whoever she was, again either. Maybe it was the spook equivalent of not leaving a comrade on the battlefield. More likely it was engineered to ensure that the investigation into who Jennifer Bowe really was would be dead in the water. He couldn't imagine anyone at headquarters being bothered by the disappearance of a body. In fact, their approval for the operation might have been sought. He realised that his request for a copy of the CCTV was perfunctory. Jennifer Bowe was gone. He hoped that whoever had her would give her the decent burial she deserved. He shook hands with Donaghy, gave him his card and ushered Reid out of the security control room.

They walked back toward the morgue. 'I should have anticipated this,' Wilson said. 'When O'Neill started poking around looking for background on Jennifer Bowe, bells must have started ringing somewhere. We've probably been monitored from the start of the disinterment of the bodies. They knew exactly where they were stored and they mounted an operation within a matter of hours. Impressive.' For no reason at all a picture of Jack Duane crossed his mind.

'I suppose that screws up your investigation,' Reid said as they entered the morgue.

'On the contrary, Bowe was a distraction albeit a very interesting one. Now, we can concentrate on finding who murdered Evans, and why. And if we can match the DNA of the third body to Cummerford we might put another crime to bed.'

CHAPTER SIXTY-THREE

Chief Superintendent Yvonne Davis was trying to compute the information that she was receiving. She knew that she was staring at the man facing her. It could have been because she found Ian Wilson attractive and charming but the real reason was that her mind was reeling from the words that were coming from his mouth. She had been told that Wilson was just about the most dangerous employee she could have been given. The word on him was that he was unmanageable. But looking at his handsome face and listening to his soft Ulster accent could beguile a woman, except Yvonne Davis wasn't easily beguiled. She was beginning to understand the veracity of the rumours. Wilson had just finished briefing her on the disappearance of the body from the Royal Victoria and the possibility that the woman in the second grave was Francis McComber. His briefing was full of words that sent shivers up her spine. She almost fainted when he expanded on his theory that it was either the British or Irish security services who had stolen the body of the woman they knew as Jennifer Bowe. Davis didn't live in a world where bodies were stolen by people who were effectively spies.

Wilson was the one who was bringing these kind of people into her life.

'You'll have to report it to HQ.' He leaned back in his chair. Davis's face was several shades whiter than it had been when he entered her office.

Davis made an effort to pull herself together. She pulled a few strands of hair away from her face and brushed them to the side. 'How am I going to explain that we've lost a body that might be important in our investigation? That bastard Nicholson is watching every move I make. I'm beginning to feel that they're waiting for me to screw up so that they can get rid of me.'

'Now you're being paranoid,' Wilson said. In general, it was the boss's job to calm the staff. The boot was on the other foot here. 'You've only been in the job a wet week. Even an arsehole like Nicholson knew that it took time to master a new job. So a corpse was taken from the Royal Victoria, so what? You can put the blame on me for not putting a guard on the morgue. But even I didn't think that they had the capacity to put an operation like that together so quickly. If we really wanted to follow up, we could check the arrival of a military transport at the airport last night and departures sometime around five o'clock in the morning. But that's not going to happen. The corpse that was taken disappeared thirty odd years ago and nobody even reported her as a missing person. It'll go down as a black mark against me. Now we can concentrate on Evans and Francis McComber.'

'We already know who killed McComber. What more can we learn?'

'I interrogated Maggie before Jennings pulled me off the case. One of the memories she has of the day was a big man loading something like a body into the trunk of his car before dropping her in the middle of a housing estate. We can suppose that whoever that man was, and I already have my suspicions, knew about Ballynahone bog. And it might even be his own private burial ground.'

'Who are we talking about?'

'Who would Lizzie Rice turn to in order to get rid of a body? Her husband was one of the main Loyalist paramilitaries at the time. I think Maggie's "big man" was Willie Rice.'

'You can think what you like but what can you prove?'

Wilson smiled. 'You're right. I'm waiting for the forensic report. We have the bullet, which we'll be able to match to a gun. If the gun still exists. I doubt we'll find any of Rice's DNA on the bodies. It would have degraded by now. So there's no real evidence linking Rice to the murders of Evans and Bowe. But he doesn't know that. I'm going to get him down to the station and grill him. We'll let him think we have a little more than what we actually have. I don't expect him to break down and admit the murder but we might learn something that will be useful to us.'

Davis was gradually regaining her composure. Wilson was right. She had no role in the disappearance of the body. She could lay that at his feet. His theory of the involvement of the security services was just that, a theory. There was less than one minute of video footage and no one could be clearly identified. Jennifer Bowe had disappeared once before, why shouldn't she disappear again? 'Sounds like a plan.'

'What's the story on Simpson?' Wilson asked.

'I almost forgot. Headquarters has agreed to his request. They've already contacted the witness protection programme and there's general agreement that if he co-operates, he'll be looked after.'

I hope he likes sheep shearing, Wilson thought. 'Good, I'm expecting a call from him. I'll pass the message on and I'll send Browne and Graham to pick him up.'

'What's you next step on Evans?'

Wilson stood up. 'I'm going to see Maggie Cummerford tomorrow. I need to tell her that we've found her mother.'

'The DNA is confirmed.' 'No, but it will be.'

CHAPTER SIXTY-FOUR

Wilson stood in front of the whiteboard for the six o'clock briefing. He outlined his theory concerning the disappearance of Jennifer Bowe from the Royal Victoria. DC O'Neill had already pinned up a still photo of the hooded figure that exited from the SUV. 'My guess is that we'll be able to clean Jennifer Bowe off the board in the next few days. Someone at HQ will decide that despite the photos taken by FSNI at Ballynahone, and despite the photos taken at the autopsy, she was a figment of our imagination. She never existed.' He tapped the photo on the whiteboard. 'And this guy also never existed.'

'What a crock of shit, boss,' Harry Graham said. 'Makes you wonder why we bother when some arseholes can wander around doing pretty much as they please. And all because it's in the interest of national security.'

I suppose that I can stop looking for information on her?' O'Neill asked.

'No matter how hard you tried you wouldn't find anything,' Wilson replied. 'Jennifer Bowe was a made-up person. She was a waste of our precious time and we have enough on our plate. Don't think that I'm not pissed with what happened. I'd love to drag those guys in the SUV into the light but I have to accept that it's not going to happen and move on.'

'What about Evans?' Harry Graham asked. 'If Bowe was on him, the murder could have something to do with the spooks.'

'They're arseholes,' Wilson said. 'But I don't think they would kill one of their own. Evans was being monitored. I haven't got a clue why. His politics were flaky at best.' He glanced at the white board, but there was nothing new on Evans. 'I suppose that we're lucky that the guys who took Bowe didn't want him. He's still in a compartment at the Royal Victoria, so we continue to examine the evidence. Nothing from FSNI?'

'I'm on the phone to them all day,' Graham said. 'It's coming, but so is Christmas.'

Wilson smiled. 'It looks like Harry and I are not making any great advances on our case.' He turned to Browne. 'Rory, anything from the CCTV?'

'Nothing so far, boss,' Browne said. 'But now that Siobhan has been freed up we can get ahead a bit faster. We've collected the CCTV from all the industrial buildings in the area. It's of variable quality. Some of it can go straight in the bin. Peter and I have been examining it but so far we haven't hit pay dirt but there are still plenty of disks to go through.'

'We know that Best was in that warehouse,' Wilson said. 'We just need to place him there around the time Sammy disappeared. I hope that we haven't let out the news that the large bloodstain has been attributed to Sammy?'

All four members of the team shook their heads.

Harry Graham's phone rang and he moved away from the group. He spoke for several minutes and then moved back to the whiteboard. 'That was FSNI.' He picked up a black felt pen and wrote under the picture of Alan Evans, "*Bullet.22 calibre, gun probably Beretta 70 used in five sectarian murders in 1970s and 80s.*"

Wilson remained silent as he assimilated the new information. He had dismissed the idea that Evans was a sectarian murder. Now it appeared to be back on the table. What had Evans done to attract the attention of a sectarian hitman? Given that it was a thirty-year-old crime, it was entirely possible that the man who pulled the trigger might be as dead as Evans. And it was equally possible that the gun was probably lying at the bottom of the Lagan. They would take the investigation as far as they could but unless they located some evidence he doubted that they would put anyone in the dock for the murders of Alan Evans and Jennifer Bowe. He didn't like mysteries that could not be resolved. 'I don't want anyone outside this group to know any details on either of our investigations until I'm ready to tell them,' Wilson said. His mobile phone started to ring. He took it from his pocket and saw that it was Richie Simpson. 'Richie.' He started moving towards his office and motioned for Browne and Davidson to join him. As soon as he entered, he set his mobile on speakerphone and put it on the desk. 'I've put you on speaker,' Wilson said. 'DS Browne and DC Davidson are listening in.'

'Enough of the chit-chat, what's the story on protecting me?' Simpson's voice was laced with tension.

'Castlereagh has agreed,' Wilson said. 'We'll bring you in, take a statement and then you'll be in taken into protective custody.'

'No can do, I'm not going back to Belfast. McGreary and Best will get to me.'

'Think about it, Richie,' Wilson said. 'We'll get you out of Northern Ireland as quickly as possible but we need to interview you locally. We'll keep you well away from McGreary and Best. And as long as you keep your end of the bargain, we'll keep ours.'

There was silence on the phone and the three police officers looked at each other. The silence lasted so long that Wilson wondered whether the line had gone dead.

'OK.' Simpson said at last.

The men listening let out a collective breath. 'We need to pick you up,' Wilson said. 'DS Browne and DC Davidson will do it personally. Where are you?'

Simpson gave them the address of the B & B in Atlantic Way. Wilson quickly estimated the best route and the time. 'They'll be with you in about two and a half hours. Stay in your room and don't contact anyone else. You'll be in the station tonight and transferred to the mainland tomorrow.'

'Don't get me killed.' Simpson's voice was shaking.

'You've done the right thing, Richie,' Wilson said. 'You won't be safe until McGreary and Best are put away. Sit tight, my team are on the way.' The line went dead. Wilson turned to Browne and Davidson. 'Pick up a car downstairs. The quickest route is through Omagh. For God's sake get there before he changes his mind. Call me as soon as you pick him up, and again when you're almost back in Belfast. And remember no interrogation in the car. You can talk about football, politics, women. Anything but what happened in the warehouse. Got it?'

Both men nodded.

'What the hell are you waiting for? On your way.'

Browne and Davidson left the room quickly.

Wilson sat in his chair behind his desk. They were finally going to clear up Sammy Rice's disappearance and his probable murder. Simpson would place McGreary and Best at the scene of Rice's murder. It would be direct evidence. He would immediately get a search warrant for McGreary and Best's homes. He needed to find the weapon that had been used to kill Rice and he needed to find the body. McGreary would hire the best barrister available and only a watertight case would put the two of them away. Step one was getting Simpson back to Belfast.

· · ·

As soon as Simpson finished the phone call with Wilson, he needed to use the toilet. He was still wondering whether he had done the right thing. There was still two hours to change his mind. He could clear out of Bundoran and head south. He could disappear for a second time only this time he wouldn't contact Wilson. But how long could he stay ahead of the posse? Wilson would still be looking for him and McGreary would be right behind him. He lay down on the small bed in his room. In two and a half hours the die would be cast. It was all about survival. He prayed that Wilson would be his best shot.

CHAPTER SIXTY-FIVE

Willie Rice was sitting in the living room of his son's house in Ballygomartin Road. He was staring at two photographs that had been taken by the cleaning lady from the whiteboards in the murder squad room. His son's photo was at the top of one of the whiteboards. Underneath was the legend *"wanted in relation to the murders of David Grant and Brian Malone currently missing"*. Willie had no idea whether his son was involved with the murders but Sammy had been off the rails for months and was liable to do something stupid. Under the legend was a photo of the warehouse in East Belfast and a close-up of the bloodstains on the floors. The smaller bloodstain had been identified as belonging to Davie Best, Gerry McGreary's right-hand man. The larger one had Sammy's name on it. He wondered how that had come about. Despite his reputation as one of the main gang leaders in Belfast, the police had never lifted Sammy. Willie knew that his son had protection at the highest level. To his knowledge Sammy's DNA had never been taken. So, how could the police have identified the larger bloodstain as Sammy's? Willie had been on the dry for almost six weeks. He knew that he needed to have his wits about him if he was going to keep things together until Sammy returned. He stared at the large bloodstain. What the hell was he thinking? If that was Sammy's blood, he wasn't coming back. Sammy's disappearance and McGreary's encroachments on his territory weren't his only problems. Three months previously he'd noticed blood in his piss. He'd waited a month until he visited a doctor and when he did it was bad news. In the course of a year, his life had turned to shit. His wife, Lizzie, had been murdered and was now in the ground in Roselawn Cemetery. His son had disappeared and was almost certainly dead. Then he was given a death sentence by the oncologist. Maybe there was such a thing as karma. Perhaps his wife and his son were paying the price for his misdeeds. He'd followed the progress of the dig in Ballynahone. They'd managed to unearth Evans and the tart that was with him. Evans and the woman weren't the only two that he'd killed. He never thought of his victims. They didn't swirl around in his head and keep him awake at night. That was the stuff of films. Now he was on his way out, he wondered whether Evans, the tart and the others would be waiting for him on the far side. Maybe there was time for one last fling. There was no great enthusiasm within his crew for a war with McGreary. But if it were ever confirmed that McGreary had murdered his son, there would be hell to play. He looked at the bottles of booze sitting on the sideboard. He would give anything to get off his head but he knew that would get him nowhere. He missed Lizzie and he missed Sammy. They hadn't been much of a family but things might have been different if they hadn't been consumed by the "Troubles". But that was all water under the bridge. He was alone and he was dying. His future consisted of a hospital or hospice bed and a nation of pain. That wasn't going to happen. He stood and went to the corner of the room. Pulling back the carpet he lifted the two loose floorboards and took out a chamois bag. He replaced the boards and sat down. The chamois bag was in his lap. He opened it slowly and revealed a Beretta 70 .22calibre pistol. It was his favourite weapon for over thirty years and had been used in seven murders. It was about to be used again.

CHAPTER SIXTY-SIX

Sir Phillip Lattimer was driving towards the family pile outside Ballymoney. He had spent a very pleasant evening in the company of some German businessmen. They had dined at EIPIC in Deane's and enjoyed a very good meal. There was only one problem. His driver had texted earlier in the evening and called off sick. It was too late to arrange an alternative driver. Lattimer didn't mind driving himself to and from Belfast. In fact, at this time of year he positively enjoyed it. However, when he entertained potential business partners, he was fond of having a few glasses of wine with his meal. The current police approach to drink driving precluded him for imbibing his usual amount of alcohol. Still, it had been a productive dinner and Lattimer was sure that he would soon be adding another directorship to his already long list and depositing a six-figure sum in his bank as a result. He was therefore in a very good mood and didn't notice the Toyota Landcruiser that slid in behind him as soon as he left Howard Street. He had arranged some female companions for his new German friends, and he was looking forward to their golf game at Royal Portrush the following day. All was well in Sir Phillip's world as he steered his BMW 750 north and out of

Belfast. He turned on the radio and chose a disk of Karajan and the Berliner Philharmoniker playing *Beethoven's Symphony No 7*. He decided to take the M2 and drove north listening to the music and watching the evening light fade. With a bit of luck he would be at Coleville within the hour where he would enjoy a stiff brandy in the study before retiring. He would limit himself to a single drink since he was due on the tee at ten in the morning. The road was relatively clear and he made good time to the junction of the A26 heading north. The Landcruiser had kept pace with him on the way out of Belfast but dropped back by fifty metres when they moved onto the A26. Lattimer kept the BMW just under the speed limit although the car occasionally tried to power ahead like a racehorse that was being held back. He skirted the town of Ballymena and kept moving north. Just outside the town of Cloughmills, he turned onto the A44. Darkness had already descended and the trees that lined the road cast ominous shadows. In many areas the tops of the tress had grown over the road joining their colleagues on the other side giving the effect of driving through a dark tunnel. He was five miles from Coleville Hall when he noticed a large four-by-four closing rapidly on him. *Some of the young bucks in the area should never have been given a driving licence*, he thought as he watched the dark shape approaching in the rear mirror. He smiled when he thought about the way he and his friends used to drive around these quiet country roads. The four-by-four was now directly behind him and he could see two dark shapes in the front seats. There was a straight road coming up and it would be the ideal place to let them past. As soon as he hit the straight, he dropped his speed. The four-by-four overtook him and pulled in front. Suddenly it stopped and if it hadn't been for the fantastic brakes on the BMW he would have driven into the other car. The passenger door of the four-by-four opened and a man got out. Lattimer almost wet himself when he saw that the man was wearing a balaclava and holding a pistol in his right hand. He dropped his hand down to the gear lever to put the car into reverse. There were two reasons he didn't engage. First, he would have to reverse at speed around a sharp corner, and secondly the man who exited the car was pointing the gun directly at him. *Oh Christ*, he thought, *I'm going to die, just when everything was going so well.*

The man with the gun opened the driver's side door. 'Out,' he said simply

The driver from the four-by-four got out of his car carrying a black bin bag. He joined his colleague. Both men were well built and their features were totally covered by the balaclavas. They were dressed all in black and wore beanies on their heads. Only their eyes showed.

Lattimer got out of the car. 'Please don't kill me,' he pleaded. He was about to fall on his knees but the driver grabbed his sleeve and kept him standing. His whole body was shaking uncontrollably.

'Take your clothes off,' the driver said.

Lattimer started undressing but his hands were shaking so much he had difficulty undoing the buttons of his shirt. He stopped and looked at the two men. 'I have money. I'll pay you well.'

The man from the passenger side pointed the gun at him. 'He said get your clothes off.'

Lattimer returned to unbuttoning his shirt. He wanted to cry. The driver held out the bin bag and Lattimer dropped his jacket and shirt into it.

'The rest,' the driver of the four-by-four motioned at his trousers. 'You can leave your underpants on.'

Lattimer was working hard at controlling his sphincter. After all, he came from good stock. His ancestors had fought with King William at the Boyne. He removed his trousers, then his shoes and stockings and placed them in the bin bag. Finally, he stood on the side of the road in his underpants.

The driver closed the bin bag. 'Your watch.'

Lattimer stared at the gold Rolex Datejust on his left wrist. He started to unfasten the clasp. At this moment, he would have handed over his wife for their pleasure. He handed over the watch. £25,000, he thought as he passed it over. It would have been cheap at twice the price. Phillip Lattimer's skin was valuable, to Phillip Lattimer.

The driver of the four-by-four dropped the watch into his pocket and took out a mobile phone. He took a picture of Lattimer standing on the side of the road in his underpants with his ample stomach hanging over the waistband. He then started walking back towards his vehicle.

The man with the gun motioned Lattimer into the BMW.

Lattimer took his place behind the steering wheel and waited.

The man with the gun retreated down the road and climbed into the four-by-four. The car moved off at pace down the straight.

Lattimer fell across the steering wheel and tears of relief streamed down his face. What the hell had that been about? It didn't matter. He had survived. It wouldn't just be a small brandy in the study. It would be several large brandies. He wondered whether his wife was in bed. He wouldn't like her to see him arriving in his underpants. There would be too many questions. After he composed himself, he started the car and moved slowly forward. His hands were still shaking.

CHAPTER SIXTY-SEVEN

W ilson spent the evening at his desk. The thought that he hadn't eaten in seven hours never came into his mind. The results of the DNA had confirmed that the woman in the single grave was indeed Francis McComber. He was still waiting on the DNA confirmation on Alan Evans. A mountain of paperwork had built up over the past week. Most of it was rubbish but there were a couple of minor fires that if left undone, might graduate to fully-fledged blazes. He kept his eye on the clock as he ploughed through the emails and the reports that had piled up on his desk. It was almost eight thirty when Browne called and confirmed that they had picked up Simpson and were on their way back to Belfast. Their estimated arrival time was eleven o'clock at night. Wilson looked at the pile of papers before him. It was going to be a late night. He decided to work until ten o'clock and then take a short nap.

The sound of his mobile brought him out of his nap. Browne and Graham were ten minutes away. Wilson had arranged for the interview room. He rose slowly from his chair and stretched. He went downstairs and waited in the reception area.

'Late night, boss?' the duty sergeant said.

'It's going to be a lot later. You have any tea on?'

'We always have a pot on brew during the night.'

'Organise four cups of tea for the interview room.'

Five minutes later Browne and Davidson entered the station with Simpson between them. Wilson led the three towards the interview room. Simpson looked like a wet rag. His hair was lank and looked stuck to his head and he was gaunter than Wilson remembered him. The four men entered the interview room. Simpson wasn't shackled. He was a witness not a criminal. He slumped into a chair on one side of the table. Wilson and Browne sat opposite him while Davidson stood at the door.

'You look like you could do with a good night's sleep,' Wilson said when they were seated.

Simpson lifted his head. 'You don't sleep too well when you're being pursued by the Peelers on one hand and Davie Best on the other.'

'You made the right choice,' Wilson said. 'We're going to record and video this interview. I'm going to ask Detective Sergeant Browne to do the preliminaries.'

Browne turned on the recording equipment and identified the four men in the room. When he had finished, the door opened and a uniformed constable entered carrying a tray on which there were four cups, a jug of milk, a plate of digestive biscuits and a few sachets of sugar. He placed the tray on the table. Then he left.

'We wish to ask you some questions relating to events that took place in a warehouse at ...' Wilson looked at Davidson who gave the exact address. 'Do you wish to have a solicitor present?'

Simpson shook his head.

'Please speak for the tape,' Browne said.

'No,' Simpson said. 'I want to place it on the record that I have been promised police protection and entry to the witness protection programme for my evidence.'

'Would you like to tell us in your own words what happened in the warehouse?'

'Gerry McGreary and Davie Best had lured Sammy Rice to the warehouse on the pretence that he was going to meet Big George Carroll. Instead McGreary, Best, Ray Wright and me were waiting there. As soon as Rice arrived, they disarmed him. Best had something personal against him. He hit Rice and knocked him to the ground. Then Rice was shot in the head.'

Wilson frowned. The statement was just one step above "no comment". It was going to be a long night. 'Who was present when Sammy Rice was shot?'

'Best, Wright and me.' Simpson took one of the cups and poured three sachets of sugar into the tea.

'Where was McGreary?' Wilson asked.

'He left just before Rice was shot.' Simpson sipped his tea.

Davidson moved from the door and placed a cup in front of Wilson and Browne and took one for himself.

'But he gave the order?' Wilson put a shot of milk into his tea. It wasn't good news that McGreary wasn't present. He would claim that the others acted without him.

'I don't remember.'

'OK, why did they decide to kill Rice?' Wilson asked.

'They didn't say. Maybe it had something to do with business.'

Wilson leaned forward. 'You're standing in a warehouse in East Belfast and one of the city's main gang leaders is lying on the floor. Who made the decision to shoot him? Was it McGreary or Best?'

'I don't remember.'

'We have a real problem here, Richie,' Wilson said. 'To join the witness protection programme you have to be a witness. It's in the title of the programme. So far, you're falling short of that description. You better start remembering something soon or I'm going to toss you out on the street, and you know what that will mean.'

Simpson rubbed his forehead. He hadn't thought that telling the truth would be so hard and there were parts of the story of what happened in the warehouse that he would rather keep to himself. However, it was becoming clear to him that Wilson was going to keep on probing until he had every scrap of the story. He had two choices: he could let Wilson drag the story out of him or he could start telling what he knew. Whatever choice he made the results would be the same. Wilson would have the truth. 'Maybe I should start at the beginning.'

Wilson could see that Simpson had decided to tell the full story. The only need for questioning would relate to clarification.

'It all began with a visit to Jackie Carlisle,' Simpson began. He related how his former mentor had paid him £5,000 as a down-payment to arrange the killing of Sammy Rice. He had tried to enlist the Fenians but had failed. Davie Best had got wind of his search for a hit man to kill Sammy. So, when Sammy had tried to kill Big George Carroll, Best and Wright had lured Sammy to the warehouse on the pretext of meeting Big George. There they had outmanoeuvred him and taken away his weapon. McGreary had left before Rice was dispatched. Simpson had left before Best and Wright had dealt with the body.

'Good man, Richie,' Wilson said when Simpson finally stopped speaking. 'You were there when Rice was shot. Who pulled the trigger?'

Simpson remained silent.

'Come on, Richie,' Wilson said. 'We're almost there. Best or Wright, which one pulled the trigger?'

'They made me,' Simpson shouted. 'They put Sammy's gun in my hand and told me if I didn't pull the trigger I'd go first. I had no choice, they were going to kill me if I didn't do what they said.'

Wilson, Browne and Graham looked from one to the other. This was a twist that they hadn't planned on. 'You fired the shot that killed Sammy Rice?' Wilson said after a short delay.

Simpson didn't answer.

'Where's the gun?' Wilson asked.

'Best took it.' Simpson's eyes looked glazed. 'He dropped it in a plastic bag. It's still got my fingerprints on it. He called it his "insurance" on my silence.'

Wilson was running through the possibilities in his mind. McGreary was almost certainly going to slide. They could try to get him for conspiracy but he doubted if the CPS would go ahead with a case. He wasn't present when the deed was done and he didn't give the order to Simpson. Best would contest that he instructed Simpson to shoot Rice and Wright would back him up. He could certainly get them for moving the body but when the gun was produced and the fingerprints checked, Richie Simpson would be in the frame. Richie had walked into the interview as a witness to a murder and was now the prime suspect. 'Sergeant Browne, would you please do the necessary.'

Browne stood. 'Mr Simpson would you please stand.'

Simpson stood up slowly.

'Richard Simpson,' Browne said. 'I am arresting you for the murder of Samuel Rice. You do not have to say anything but it may harm your defence if you do not mention when questioned something that you later depend on in court. Anything that you do say may be given in evidence.'

'You're entitled to a solicitor.' Wilson was genuinely sorry for Simpson. He believed him that Best and Wright had threatened him with death if he didn't fire the fatal shot into Rice. But it was going to be hell to prove. Best and Wright were well-known hard men. They would be difficult to crack, if not impossible. They would do time for interfering with the body but only if Rory and Peter could find CCTV footage of them removing the body from the warehouse. It was going to be a very difficult case but that wasn't his problem. He was paid to collect and present the evidence. The CPS would have to make the decision about whom to prosecute and for what. 'I suggest that you take up the option.'

Simpson sat down heavily. He looked dazed. 'What about our deal? I'll give evidence against the others but you can't put me in jail in Ulster. I wouldn't last a week. What about witness protection? I wouldn't have come here without assurances that I'd be protected.'

'But you weren't just a witness, Richie,' Wilson said. 'You were the shooter. For God's sake, I understand that they forced you and I'm sure that your brief will make that case. But I'm equally sure that Best and Wright will point the finger at you.' He looked at his watch and nodded at Browne.

'Interview suspended at 23.45.' Browne switched off the recording equipment.

Peter Davidson collected the cups and replaced them on the tray. 'Richie, come with me,' he said. 'I think a rest in one of the cells would do you a lot of good.' He put his right hand under Simpson's left arm and lifted him up gently.

'Peter.' Wilson stood. 'Book Richie in and my office in fifteen.'

Davidson nodded.

FIFTEEN MINUTES later Wilson sat in his office with his ergonomic chair tilted back as far as it could go. He had pulled a lot of late nights during his career but he had been younger and keener then. He had been on the job for more than sixteen hours and the thought of his bed was pre=eminent in his mind. The Rice case was in the toilet. The man who had fired the shot would probably go down and so would Best and Wright but on much reduced charges. The latter two would serve a relatively modest sentence and then only if Browne and Davidson could find CCTV of them moving the body. McGreary would walk. Best and Wright would never divulge the whereabouts of Rice's body. It was a toxic cocktail for him and the team and a disaster for Richie Simpson. Browne and Davidson sat across the desk from him. They looked as shattered as him and Peter, in particular, was beyond the age for handling sixteen-hour days.

'We need that CCTV footage.' Wilson was afraid that Browne and Davidson's motivation would dip with the uncertainty of a decent conviction.

'I'm all in, boss,' Davidson said. 'My brain has turned to mush. At least it's a result. Simpson was stupid and he's going to pay the price. McGreary and his crew will be laughing up their arses at us. Sammy's been removed from the scene and the damage will be minimum. '

'It is what it is, Peter.' Wilson flipped forward in his chair. "It's time to go home. Rory will continue with the interview of Simpson tomorrow morning. Call the duty solicitor. We need someone in the room with him. Find some bloody CCTV footage of Best and Wright moving the body. We're probably not going to get them for murder, but I want them banged up for the most time possible. Rory, we need a search warrant for the houses of Davie Best and Ray Wright. We'll pick them up tomorrow. And I want everything we have on both of them. If I remember correctly, Wright has a sheet as long as my arm. I'm off to Hydebank in the morning. I have to give Maggie Cummerford the bad news about her mother.'

CHAPTER SIXTY-EIGHT

Hydebank Wood is the principal women's prison in Northern Ireland and is located in a leafy suburb of south Belfast. Wilson's meeting with Maggie Cummerford was scheduled for ten am, which gave him just enough time to brief his boss about the events of the previous evening. Davis was of one mind with Peter Davidson: identifying Simpson as the murderer of Sammy Rice was a result and would save the taxpayer the cost of putting him in the witness protection programme. Wilson wasn't so happy with the turn of events. Simpson fired the fatal shot but somewhere in the background was Jackie Carlisle. What interest had Carlisle in having Rice assassinated? He could see why McGreary and Best might want to see the back of one of their main competitors. But Carlisle was a different matter. Sammy Rice held the key to the deaths of Grant and Malone. He was the ultimate paymaster for the murderers, Baxter and Weir. With Rice gone the motive for the murder of Grant and Malone might never be known. If Rice's body wasn't located, Best and Wright might possibly walk alongside their boss. That wasn't a result. It was a bloody disaster. And that wasn't the only disaster he was facing. The news on the use of a well-known

weapon in the Evans murder would send the investigation
back to the sectarian track which both Wilson and his superior
knew was a rat's maze that would probably lead nowhere.
Wilson wasn't in the best of moods when he arrived before the
gates of the prison ten minutes before the appointed time of
his meeting. The prison consisted of two sections, Ash House
contained women prisoners who had been either sentenced or
were on remand while the other section housed male juvenile
prisoners. The prison, as its name would suggest, was situated
in a wooded area and was surrounded by green fields. Wilson
showed his warrant card at the gate and was directed to the
visitors' car park to the right of the female section of the
prison. Hydebank Wood was not the kind of maximum-secu-
rity female prison that watchers of TV programmes might
recognise. Wilson was aware that one murderess was
currently on the run after failing to return from a day release
job. He checked in at the reception and was led through a
series of gated corridors to an interview room. Like the interview rooms at the station it was antiseptic and sparsely
furnished with only a steel table and four chairs. A female
warder entered and opened the door permitting Maggie
Cummerford to enter. He had forgotten how slight she was.
Her red checked shirt looked baggy on her small frame and
her hair had been cut short. She was wearing a pair of cheap
jeans that were a little too long with the bottoms rolled up.
She didn't look like the person who had murdered three
women by cracking their skulls open.

She smiled as she entered the room. 'Hello, Ian, couldn't
live without me?'

Wilson stood up. The bad mood he had when he entered
the prison was dispelled somewhat by Maggie's smiling face
and cheery manner. Knowing her as he did, he knew that
initially prison wouldn't dampen her spirit. But ten years was a
long time inside and he knew the Maggie Cummerford who
eventually walked through the gate to freedom would bear

little resemblance to the woman who had entered. 'Good to see you, Maggie.'

They sat down on opposite sides of the table and watched as the female warder closed the door and stood beside it.

'How's it treating you, Maggie?' Wilson said when they were settled.

'It's prison, Ian, not Club Med. It's all about treating us badly so that we won't want to come back here. Quite honestly, there are a lot of places I'd rather be but I suppose I shouldn't have murdered those three bitches. So, this obviously isn't a social visit, otherwise you would have waited until visiting hours. What can I do for you?'

'We're pretty sure that we've found your mother's body.'

Cummerford started to breathe deeply. She sat up straight but couldn't fight back the tears that started to run down her face. Wilson reached into his pocket and took out a handkerchief and passed it to her. The female warder came forward, took the handkerchief and shook it loose before passing it to the tearful woman.

'Where was she?' The words came out hesitantly accompanied by sobs.

Wilson explained how the search for Evans's body had led to the discovery of a second grave, which contained the body of a woman who they had identified as Francis McComber from a DNA match.

'They put her in a hole in a bog.' Cummerford dabbed her face with the handkerchief and pushed it across the table. 'I want to see her.'

Wilson pushed the handkerchief back. He felt that she would need it later. 'There's not a lot to see. You might find it distressing.'

She smiled. 'You're talking to someone who cracked open the heads of three old ladies. I don't distress easily.'

'It's your choice. I'll talk to the powers that be. I'm sure something can be arranged.'

'Who will arrange the funeral?'

'I don't know. But I'll find out. Have you thought about the big man in your story?'

'I was a child. Every man was big.'

Wilson removed a picture from his pocket. It was a thirty-year old photo of Willie Rice. At that time, he still had a head of bushy black hair and a drooping Viva Zapata moustache. He pushed the photo across the table. 'Do you recognise this man?'

She took the photo in her fingers and raised it. She stared for several moments before replacing it on the table. 'I really want to say that he's the "big man" that put me in the car, but I'm not sure. Who is he?'

'His name is William Rice. Lizzie Rice was his wife.'

'Maybe it's time to let this one go, Ian.'

'Your mother was murdered and her body hidden. The people who murdered her have escaped justice. So did the man who buried her. We failed you once, I'd like to redress that failure by putting the man that buried her behind bars.'

'Let it go.' She stood up. 'When can I see her?'

Wilson stood up. 'Call your solicitor. She'll be able to help.'

She turned towards the warder. 'Can I hug him?' she asked.

The warder nodded.

Cummerford hugged Wilson. He could feel the wetness of her tears on his shirt. She looked up into his face. 'You're a good man, Ian. Under different circumstances I think we might have been friends.'

He moved away from her. 'Take care of yourself, Maggie. I'll make sure your mother is laid to rest properly.'

He walked back through the corridors to the front of the building. Maggie was a survivor. He wouldn't be surprised to hear sometime in the future that she had done a runner, but for now she looked settled. There was still plenty of money in his bank account from the sale of the Malwood Park House. Some of it would go into making sure that Maggie's mother didn't end up in a pauper's grave. He stood by the car and removed Willie Rice's picture from his pocket. Deep down he knew that Rice was the "big man" that had loaded Francis McComber into the boot of his car before putting her into a hole in Ballynahone bog. If that was the case, Rice could also have been involved in the murder of Alan Evans and the mysterious Jennifer Bowe. The question was, how was he going to prove it?

CHAPTER SIXTY-NINE

'The drinks and lunch are on me.' Sir Phillip Lattimer deposited the trolley holding his Callaway golf clubs on the gravel area in front of the clubhouse of Portstewart Golf Club. It had been both a pleasurable, and profitable morning for Lattimer. The morning was spectacular, the sun set off the wild north coast of Northern Ireland perfectly and the walk around one of the outstanding golf courses in the British Isles was absolutely delightful. Despite the fact that he hadn't slept very well, he was on his game and had trousered a cool grand from his playing companions having won the front and back nines, and the overall score. However, every time he looked at his left hand he was reminded of how scared he had been for his life the previous evening. But that was all in the past. He was desperately in need of a drink and he ushered his German guests into the imposing clubhouse and in the direction of the bar. He nodded at several of the members and passed a word with some of them. Each generation of Lattimers had been members of Portstewart Golf Club since it was founded in 1894. Phillip Lattimer was known by and knew every member of the club. He made his way to the bar and gave his and his companions' order. His new colleagues were in raptures about their morning's golf and Lattimer would use the afternoon to cement their business relationship. As he turned away from the bar with three drinks in his hand, his eyes were drawn to a well-dressed lady sitting by the window overlooking the eighteenth hole of the Strand course. He almost dropped the drinks when he recognised Helen McCann sitting alone and staring directly at him. He quickly deposited the drinks with his business associates and made his way to Helen's table. He sat down and put his drink in front of him. "I didn't realise that you were a member here?'

Helen smiled. 'I'm not.'

His sipped his gin and tonic. 'So what brings you here?'

She crossed her legs showing a pair of shapely knees. 'I came to see you.'

'I'm impressed. You actually took time out to catch me at my golf club.'

She smiled. 'I've been reflecting on our last meeting and I've been somewhat upset that you were beginning to think that I might be irrelevant.'

'Not at all,' he interjected and then smiled.

He was about to continue when she put her hand up to silence him. 'So, I wondered what I could do to show you how mistaken you were.'

The smile faded on his face. His father had warned him about Helen McCann but that had been twenty years ago. Although she was well preserved, her powers had certainly waned in the meantime.

She opened her bag, produced a gold Rolex watch and held it dangling in the air by the wristband. 'I understand you lost this last evening.' She dropped the watch on the table and pushed it across to him.

He didn't have to pick it up to see that it was indeed his. 'Where did you get this?'

'Does it matter?' She opened her mobile phone and showed him a picture of himself standing on the side of the road wearing only his underpants. 'Do you still think that I'm irrelevant?'

He looked around quickly to see if anyone in the bar was looking in their direction. Luckily everyone seemed blissfully ignorant of the photo on the mobile phone. 'You bloody bitch.'

'Now, now, Phillip, remember all that noble blood coursing through your veins. Remember you're a gentleman. You, and the tawdry toadies that you call friends, will never make me an irrelevance as long as there is breath in my body. Last night was just a little demonstration. You pleaded and cried, and you survived. You should rejoice. The next time you might not be so lucky.' Her face suddenly took on a hard look. 'You do not make any decisions regarding the Circle without my express approval. You will not throw my husband to the wolves. And you will tell the young Turks in the Circle that the organisation is in good hands. Now, Phillip darling, your Kraut friends are wondering why you left them for an old bitch like me. Take up your watch like a good man.'

He lifted up his watch and slipped it onto his wrist. It used to be his pride and joy but now it was a symbol of his weakness in the face of Helen McCann's strength. He stood up and went to the bar. He ordered a double brandy and put on his business face. The prospect of an afternoon of Teutonic conversation suddenly didn't seem so appealing. He would have preferred to crawl into some dark spot and lick his wounds. But there was money to be made. He forced a smile onto his face as he made his way to the Germans' table. As he reached it, he glanced at the spot where Helen McCann had been sitting. There was no one there.

CHAPTER SEVENTY

I t was after eleven o'clock when Wilson returned to the
station. He went immediately to the squad room. He saw
O'Neill and Davidson hunched over their computer screens
watching grey images from CCTV cameras. He hoped that
sooner or later they'd chance upon some footage of Sammy
Rice being loaded into the boot of a car. It would be their only
hope of nailing Best and Wright. When he entered his office,
he saw that there were two files on his desk. One bore the
legend *Davie Best* and the other *Raymond Wright*. He sat at
his desk and picked up the file on Best. It consisted of ten A4
pages most bearing official logos associated with the British
Army. Best was born in Belfast and had a non-descript
upbringing until he hit eighteen. He was picked up for selling
drugs and at his hearing it was suggested that if he entered the
army the charges would be dropped. It was ten years later that
he reappeared in Belfast. In the meantime, if the documents in
the file were accurate, the army had turned him into a killing
machine. He had completed one tour in Iraq and two in
Afghanistan. In both theatres he had seen considerable action.
Before being demobbed in 2013, he was awarded the Opera-
tional Services Medal for Afghanistan. For the past three

years, he had been rising through the ranks of McGreary's organisation while at the same time keeping himself below the PSNI radar. It was apparent that Davie Best was someone not to be underestimated Ray Wright fell into a totally different category. He was as far above the radar as Best was below it. Wright was a prominent member of the UDA and had been arrested on no less than fourteen occasions for intimidating Catholics and making threats on the lives of several individuals. Despite the high number of arrests, Wright had only served one custodial sentence, two years for GBH. Whenever Wright was about to go to court, witnesses had a tendency to change their evidence. He could see no connection between Best and Wright in the paperwork. The latter had never been recognised as a member of McGreary's crew. However, they were both hard men and hardened criminals. He didn't relish the task of trying to break them down.

'Boss.'

Wilson looked up and saw Browne at the door.

'We have Ray Wright downstairs. We haven't located Best yet but we have the uniforms looking out for him. We'll have the search warrants by this evening.'

Wilson picked up Wright's file and stood up. 'Let's not keep friend Ray waiting.'

Ray Wright was lounging in one of the chairs when Wilson and Browne entered the interview room. Unlike a first timer, Wright was completely at ease. From his file Wilson knew that Wright was fifty-four years old although his rugged features gave the impression that he was older. His nose was bulbous and blue and his skin was pitted and mottled. His red hair was cut close to his scalp and his ample stomach hung over the belt of his cheap jeans. He wore a royal blue Glasgow Rangers hoodie.

Wilson dropped the file on the table and sat down facing Wright. Browne took the seat beside Wilson. 'Thank you for coming in today,' Wilson said as soon as he was seated.

Wright sat forward. 'I wasn't given much choice.'

Wilson ignored the remark. 'Rory, the preamble please.'

Browne switched on the recording equipment, gave the time and date and the participants.

Wilson opened the file and flicked through the papers. 'Not your first dance.'

Wright didn't respond.

This is not going to be easy, Wilson thought. 'Can you tell me where you were on the evening of April 26th?'

'No idea, I'd have to look at my diary.' Wright smiled.

'We have reason to believe that you were in East Belfast on that evening.'

'No comment.'

Wilson took out a picture of the warehouse. 'Have you ever been in this building?'

Wright looked at the photo. 'No comment.'

'We have reason to believe that a man was murdered in this warehouse on that evening. And that you were present at that murder.'

'No comment.'

'Did you along with Davie Best remove a body from that warehouse?'

'No comment.'

Wilson had only one tactic left. 'We already know who pulled the trigger and killed Sammy Rice. We're just filling in the gaps. We're going to place you in that warehouse and we're going to find CCTV footage of you and Best removing a body from that location. Whoever gives us the first information is going to get the best deal. We have the murderer. You only moved the body. That's interfering with a police investigation. At most you'll get a year. You help us out and it might be less.' Wright was staring at the ceiling as he spoke.

'No comment.'

Wilson closed the file. 'Your choice.'

'I'm leaving,' Wright stood up. He bent down over the

recorder. 'The next time you bring me here I'll be under arrest, or I won't be here,' he shouted. He smiled at the two police-men. 'I hope your recording got that.' Then he marched to the door and was through it.

Wilson and Browne watched the door close behind Wright's back.

Browne shut off the recording equipment. 'I'd give a month's pay to take that smirk off the bastard's face.'

Wilson stood up. 'Like I said it wasn't his first dance. As long as he and Best sing dumb, we're not going to find Rice's body. And if we don't find the body, neither of them is going to jail. From reading the files, I thought that Wright might be the easier to break. But now I'm not confident that either of them is going to break.'

'What can we do?' Browne asked.

Wilson started for the door. 'Find Rice ourselves.' A lot easier said than done, he thought as he opened the interview room door.

CHAPTER SEVENTY-ONE

Thus far it had been a bad day and the prospect was that it wouldn't get better soon. Cummerford had failed to identify Willie Rice as the man who had deposited her in the housing estate where she had been found. The identification would have confirmed Wilson's theory that Willie Rice was the person who had buried Cummerford's mother in Ballynahone bog. That in turn would help to confirm his theory that Rice might somehow be involved in the Evans and Bowe murders. It was such a neat package that Cummerford spoiled. But Wilson wasn't about to ditch his theory that easily. To his mind, Willie Rice would be the obvious person that Lizzie would turn to in order to dispose of a body. The involvement in the Evans and Bowe murders was a leap in the dark but it wasn't inconceivable. On his return to his office in the murder squad room, he ploughed through his emails. It was comforting to see that there wasn't a word from HQ concerning the disappearance of Jennifer Bowe's body. He hated being right when it meant a further drop in his respect for the venal arseholes that inhabited the upper reaches of the organisation he served. He picked up the phone and called Reid. She was enthusiastic about his invitation to lunch and it was the first positive response he had all morning. They settled on the Lantern in Wellington Place ostensibly because it was equidistant from the station and the Royal Victoria. Another reason for his agreement to the venue was the fact that Kate had never mentioned a desire to go there. They arrived more or less together just before twelve-thirty and were immediately shown to their table by a pleasant young man.

'What's the event?' Reid said as soon as they were seated and menus were being examined.

'Bad day at the office.' Wilson liked the look of the menu but he was seriously not hungry.

She put down the menu and leaned forward. 'Tell mother about it.'

He smiled and tried to tear his eyes off her cleavage. 'It started at Hydebank Wood this morning.' His story was only interrupted by the waiter taking their order for lunch. He settled for a club sandwich and Reid asked for a Caesar salad. They both opted for still water as the liquid accompaniment to their food. He finished his description of his interview with Ray Wright before touching his sandwich.

'Don't you ever get a case of a husband murdering his wife or vice versa?' she said when he finished.

He looked around the restaurant, which was full. At the tables, people were conversing and laughing while enjoying a meal together. 'Look around you. This is normality. People enjoying themselves with their friends, loved ones and colleagues. Everybody just wants to have a decent life. I bet I'm the only one here who was digging up dead bodies in Ballynahone bog a couple of days ago. And I bet none of these people has ever looked at a thirty-year old corpse that's had its face shot off or its head cracked open. For Christ's sake, some-times I get fed up dealing with the shit end of life.'

'It's what we do, Ian.' She forked some salad into her mouth. 'When I was in the Congo, when something outra-

geous happened we used to say TIA. It stood for This is
Africa. Here we should just say TINI and continue doing our
jobs.'

'OK.' He bit into his club sandwich. 'I'll get down off the
soapbox. There's a reason I asked you for lunch today.'

She leaned forward. 'You've booked a hotel for the
afternoon.'

'I wish.'

'I would have had to refuse anyway. I have a busy afternoon. What's the problem I can help you with?'

'When will McComber's body be released?'

'I'm finished with it. There'll be an inquest but I doubt if
the coroner will want the body kept. It mightn't be for months.
Why?'

He was always amazed how pathologists could be so cold
when speaking about corpses. 'I want to make sure she has a
proper burial. We let her down all those years ago and I want
to make up in some small way.'

She slid her hand forward on the table until it covered his.
'You're like one of those sweets that's hard on the outside but
has a soft centre. I'll call the coroner this evening and convince
him to release the body immediately.'

It felt good with her hand on his. 'Hold on a while, I have
to make some arrangements. And Maggie wants to see her.'

'That won't be fun for her.'

'I already told her that.'

'I have all the contacts with the undertakers. Leave it with
me to make the funeral arrangements. Have you spoken to the
governor of Hydebank yet?'

'It's on the agenda for this afternoon.'

'So, we'll never know who buried her in Ballynahone.' She
pushed her empty plate away.

'I already have a theory about that.' He had only eaten half
his sandwich.

'And he's still alive?'

'He is and I intend to get him.'

The waiter came to their table. Reid looked up into his face. 'We'll have two black coffees and pack up the half sandwich. My friend will get peckish before the evening is out.'

CHAPTER SEVENTY-TWO

D avie Best's inside man at the PSNI had informed him that Richie Simpson was sitting in a cell having spilled his guts on what he knew of Sammy Rice's murder. At midday, he received a call from Ray Wright, which caused him to detour past Ray's base in Portadown. They met in the Orange Hall on Carlston Street, a fine, old red-bricked building inaugurated in 1908. It is one of the most prestigious Orange Halls outside Belfast. The Portadown Room at the hall was Wright's favourite meeting place. It was a place where it would be impossible for their conversation to be overheard. Best wasn't as much into the Loyalist crap as Wright. He would have preferred to meet in a quiet pub or restaurant. Wright was still old-school, he wasn't. Plan A had failed. He would have preferred to find Simpson and silence him permanently. It was time to move ahead to Plan B and that entailed the Peelers never discovering where Rice's body was. It wasn't part of Best's career plan to spend time in jail. It might be a rite of passage for some of the idiots who bought into the professional criminal mystique. He wasn't in the McGreary gang to play at being a hard man. He was there to make money, lots of money. He didn't give a shit about the preservation of the Union. The

only preservation that interested Best was his own. He realised
he had to play the Loyalist card to keep guys like Wright
onside but he had zero interest in the politics of the province.
They met in a room that was festooned with Loyalist parapher-
nalia. A Union Jack sat on the table at the head of the room
and the Red Hand flag of Ulster and the Lodge flag adorned
the back wall on either side of a picture of Queen Elizabeth II.
Wright looked like he had spent a sleepless night. It was
always the same with the first man pulled in. Although Best
knew that Wright had probably never heard of the prisoner's
dilemma, his colleague knew instinctively that when things
were going ass-over-tit, it was wise to be the first to jump ship
in an effort to land in the closest lifeboat. Wright had insisted
that in his interview with Wilson, he had played according to
Best's instructions. For sure Simpson would put him and
Wright at the warehouse on the night Sammy was murdered.
If he and Wright kept to the script, they were there but they
had nothing to do with Sammy's murder or the disposal of the
body. For the moment, the script suggested that they stay
dumb. The 'no comment' strategy gave them the opportunity
to find out what the Peelers knew while giving nothing away.
After leaving Wright, Best drove to Belfast and instead of
checking in at the Queen's Tavern he decided to go straight to
Tennent Street and present himself for interview. When he
got there he found that Wilson was out somewhere and some
dogsbody put him in an interview room. McGreary would be
doing his nut if he knew that Best was being interviewed. 'Slim
Ger' had been inside and it had the desired effect on him.
There was no way he was going back. Best knew that he was
playing a dangerous game with McGreary. But ten years plod-
ding around Iraq and Afghanistan had taught him that life was
a dangerous game. McGreary had dropped the Loyalist shit a
long time ago. As soon as peace was declared, McGreary had
gone from Loyalist paramilitary leader to criminal gang boss.
And while McGreary was not a man to be trifled with, he had

grown fat and complacent. Best knew that with his own crew and his contacts in Europe the sky would be the limit. He also knew that confrontation with McGreary was just around the corner.

Wilson received a text as he was leaving Wellington Place. Davie Best had walked into Tennent Street and presented himself for interview. *The cocky wee bastard*, Wilson thought. But he knew that Best had every reason to be cocky. They needed Sammy's body to put Best and Wright behind bars and they were a long way from having it. Sammy had probably been murdered some two months previously. Depending on where the body was there would already be substantial decomposition. Any DNA that might be on the body would be disappearing day-by-day. A point would be reached where even if they found the body they would not be able to tie Best and Wright to it. The outlook was not favourable but that didn't mean that they had to stop trying. Wilson looked through the small glass panel in the door to the interview room. Davie Best sat at the table. He wore a light leather jacket over a black polo neck shirt and jeans and he was totally at ease. He was a man without a problem in the world. Breaking Davie Best was going to be very difficult indeed. Wilson turned to Browne and Davidson. 'You're on.'

'You're not taking this interview?' The tension was obvious in Browne's tone.

Wilson turned the handle on the door. 'This is your ball game. I'm sure that you and Peter can handle it.' He pushed the door open and moved to the next room where he could watch the proceedings through a two-way mirror.

Browne and Davidson entered the room and sat at the table directly across from Best. 'I'm Detective Sergeant Browne and this is Detective Constable Davidson.' There was a nervous catch in Browne's voice. 'Do you wish to have a legal representative present?'

'Do I need one?' Best's body uncoiled and he leaned forward towards the two policemen.

Browne looked at Davidson who stared straight ahead. He was on his own. 'You are not being arrested but we think that you may be able to help us with our enquiries into the apparent disappearance of Sammy Rice.'

'Then I won't be needing legal representation.' Best was wondering why the big boss wasn't taking the interview.

Browne opened a file. 'Where were you on the evening of April 26th this year?'

'No idea, probably playing snooker or watching football on TV.'

Browne took out a photograph of the warehouse and placed it on the table. 'What would you say if I told you that we have evidence that you were in this warehouse?'

Best looked carefully at the photo. It was the same one Wilson had shown him. 'I've been in that warehouse. In fact I had a bad nosebleed there. Maybe it was on the evening you said.'

'So, you were there on the evening of the 26th.'

'That's not what I said.'

'What would you say if I told you that we have evidence that Sammy Rice was murdered in that warehouse on the evening of April 26th and that you were present?'

Best sat up straight with a look of indignation on his face. 'Are you having a laugh? I don't care who told you that bit of fiction but I know nothing about any murder.'

'We have blood evidence that places you in the warehouse,' Browne continued. 'And we have direct evidence that you were present when Sammy Rice was murdered.'

Best decided to throw his ace card onto the table. 'How do you know that Sammy was murdered? Do you have his body?'

Browne looked at Davidson but got no encouragement.

Best stood up. 'When you can prove that there was a murder that I'm supposed to have been present at, you can give me a call. I'll be more than happy to drop by to answer any of your questions.' He sauntered slowly to the door and left the two policemen sitting with egg on their faces.

One minute after Best left, the door opened and Wilson entered the room.

'I'm sorry, boss.' Browne fumbled with his file. 'I screwed it up.'

'It was a no-win situation,' Wilson said. 'Best isn't the usual Belfast headbanger. Read his file. He probably had training in the army to resist interrogation. Keep working on the CCTV. It won't take us all the way but it will increase the pressure.' He could see from Browne's face that he wasn't a believer. 'We may not get a result on Sammy but we're going to give it everything we've got.'

Browne could see that the remark was aimed at him. He wanted so badly to bring Best down. 'Sorry, boss, I thought I could have done better. I'm so bloody frustrated knowing that the bastard was involved but not being able to prove it.'

Wilson slapped his new sergeant on the shoulder. 'Believe me, you couldn't have done better. We may not be able to prove that Best was involved today but that could all change tomorrow. I always thought that Wright would be the weak link but Best has obviously trained him. Wright will continue with the "no comment" strategy while Best will talk to us in order to find out what we know. He's holding all the high cards. As long as Sammy is hidden away somewhere, we're on the losing team. We find him and the roles are completely reversed. Now find me some CCTV footage.'

CHAPTER SEVENTY-THREE

William Rice hadn't slept well. In fact, he had hardly slept at all. Every time he closed his eyes films seemed to be playing on the inside of his eyelids. Sometimes they were in black and white, and sometimes a vivid colour splashed across his vision. The black and white films contained people that in general he didn't recognise. When he opened his eyes the films stopped but they started again as soon as he closed his eyes again. He was sure that there was something wrong with his brain. About two o'clock in the morning he finally gave up on the idea of sleep. He had no idea what was happening to him but he knew that he didn't like it. Maybe he was going loony. Perhaps all the drinking he had done was catching up on him. He wondered whether this was the delirium tremens that he heard about. Next he'd be seeing giant spiders climbing the walls and pink elephants in the corner of the room. He wasn't going that route. Over the past few days he had been coming to a conclusion. In the middle of the sleepless night, he had finally made the decision. He was surprised how good it felt when he saw the road ahead clearly. For the first time since Sammy disappeared, he felt calm. All he had to do now was to follow the course of action he had decided on. He had spent the night in the old house in Malvern Street, for much of the night he sat in the front room staring at the spot where Lizzie had been murdered. He had sworn that he would kill the bitch that murdered his wife but it was a promise that would go unfulfilled. But that didn't mean he had to check out like a wimp. It was funny. He'd lost interest in Lizzie years ago. It was around the time that Lizzie lost interest in him. He couldn't remember when they'd last had sex. Then there was Sammy. They'd been growing apart for years. Lately, his son had developed the habit of treating him like the village idiot. But Willie Rice was no village idiot. He'd been the leader of men in the most violent era of Ulster's history. Now, he was a physical and mental wreck. In two weeks, he would be sixty-five years old. At least he'd made it further than a lot of the lads he'd grown up with. There was one more decent thing he had to do before he checked out. He downed a fistful of painkillers and picked up his Beretta. He checked that there were eight cartridges in the magazine. Today was the day he was going to put things right.

GERRY McGREARY also had a sleepless night. Something was bothering him but he couldn't quite put his finger on it. Business had never been better. He'd always felt that some day Sammy was going to launch a war against him to get control of the drugs business in West Belfast. But Sammy was pushing up daisies somewhere or feeding the fish in the Irish Sea. McGreary didn't much care where he was. He was making money hand over fist and soon he would get rid of the last vestiges of the Rice gang. Everything in the garden was rosy. So what was with the sleepless night? When he played for Linfield and was less than half the size he was now, he was famous for being able to smell the wind during a game. He seemed to have an instinct for finding the opponent's weakness and putting the point of the attack at that specific spot. It was a gift that he carried into his criminal career. His career was approaching its zenith. The big gangs from across the water and Europe were already courting him. So much money was flowing in that he didn't know what to do with it. The only cloud on the horizon was the pressure from below. He knew from his limited grasp on history that the higher you climb the more arseholes there were who want to take your place. He went into the kitchen and put the kettle on. A nice cup of tea would settle him down. He was beginning to tire of the bull-shit and the banter with the old crowd in the Queen's Tavern. He'd heard that the head boys in the drugs trade down south all lived in Spain. The business in Ulster was almost running on autopilot. Maybe it was time to buy the mansion and put himself beyond the reach of some toerag who wanted to take him out. It was an idea that was worth serious consideration. What was the point of having a shedload of money if you couldn't enjoy it? He dropped a teabag into a mug and poured in some hot water. He'd start working on putting himself out of harm's way today.

CHAPTER SEVENTY-FOUR

Willie Rice was in the zone. It was like he had travelled back in time and discovered the strength and clarity of mind of his younger self. He sat in the rear of a black cab as it passed the Queen's Tavern. He was surprised to see that there was no guard standing outside. It was his son's policy that one of the crew was on duty at the Brown Bear whenever he was in residence. McGreary was becoming complacent. The bastard thought that the Rice family was finished. That might be the biggest error he had made in his life. Rice ordered the cab to turn around and drop him off in front of the pub. He tossed a £20 note onto the front seat and slid out of the rear of the cab. He walked up to the pub and put his hand on the door. Once he pushed it in there would be no turning back.

McGreary and his cronies were at their habitual table deeply engrossed in a game of twenty-five. None of them looked up when the door opened. A loud shout went up from their table as McGreary claimed a trick and the game. He was sitting with his back to the door and as he pulled the cards in from the centre of the table he saw the look on the face of the man across from him. Jamesy Sutton was the first at the table to react to the arrival of Willie Rice. Sutton had been

McGreary's bodyguard for more than ten years and was the only member of the crew who carried a weapon. He half stood and reached for his pocket but the bullet caught him in the face and flung him back against the wall.

'The next man that moves will get the same treatment,' Rice said. He was amazed at the way his body and mind had acted in perfect harmony in the killing of Jamesy Sutton. He almost hadn't thought about pulling the Beretta from his pocket, raising it and firing in almost the same movement. It was like the old days all over again.

McGreary remained seated and turned around slowly. 'Now, now, Willie, there was no need for that. Jamesy shouldn't have stood up like that. He got everything he deserved.' Over Rice's shoulder, he could see the barman dialling on his mobile. It wouldn't matter if he were calling Davie Best or the Peelers. It was going to take some time before anyone got there. And Gerry McGreary was smart enough to know that he didn't have that much time. Although Rice looked calm, his eyes were red and bloodshot. He was a man on the edge and men on the edge who had made their minds up didn't normally wait long before acting. He ran through a list of options, none of them saw him living too long. He stared into Rice's face and knew that he was already dead. 'Willie we can sort this out.' The bullet ripped through his face and ricocheted around his skull ripping his brain to shreds in a matter of seconds. He slumped in his seat.

Willie Rice pulled out a chair at an adjoining table and sat down. He kept his gun pointed at the four men seated at the table. 'I have six shots left. You can try to rush me but I'll get at least two of you. Who feels like dying today?'

None of the men spoke.

Rice smiled. 'Now, all we have to do is wait for the Peelers. No one else needs to die.'

Wilson was sitting in his office struggling with another questionnaire from HR when Harry Graham burst into the squad room. He rushed to the door of Wilson's office. 'Boss, quick, there's been a shooting at the Queen's Tavern.'

Wilson stood up. The Queen's Tavern was the McGreary gang's hangout. 'How many casualties?' He took his Glock from the drawer of his desk and slipped it into his jacket pocket. 'Are there any uniforms on the scene?'

'No news on the casualties,' Graham said. 'The uniforms are on the way.'

'Tell them not to do anything until we arrive. Get two flak jackets.' It looked like the gang war that he had been anticipating had just broken out.

Graham pulled out his mobile phone and made a quick call. 'The jackets are in the car and the uniforms have been told to stay outside. As far as we can tell from the message that was phoned in, it's not a hostage situation.'

Wilson quickly followed Graham and they both rushed down the stairs and out the front door of the station. A car was waiting in the courtyard, and as soon as they were inside it sped off in the direction of the Woodvale Road.

Two police Land Rovers were blocking the street from both ends when Wilson's car arrived. A uniformed officer cradling a machine gun waved them through and they stopped fifty-feet from the Tavern. Wilson got out of the car and approached a group of uniformed officers standing outside the pub. Wilson saw that one of them was wearing the two diamond flashes on his shoulder indicating that he was an inspector. 'What's happening?' he asked.

The inspector turned to face him. 'We have instructions to wait for your arrival.'

'No further shooting?' The outside of the pub had been cordoned off.

'Not since we arrived,' the inspector said. 'How do you want to play this?'

'We need to know what's going on inside.' Wilson looked at Graham who nodded in return. 'DC Graham and I will go and have a look. You keep your people back. If we need help, you'll hear us.' He started walking towards the pub closely followed by Graham who already had his Glock 17 in hand. He pushed open the front door of the pub and walked inside. It took a few moments for his eyes to acclimatise to the low level of lighting. An unnatural silence hung over the large room. The barman was still standing behind the bar and he motioned with his head towards the rear of the room. Wilson looked along the bar until his eyes came to rest on a table at the rear. The first thing he noticed was a man directly facing him was lying back in his seat staring at the ceiling. A second man who had his back to Wilson was slumped over on the table where playing cards had been scattered about. *Two casualties minimum*, Wilson thought. There were four men seated at the table with the two corpses. He recognised them as members of McGreary's crew. He turned to look at Graham who was surveying the scene. He noticed the pistol in his hand. Wilson walked forward slowly. There was an alcove to the right of the rear and he could see a pair of legs extended from the side. He motioned Graham to move to his left while he moved forward. Gradually, the body of the man sitting in the alcove became clear. Wilson recognised it as belonging to Willie Rice. As he drew level with the alcove, he saw that Rice was cradling a pistol with the muzzle pointed at the four men seated across from him.

'Jesus Christ, Willie,' Wilson said still ten feet away from the alcove. 'What have you gone and done?'

'He killed my son.' The gun never wavered in Rice's hand. 'The stupid bastard forgot that I once had the biggest set of balls in the Shankill. He thought he could take my only son from me and I wouldn't fight back. Well, I showed the bastard.'

'It's all over now, Willie.' Wilson could see out of the corner of his eye that Graham had taken up a position at the far side of the room. All his team trained regularly at the shooting range and he knew that if Rice made a wrong move,

Graham would kill him. The last thing he wanted was Willie Rice dead. He walked forward until he was almost level with the alcove. He was aware that he would be impeding Graham's shot but it was a risk he had to take. He walked forward and put a finger on McGreary's neck. There was no sign of a pulse. He turned back towards Rice. 'He's gone. You've accomplished what you came here to do.' He moved forward aware that he was totally obstructing Graham's view. He extended his hand towards Rice. 'Now, be a good man and give me the gun.' He could almost see the wheels turning in Rice's mind. He was convinced that the seemingly helpless old man sitting before him was an ice-cold murderer and he was aware that at any moment the muzzle of the gun could be turned towards him and it would be the last sight that he would ever see. All his instincts told him to get out of the way and let Graham finish off what had been a mad dog. But Willie Rice held the key to the death of Alan Evans, Jennifer Bowe and even Francis McComber. He wasn't about to let him die. He walked forward until he was only a few feet from Rice. 'You look tired, Willie. You should let me take the gun and we'll get you back to the station where you can have a nice cup of tea.'

Rice looked up. 'I did Sammy proud, didn't I Mr Wilson?' He moved his right hand forward.

Wilson could feel Graham's Glock trained on his back. He extended his hand forward and wrapped it around the muzzle of Rice's pistol. 'Good man, just let it go. You did Sammy proud.' He felt Rice's grip go slack on the handle of the gun and he pulled it away sharply.

Immediately, the four men at the table stood up and made for the door. Wilson had no interest in them. The uniforms outside would corral them. Rice had collapsed forward in the chair. Wilson motioned Graham forward. 'You can put the gun away now, Harry. Put handcuffs on him and let's get him to the station. He took a plastic bag from his pocket and dropped the Beretta 70 into it.

Graham heaved Rice to his feet and handcuffed his hands behind his back. The two police officers and their prisoner made their way through the pub and towards the light spilling through the front door. Outside, Wilson's car had been pulled up to the door of the pub and Graham bundled Rice into the rear before climbing in after him.

'Good job, sir.' The uniformed inspector came to stand beside Wilson. 'Sectarian?'

'No, money,' Wilson said. 'And revenge, two of the oldest motives in the world. The crime scene guys will be along. Make sure nobody contaminates the scene.' The inspector started to move away. 'And lend me one of your guys to drive the car back to the station,' Wilson shouted after him.

It was one of those times that he really wished he hadn't given up smoking.

CHAPTER SEVENTY-FIVE

W ilson nodded at Harry Graham who then turned the recording equipment off. The table between them and Willie Rice was littered with plastic cups containing the dregs of cold tea. Wilson had insisted on a solicitor being present during Rice's interview. The man had done his best to protect his client but Willie had wanted to talk and Wilson had wanted to listen. It was now almost six o'clock in the evening and Rice had finally run out of steam. As soon as they had reached the station, Rice had been cautioned and placed in the interview room. When the solicitor had arrived, the interview began and continued for four hours. Rice had immediately put his hand up for McGreary and Sutton. He would certainly go down for that. After all, the murder had been witnessed by the patrons of the Queen's Tavern and Wilson had taken the murder weapon from Rice's hand. The admission to the murder of McGreary had opened the floodgates and during the rest of a rambling interview Rice had admitted to killing Evans and Bowe along with five other unsolved sectarian murders. He put Jackie Carlisle firmly in the frame as the man who wanted Evans dead. He had no idea why. That wasn't one of the questions that interested him. He was only required to pull the trigger. He had told his story of the last hours of Francis McComber and explained his part in disposing of her body. In one fell swoop, Wilson had cleared up five murder cases. He was elated but exhausted. Listening to Rice's catalogue of crime made him angry. Rice had unleashed his own reign of terror on the people of Belfast and his son hadn't fallen too far from the tree. It was a miracle that neither man had thus far been made to answer for their crimes. Or maybe it wasn't so much of a miracle. There was more than one serial killer walking the streets of Belfast. Wilson was an old-style copper. Murderers belonged in jail not walking the street. He didn't believe in "political" crimes and he certainly didn't believe in a process that put convicted murderers back on the streets. The four men in the room stood up. The solicitor packed up his briefcase and a uniformed officer led Rice away to the cells. Rice would have a short court appearance the following day but there was still a lot of paper to prepare.

'You get off home, Harry,' Wilson said as they left the interview room. 'I'll handle things here.'

'I'm OK to stay on for a few hours, boss.'

'Thanks, but I can manage. Go home. I'll see you tomorrow.' Wilson walked off in the direction of the squad room. It had been a hell of a day. The room was in darkness when he entered except for a light in his office that he didn't remember leaving on. He could also see a figure sitting in the light. He walked the length of the room and pushed open the door to his office.

Jack Duane sat in his visitor's chair. A bottle of twelve-year-old Jameson and two glasses were on his desk. Duane didn't bother to look around. He unscrewed the top of the whiskey bottle and poured two large measures. He pushed one of the measures across the desk towards Wilson's seat. 'I'd say that you need a drink.'

'How the hell did you get in here?' Wilson moved to his side of the desk and sat down.

'Your boss and my boss, that kind of thing.' Duane lifted his glass and toasted Wilson. 'You're a good copper, Ian and you've got the luck of the devil.'

They touched glasses and drank. Whiskey never tasted so good to Wilson. He felt like he could drink a lake of it.

'We've got the man who killed Alan Evans and Jennifer Bowe,' Wilson said.

'I know.' Duane refilled their glasses. 'I was watching in the room next door.'

Wilson smiled. 'Who the fuck are you, Jack?'

Duane smiled. 'A simple Irish bogtrotter, the good news is that the killer was one of your bad men and not one of ours.'

'Simple Irish bogtrotter my arse. That's the problem with this province. We've had every organ of the British security apparatus operating here and I have no doubt that there were plenty of guys like you from the south putting your oar in. Maybe somebody might have thought that if you had all fucked off and left us alone that we might have been able to manage our own problem.'

Duane raised his glass again. 'I'm only the monkey. Somewhere behind me is the organ grinder. And I'm not talking about Nolan, or Nicholson in your case. We're the foot soldiers and you know what foot soldiers are worth in a war. So, tonight we both probably dodged a bullet thanks to Mr Rice. All the organ grinders will be happy. The murderer will be in the dock and we can all sleep sound in our beds.'

Wilson sipped his second whiskey. He would not be driving home tonight. 'But we still don't know why. Why did Jackie Carlisle, a respected if dubious politician, want Alan Evans dead?'

'Unfortunately, we can't ask him. But I bet that there's a very good reason.'

'You haven't been dealing with us very long, Jack,' Wilson said. 'Up here, there doesn't have to be a very good reason.'

'What's your problem? You've cleared up a half a dozen

crimes. You're going to be a hero. One gang boss is dead and another is going down. It's a hell of a result.'

'You heard what Rice said at the end of the interview.'

'Remind me.'

'Rice and McGreary were old school. The people that are coming up have been raised differently. Rice said that we might be happy to get rid of McGreary and him today but that we'd be sorry tomorrow when we see the guys who are going to replace them. Now, fuck off and let me finish my paperwork. I hope it's the end of a beautiful friendship.'

Duane stood up. He pushed the Jameson bottle across to Wilson. 'You never know.'

DAVIE BEST POURED the end of a bottle of champagne into his glass. Three young men who could have been his doubles surrounded him. They were fit and sported short haircuts and their friendship had been honed in battle. They were sitting in the VIP area of the El Divino nightclub in Mays Market in the centre of Belfast and they were celebrating. Willie Rice had ripped the torch out of McGreary's hand and had passed it to Best. Tomorrow, Best would declare himself the *de facto* head of the old McGreary crew. Within a week he would amalgamate the McGreary and Rice crews and a new era in the history of crime in Belfast would be written. He had every reason to celebrate.

CHAPTER SEVENTY-SIX

The mood in the murder squad room was cheerful. The whiteboard section dealing with the murders of Alan Evans and Jennifer Bowe had been marked "solved" and Willie Rice's photo had been added to the board. The section under Sammy Rice's name was not looking so positive and that was reflected in the only non-smiling face on the team. DS Rory Browne didn't like failure. He was beginning to wonder whether Wilson gave him the Rice disappearance because he knew it was going nowhere. Earlier in the day a solicitor had arrived at the station and indicated that he was now representing Richie Simpson. Two hours later, Simpson was retracting his testimony with regard to Rice's murder and disappearance. He had been delusional when he had spoken to Browne and Wilson. There was no body and no murder weapon and without either or both there would be no case. Simpson was going to be bailed and would not be available for future interview without the presence of his new legal advisor. Wilson would now be seen as the hero of the piece while he would be cast as the idiot who let Simpson fade away.

Wilson noted that his new sergeant was not a happy camper. All the graduate fast-track officers were the same.

They came from a background where they had performed. They were near the top of their class at school and they had earned their honours degrees at university. Their expectations were high and so was their need for achievement. Browne was no different. He'd made sergeant in quick time and looked forward to being an inspector as quickly. He could see that he was worried by the lack of a result in the Sammy Rice case. Perhaps Wilson should suggest that he examine the unsolved crime statistics. He scrubbed the section of the board dealing with Alan Evans's murder. 'Now we concentrate on Sammy Rice,' he said.

'What's the point?' Browne said.

'Because we know what happened in the warehouse,' Wilson said. 'We just can't prove it. Siobhan, any news on the CCTV?'

She shook her head.

'It doesn't stop,' Wilson said. 'The body and the weapon are out there somewhere. Sooner or later, the one or the other, or both will turn up. When they do, we'll be ready. For now we keep looking at the CCTV. We keep an eye on Simpson. He's no great loss. Without a body and a weapon, his evidence would have been useless.'

'So where does that leave us?' Browne asked.

'Waiting for a break. Where we were with the Evans case thirty years ago. There's a reason they call us "the plod". Because that's what we do. We're not Hercule Poirot or Sherlock Holmes. We're PSNI officers. Some we win and some we lose and some we keep at in the hope of winning. Rory, you and Harry do the paperwork on Willie Rice. Peter and Siobhan will follow up on Sammy's disappearance.'

'And what will you do, boss?' Harry Graham said laughing.

Wilson thought of the paperwork on his desk and the emails on his computer. 'What they pay me for.'

CHAPTER SEVENTY-SEVEN

Wilson had never been for drinks in the Chief Constable's office. So he was surprised when the CC's personal assistant told him to be at HQ in Castlereagh at 20:00 sharp. Ten minutes after he received the call, Davis phoned and told him that she too had been invited. They could travel together. When they arrived, they found that they were members of a select group of four. The only other people present were Chief Constable Baird and Assistant Chief Constable Nicholson. Wilson was handed a whiskey and Davis opted for a sherry. When they were settled with their drinks, Baird drew himself up to his full height. 'Cheers!' He lifted his glass in a toast. 'I want to congratulate our new Chief Superintendent on a job well done. You've only been the boss of the station a few weeks but you've already produced a stunning result.'

'Excuse...,'Davis tried to interrupt. She'd done nothing. It was all down to Wilson's team.

'Now, now, Yvonne,' Baird continued quickly. 'There's no need for false modesty here. You've done a brilliant job and if I'm any judge of character you'll be joining us here in HQ in a very senior capacity. You won't just break the glass ceiling, you'll shatter it.' He cast a glance in Wilson's direction. He noticed a smile flitting across the head of the murder squad's lips. He was fully aware that 90% per cent of the credit should go to Wilson and his team but they needed to push bright female officers. And Yvonne Davis was bright.

Wilson toasted Davis with his glass of whiskey and then drank half the contents. He knew exactly where Baird was coming from and he expected that most of the credit for the Alan Evans's case would fall on Davis. The press office would be cranking out copy outlining the "stunning result". Wilson might get a mention but he didn't really care. He wasn't as happy with the result as his big boss. Rice might go to jail but if he was as ill as he said he was, that was unlikely. They would never know why Jackie Carlisle was so anxious to have Evans murdered. And nobody was mentioning the body that had been removed from the morgue at the Royal Victoria. In Wilson's eyes the result wasn't so "stunning". He looked at his watch and when he looked up he saw that Baird was staring at him. The Chief Constable put his hand on Wilson's shoulder and ushered him aside from Nicholson and Davis.

'No hard feelings,' Baird said.

Wilson shook his head.

'We need her to be a star.' Baird dropped his hand from Wilson's shoulder. 'Donald was right. You have a talent for getting results. I'm glad you decided to come back.'

'I wish I was as happy as you.'

'Refill?' Baird nodded at the bottles on his desk.

'Thanks, but these kind of events are not my thing.'

'We should have a drink soon, just you and me.'

'Why not?' Wilson felt the sentiment was genuine but he wouldn't be waiting on Baird's call.

Baird looked across at Davis. 'Keep her out of trouble.'

'I'll do my best.'

Baird looked at his watch. He walked back to where Nicholson and Davis were standing. 'I'm sorry to break up our little gathering. I have a meeting with the Minister in fifteen and he doesn't like to be kept waiting.' He finished his drink.

'I'm so embarrassed,' Davis said when she and Wilson were in the car. 'The credit was yours. I tried to interrupt but he cut me off.'

Wilson smiled. He was beginning to warm to his new boss. 'Don't worry about it. You did your job and I did mine. We don't do it for the praise.'

'It's not correct.'

'It is what it is. You should be flattered. They want you at HQ.' He sat back. Working at HQ would be Wilson's worst nightmare. The administration associated with managing his small team was just about as much as he could handle. A day crammed full of meaningless meetings discussing reports that would never be implemented with individuals as bored as he would be was his version of Hell. If that's was Yvonne Davis wanted, then she was welcome to it.

CHAPTER SEVENTY-EIGHT

W ilson and McDevitt were sitting in the snug at the Crown. They were on their third pint of Guinness and Wilson had brought McDevitt up to date on the Frances McComber situation. McDevitt was excited that the book he was working on would have its final chapter and asked whether he could record the conversation. Wilson had acquiesced. Rice would never be brought to trial for his part in hiding McComber's body. The murder charges against him would be enough to put him away for whatever remained of his life. The test results on the Beretta 70 were back from FSNI. It was the gun that had killed Evans and Bowe. Willie Rice had been a busy man during the "Troubles". Wilson found it strange that he had never been hauled in for an interview on any of the murders he committed. It was clear that someone had protected him. Perhaps Jackie Carlisle had been that somebody. Unfortunately, Jackie had spoken his last word.

'You've been to see Maggie?' McDevitt asked.

'Yesterday.' The combination of tiredness and alcohol was making Wilson sleepy.

'What happens next?'

'Reid has arranged for the body to be released and she's

going to be buried tomorrow.' He thought about how much he owed Reid. She was always there when he needed someone, and she asked for so little in return. 'I managed to obtain a plot in Roselawn. The service is at ten o'clock at the Presbyterian Church in Saintfield Road.'

'Who's paying for the funeral?' McDevitt was about to push the button to order another drink.

Wilson put his hand over the button. He'd had enough. 'It's the least I could do. I wasn't about to see her being buried in a pauper's grave.'

McDevitt switched off his recorder. 'That's very noble of you. You don't owe Cummerford or her mother anything. I suppose that's not something that I can put in the book?'

'We wouldn't be best friends any longer if you did that.' Wilson stood up. 'I'm dog tired and I've a funeral to go to tomorrow.'

McDevitt stayed where he was. 'Would it be alright if I turned up tomorrow?'

Wilson opened the door to the snug. 'I'm certainly not going to stop you. I'm not expecting a huge attendance.' He walked through the pub and headed for the front door. The pub was packed and he didn't notice the two well-dressed young men detach themselves from the bar and follow him outside. It was heading on for ten o'clock and there was a sparse crowd of pedestrians on Victoria Street. He'd left his car at the station and since it was a fine evening he decided to take a short walk. He would at least go as far as Wellington Place and maybe pick up a cab there. He was just across the street from Jury's Inn when a Range Rover pulled up beside him. Two men suddenly appeared at his back and ushered him toward the back door of the car. The door opened. Wilson was about to object when he recognised the man sitting in the rear. It was the MI5 man who used the name Boag.

'Get in,' Boag said.

Wilson looked at the two men standing at his shoulder.

There were enough people on the street for him to make an issue of the invitation. However, he knew that he wasn't in any immediate danger. He smiled and climbed into the rear beside Boag. 'I was wondering when you were going to crawl out from underneath your rock,' he said as he settled himself.

One of the young men climbed into the passenger seat beside the driver and the car moved off in the direction of the centre of the city.

'You've had a rather eventful few weeks,' Boag said.

Wilson thought that Boag looked even greyer than usual. He wondered whether the MI5 man was well. 'Thanks to you, no doubt.'

'We had to retrieve the body,' Boag coughed. 'It was done professionally and with the minimum of disruption. We couldn't have you running around contacting all sorts of agencies in an effort to discover her real identity.'

'So Jennifer was one of yours?'

'Not mine specifically. But she was working for us when she was killed.'

'You were interested in Evans?'

'We were becoming interested in him. It was an initial contact. We had no idea he was about to be killed. If we had, we would have pulled our operation to keep an eye on him.'

'So you weren't the ones that ordered the hit?'

'God, no!' Boag laughed which brought on a fit of coughing. 'We're evil bastards but we don't kill our own. However, we are responsible in a way for what happened.'

'So, this meeting is in the way of a confession.'

Boag smiled. 'You're an interesting character, Ian, which is why I like you. No, I'm not here to confess either for myself, or my organisation. Have you ever heard of Gladio?'

'No, but it sounds Roman.'

Boag clapped. 'Bravo, it was an organisation set up by the CIA and MI6 at the end of the Second World War. The Americans had this irrational fear of Communism, which they saw as spelling the end of their way of life. Unfortunately, we bought into their irrationality. Gladio was a paramilitary organisation set up in several European countries like Belgium and Italy, which would rise up against any attempt by the communists to take over the country. It was the usual CIA operation. Weapons were buried in caches and of course there was lots of money floating around. A lot of people became rich on the back of Gladio.'

'What has that to do with Northern Ireland?'

'There was a branch of Gladio set up here.'

'Why the hell here?'

'I have no idea of the thinking of the time. I suppose that you were considered unstable. Anyway, it appears the local leaders of Gladio thought Evans was about to lead a communist takeover of Ulster and organised his death. We had no idea what they were up to.'

'But you know who they were?'

'They're all dead.'

A picture of Jackie Carlisle came into Wilson's mind. He'd forgotten about the diaries. 'You're not going to tell me who they were, are you?'

'No.'

'But they killed your colleague and Alan Evans.'

'Rice killed Alan Evans and our colleague. It's best left like that.'

'For you people.' Wilson wanted out of the car. He preferred criminals to these people. 'What happened to Jennifer's body?'

'She's being buried with her parents.'

Wilson looked out of the car window. They had made a loop to the right at the city centre and they were approaching Ann Street. They turned left and crossed the river.

'Has your curiosity been satisfied?' Boag asked.

'Not even remotely.'

They were approaching Queen's Quay from the south.

Boag leaned forward and said something to the driver who immediately pulled in to the side of the road. 'Its been pleasant speaking with you again, Ian.' Boag nodded at the young man in the passenger seat who descended and opened the door for Wilson.

Wilson shifted his weight to the right as he prepared to leave the car. 'I'd like to say the same. Why don't you people just leave us alone?'

Boag stared straight ahead.

Wilson climbed out of the car and the young man closed the door behind him. Wilson barely had his feet on the street when the car was gone. He started walking toward his apartment. Had he just been handed a line of bullshit or was Boag trying to explain the mess? Maybe the diaries he left with Gowan would contain the answer.

CHAPTER SEVENTY-NINE

The Presbyterian Church in Saintfield Road was a modern building that looked like a former NASA engineer had designed it. From the front it had the aspect of a rocket preparing for take off. The service had been dignified. Maggie Cummerford was delivered to the door by a police van ten minutes before the ten o'clock start time. The prison authorities had been gracious enough not to have her handcuffed. She sat in the front pew accompanied by a female warden. Reid and Wilson sat two pews back and McDevitt sat at the rear of the church. As soon as the vicar had finished the service, the five mourners accompanied by the vicar made their way to Roselawn Cemetery. The spell of fine weather had broken and the light rain, which had been falling when they entered the church, had become a full-blown downpour by the time they reached the gravesite. It was Wilson's curse that every time he attended a funeral the heavens decided to open. The mourners stood around the open grave for the final prayers and watched as the coffin was lowered into the earth. McDevitt was the first to detach himself from the group. He made the signal for a drink to Wilson who in turn shook his head. The female warden was leading Cummerford toward the prison van when they passed Wilson and Reid.

Cummerford stood directly in front of Wilson. 'Thank you, Ian. I'll pay you back when I can.'

'No need, it was the least I could do. We screwed up all those years ago. She's at peace now and I hope so are you.'

She put her arms around him and hugged him. 'See you in six years or so.' The female warden took her arm and led her away.

'It appears I have a rival,' Reid said as they walked back toward the road through the cemetery where he had parked the car.

He didn't answer but put his arm around her shoulder and pulled her to him.

She smiled and slipped an arm around his waist. It was beginning to feel natural between them. Kate McCann would always hover somewhere between them like Banquo's ghost hovered about Macbeth. But her presence was already beginning to wane. 'Do you have plans for the rest of the day?' she asked as they separated to climb into his car.

He sat behind the steering wheel. 'I hadn't thought beyond the funeral. I suppose I could go back to the station.'

'Don't be a bore. I've taken the day off. Let's have lunch and I haven't had time to visit the Titanic Exhibition. Then you might make me dinner.'

It sounded good. He'd never played tourist in Belfast. Today there were no bodies to be dug up, no murderers to interview and no spooks to spin him stories. He looked across into Reid's beautiful face. He was such a lucky man. In general, the world he inhabited was black. Today he would try to let a little light in.

Author's note

I HOPE that you enjoyed this book. You will note that there are no acknowledgements in this book. That's because I have no agent, no editor to hold my hand and no publisher. As an indie author, I very much depend on **your** feedback to see where my writing is going. Therefore, I would be very grateful if you would take the time to pen a review on Amazon. This will not only help me but will also indicate to others your feelings, positive or negative, on the work. Writing is a lonely profession and this is especially true for indie authors who don't have the backup of traditional publishers.

PLEASE CHECK out my other books on Amazon and if you have time visit my web site (derekfee.com) and sign up to receive additional materials, competitions for signed books and announcements of new book launches.

COPYRIGHT©DEREK FEE 2016
     All rights reserved.

UNTITLED

DEATH ON THE LINE

DEREK FEE

CHAPTER EIGHTY

O*utside Aughnacloy, South Tyrone*

JOCK MCDEVITT WONDERED what the hell he was doing lying on his belly in the wet grass on the side of a knoll in an open field in the middle of the night. The knoll directly over-looked the tarmac road that connected Northern Ireland and the Republic of Ireland. Although it was early September and theoretically summer was only several days ago, the air was bitingly cold and a soft drizzle was falling. In 1607 the local chieftain, Hugh O'Neill, headed to Lough Swilly with his whole kit and caboodle and took sail for France. The history books say that he did so to avoid an all-out battle with Lord Mountjoy and half the English army. But lying in a wet field with the cold penetrating his bones, McDevitt was of the opinion that he and his clan probably just wanted to get away from the horrible Ulster weather. He looked across at the man lying beside him. Thomas Kielty was a seventy-year-old local farmer, and presumably a busybody and an insomniac because who else but a busybody and insomniac would have discovered criminal wrongdoings in his area by tramping about in the early hours of the morning. Kielty appeared to be totally relaxed and at home lying on his back staring at the black clouds above their heads and feeling the misty rain kissing his face. He was wearing a flat cap of the kind favoured by the farming community and a waterproof jacket and trousers. McDevitt had supposed that they would be in some kind of covered hide and consequently he had limited his dress to a pair of jeans and a North Face jacket.

'We'll have full-on rain before the night's out, so we will, mind my words,' Kielty said.

'Fucking wonderful,' McDevitt said under his breath. That would put the tin hat on it as far as he was concerned. He was a city slicker and proud of it. He looked at his watch and saw that it was almost two o'clock. He thought of his comfortable bed and his warm house in Belfast. He had to be mad. This was the kind of craziness that junior reporters got up to. His book on the Cummerford woman would be launching in three weeks. The advance sales looked good and it had already been positively reviewed by his colleague in the arts department at the *Chronicle,* surprise, surprise. There was even talk of a film and a treatment had already been presented to Northern Ireland Screen to attract investment. So, he asked himself, what the hell are you doing lying on the ground beside some hick farmer waiting for the rain to piss down on you? He smiled inwardly. He knew exactly why he was lying there.

Jock McDevitt was obsessed with the front page of the *Chronicle*. If his byline wasn't on the front page, he was generally miserable. And if the old man lying next to him was right, McDevitt's byline would be on his favourite page of the *Chronicle* for an extended period of time. And it wouldn't only be front-page news in Northern Ireland. There was no way he was going to dump that kind of opportunity into the lap of another reporter. He lifted the Night Owl binoculars that hung round his neck and looked again at the stretch of road fifty metres in front of him. The night-vision binoculars were brand-new but would be well worth the significant investment if Kielty's information proved solid. 'Are you sure that they're going to show?'

'Are you kiddin' me?' The old man smiled. 'Do you know that the leopard is one of the most difficult animals to spot?' His gaze never moved from the sky above his head. McDevitt sighed but didn't reply. 'Well these fellas are more shy than the leopard. If they show, then they'll show. If not, then there's always tomorrow.'

No there isn't, McDevitt thought. He wasn't about to spend his time lying in a field hoping something would happen. He had much too much going on in his life to waste any more time than this one evening on what might turn out to be the ramblings of a deluded geriatric farmer. The good news was that Kielty hadn't demanded money to convey his tip. The people McDevitt normally dealt with had their hand stretched out before they condescended to open their mouths. He would give it another hour and then he'd head back to Belfast and tumble into his bed.

'Where exactly is the border?' McDevitt asked.

Kielty rolled over onto his stomach and looked over the knoll. 'Yonder to the left was where the customs post was in the old days. That was the official border, I suppose, but nowadays people have forgotten where the exact line is, don't ye know.'

'They'll know pretty soon if the Brits get their way,' McDevitt said. The border that had blighted the island since 1922 had become an invisible divider in 1973 when the Irish Republic and the United Kingdom joined the European Common Market.

The dark clouds that had been threatening since early evening had begun to send spits of rain onto McDevitt's head when he heard the first sounds of a truck coming along the road from the south. He lifted the binoculars to his eyes and sighted on the direction where the noise was coming from. He wasn't used to night-vision equipment and he had to re-focus his eyes as he saw the truck appear like a ghost through an eerie green light. He tried to make out the licence plate but was unsuccessful.

Kielty peered over the top of the knoll. 'Aye, that's them all right,' he said, looking into the darkness. 'Your luck's in.'

The truck had come to a stop about one hundred metres from their position. The rain was now falling steadily and McDevitt's jacket was almost soaked right through. However, he was oblivious to the rain now that the old man's information had been proven correct. He peered through the green mist and watched two men descend from the truck. He heard the noise of a second truck, this time coming from the northern side. A few minutes later it came into view and he sighted on it. It pulled up directly facing the truck already parked in the road. McDevitt watched as three men descended and walked forward. They reached the two men already in the centre of the road and there was a degree of hugging and back-slapping. McDevitt fiddled with the focus of the binoculars and zoomed in on the faces of the men in the road. Their faces seemed to leap forward into his vision. 'Fucking hell,' he said softly as the faces became clear. The men gathered together before one of them moved off into the field on the far side of the road. McDevitt lost sight of him as he left the road.

'Aye,' Kielty said into his right ear. 'Now that you've seen them, we'd best get out of here. That boy who went into the fields isn't lookin' for rabbits.'

'I don't believe it,' McDevitt said, continuing to watch through the binoculars.

'Neither did I,' Kielty said. 'You've got what you came for. Now, we need to be away.' He started to pull at McDevitt's jacket.

Jock McDevitt was busy looking at the scene in the middle of the road. This wasn't just one front page, it was dozens of front pages. And Tom Kielty was trying to pull him away from the biggest story of his life. McDevitt shook off the old man's hand. Why hadn't he thought to bring a camera? A photo of the scene on the road would be the clincher for his story.

Kielty had already risen and was making his way down the rear of the knoll and away from the road. There was a copse of trees sixty metres behind them and Kielty was almost there when a brace of shots rang out.

McDevitt whirled around in time to see Kielty fall to the ground. Holy shit, he thought, what have I done? Is it safer to burrow down here or to make a run for it? He could hear shouting from the road, which elicited a shouted reply from somewhere to his right. He felt an overpowering desire to urinate. His mind was refusing to operate. Kielty hadn't stirred. McDevitt tried to move but his legs refused to obey the instruction from his brain. He began to crawl away to his left, keeping the lowest profile above the ground. There was more activity on the road and he could hear footsteps coming from what seemed to be every direction. He raised his head to see if there was any clear path of escape. There was an explosion from behind him and he felt a stinging pain in his back just below his left shoulder blade. Then he heard a second shot, something impacted with the side of his head and his world went black.

The men from the trucks examined the two bodies. 'They're gone,' the eldest of the group said. 'Let's get through with the business and get out of here.' He looked over to where Kielty lay. 'Stupid old fucker, he should have minded his own business.'

A younger man standing close to him nodded. 'We'll have to look for another spot.'

After the men had left, McDevitt stirred. His body was wracked with pain and slowly the realisation that he had been shot dawned on him. He tried to move, but his limbs were not responding. He could feel the rain falling on him and he knew that if he didn't do something he would either die from his wounds or from exposure. He managed to release his mobile phone from his pocket. He flicked it open. There was only one person he knew who could save him at this point. Slowly he dialled a number.

CHAPTER EIGHTY-ONE

Ian Wilson heard the ringing noise but it seemed to be very far away. It was the middle of the night and he was sleeping the sleep of the just, having just passed one of those quiet evenings that had become part of his life over the last three months. Luckily, murder had taken a holiday from Belfast, which was just as well since he had spent an inordinate amount of time debriefing Willie Rice. As a result, he'd managed to close five open cases of murder that had been hanging around for twenty years. Willie had been more than open about his own role in the murders but tight-lipped about who else might have been involved. Wilson assumed it had something to do with honour among murderers. Either that or Willie still harboured some fear about what the other participants might do to him. All that speculation came to nothing when the oncologist confirmed that, although Rice was probably one of the most prolific psychopaths in Ulster's history, he would never be judged in a court of law. The physician had been proved right almost to the day. Willie had shuffled off this mortal coil two weeks previously. He followed his nemesis, 'Slim' Gerry McCreary, into the great beyond.

McGreary had probably counted on receiving a hero's send-off, but his interment had more of the flavour of a mobster funeral. The coffin had been draped with the obligatory Union Jack and McGreary's famous royal blue number six Linfield shirt lay on top of the flag he had professed to love so much. The biggest floral tribute had been provided by Davie Best, McGreary's former right-hand man. The words 'Goodbye Boss' had been laid out in an enormous spray of blue, red and white flowers attached to the side of the hearse. Wilson was present at Roselawn Cemetery to see the baton passed on to Best as the old McGreary mob paid homage to the new leader in front of the grieving widow and her family.

The demise of two established mob bosses in the space of a couple of weeks had led to a sea change in the organised crime scene in Belfast. The Brown Bear and the Queen's Tavern had lost their positions as the homes of the two gangs. The men who had spent their days bullshitting at McGreary's or Rice's tables had been put out to pasture. Wilson often remembered Rice's prophecy that the cops would be sorry when the new crew took over. It certainly wasn't borne out in terms of an increase in the number of murders. Wilson was aware that there had been a certain amount of consolidation in the drugs trade, the prostitution business and protection rackets. But that was a problem for the Drugs and Vice Squads. In order to keep the team focused, Wilson had ordered a complete review of the deaths of Grant, Malone and O'Reilly. It had already been established that a pair of Scottish criminals named Baxter and Weir had carried out the murders of Grant and Malone. He was sure that Sammy Rice had ordered the deaths, but that had not been proven definitively. Big George Carroll, Sammy's driver, was currently serving five years at the funny farm for tossing O'Reilly out of a fourth-floor window onto a Belfast street. The motivation for the murders had led to a shadowy conspiracy involving a group called Carson Nominees. That company had disappeared as soon as its existence had been recognised. In the meantime, Wilson's working life was consumed with the need to find either a living or a dead Sammy Rice.

Wilson turned in the direction of the phone and saw that he was alone in bed. His 'girlfriend', Stephanie Reid, had an annoying habit of spending the early part of the night in his bed and leaving as soon as she woke, regardless of what time that might be. He picked up his mobile phone and answered. 'Hello.'

'Ian?' the voice was so faint that for a few moments he wasn't sure who was on the other end.

'Jock, is that you?'

'I've been shot,' the words seemed to be forced out of the mouth. 'I think I'm dying.'

'Jock, if this is a joke, it's a pretty bad one.'

'No joke, help me. I feel like passing out again.'

'Where are you?'

There was a cough on the line as a response.

'Leave your phone on,' Wilson was already out of bed. 'Jock, Jock, whatever you do don't close the communication.'

There was no reply. Wilson went to his landline and phoned the station. He gave the desk sergeant McDevitt's number and told him to organise an immediate trace on the phone. He dressed quickly and had just finished when his landline rang. McDevitt's phone was in South Tyrone, close to the village of Aughnacloy. Wilson told the sergeant to advise the local station that there was an injured man at the location and to get an ambulance there as soon as possible. He took the number of the Armagh PSNI station and rushed to the garage to collect his car. Aughnacloy was one hour away by car. If McDevitt really had been shot, every second would count. In another version of reality, Wilson would have scrambled the helicopter but that would bring the chief superintendent down on his head over the cost. Instead he punched in the coordinates of the location of McDevitt's phone, gunned the engine of his Saab 92 and tore through the empty streets of Belfast heading west. He reached the M1 and pushed the accelerator to the floor. He would deal with the speed issues later if they arose.

CHAPTER EIGHTY-TWO

The arc lights cast an eerie glow over the fields outside Aughnacloy. Wilson's GPS guided him to the area, but he had no need of technology when he got close to the crime scene. A roadblock had already been set up on the B35 and Wilson was permitted inside the cordon when he presented his warrant card. He finally came to rest behind two police Land Rovers that effectively blocked the road. It was still dark as he made his way towards the arc lights. His mind had been in turmoil as he had driven from Belfast. What the hell was McDevitt doing in the back of beyond in the middle of the night? It had to be something dangerous if it had got him shot. Why would McDevitt place himself in danger? It wasn't part of the man's makeup. He gave his name to the officer charged with controlling access to the site and made his way to where a group of uniformed officers were standing. One of them turned as he approached and detached himself from the others. The rain had stopped, but Wilson's shoes and the bottoms of his trousers were still soaked from tramping through the long grass.

'Detective Superintendent Wilson?' the officer asked as he walked forward.

Wilson nodded and extended his hand. 'How's McDevitt?'

'I'm Detective Sergeant Darren Gibson from Armagh CID.' Gibson was maybe five years younger than Wilson. Unlike the man from Belfast, he was dressed in uniform.

'How's McDevitt?' Wilson spoke louder.

Gibson retreated a step or two. He'd heard of Ian Wilson. Who in the force hadn't? 'There were two men injured, one fatally. One man has already been transferred to Craigavon Hospital. Since the fatality was a local farmer, I assume that Mr McDevitt is the one that's in hospital.'

Wilson cursed himself. He'd been in such a hurry to get to the site he hadn't thought that McDevitt might be on his way to hospital. 'How badly is he hurt?'

Gibson could see that McDevitt was more than a casual acquaintance of Wilson's. 'The ambulance crew were here when I arrived and they were anxious to get him off to hospital. He's been shot twice, once in the back and once on the side of the head.'

That didn't sound good. 'How quickly did the ambulance get here?' Wilson was aware that cuts to the National Health Service had played havoc with response times. If McDevitt had been lying out for anything more than a half-hour, he probably would have bled to death.

'They were here fifteen minutes after you raised the alarm.'

Wilson took a deep breath. That gave McDevitt a fighting chance. 'And the fatality?'

'Also shot twice, one of the shots killed him outright.'

'Can I see him?'

Gibson didn't reply but started walking in the direction of the arc lights.

'Are Forensics on the way?' Wilson asked.

'They're trying to get a team together,' Gibson said as they walked along. 'We've covered the area as best we can in order to preserve the evidence.'

They stopped at an area that had been cordoned off with crime scene tape. Wilson went to lift the tape, but Gibson put a hand on his arm. 'We're waiting for the protective suits to arrive. We've checked him, he's dead.'

Wilson looked at the man highlighted by the crossed beams of the arc lights. The corpse was dressed in a rainproof jacket and trousers. A felt cap lay in the grass. He had been running when he had been shot and had pitched forward sending his cap to the ground ahead of him.

'Do we have a name for the dead man?' Wilson asked.

'Tom Kielty,' Gibson replied. 'He farms twenty acres less than a mile from here.'

'Any idea what they were doing here?'

'No.'

'It must have been something important if two men were shot.'

Gibson nodded. 'As soon as Forensic and the pathologist have finished with the body, we'll deliver the bad news to the Kielty family. Maybe they'll have some idea what the old man was up to.'

'I've got to get to Craigavon,' Wilson said, more to himself than to Gibson. He turned and started to walk away.

Gibson re-joined him. 'We'll need to talk to you at some point.'

Wilson's eyebrows rose.

'Just a statement,' Gibson said. He extended his hand. 'I hope your friend is OK.'

Wilson shook hands. He also hoped McDevitt was OK. He didn't have so many friends that he could afford to lose one.

AUTHOR'S PLEA

I hope that you enjoyed this book. As an indie author, I very much depend on your feedback to see where my writing is going. I would be very grateful if you would take the time to pen a short review. This will not only help me but will also indicate to others your feelings, positive or negative, on the work. Writing is a lonely profession, and this is especially true for indie authors who don't have the backup of traditional publishers.

Please check out my other books , and if you have time visit my web site (derekfee.com) and sign up to receive additional materials, competitions for signed books and announcements of new book launches.

You can contact me at derekfee.com

ABOUT THE AUTHOR

Derek Fee is a former oil company executive and EU Ambassador. He is the author of seven non-fiction books and sixteen novels. Derek can be contacted at http://derekfee.com.

ALSO BY DEREK FEE

The Wilson Series

Nothing But Memories

Shadow Sins

Death To Pay

Deadly Circles

Box Full of Darkness

Yield Up the Dead

Death on the Line

A Licence to Murder

Dead Rat

Cold in the Soul

Border Badlands

Moira McElvaney Books

The Marlboro Man

A Convenient Death